DEADLY CAMPSITE

I fetched our tent from the mule's back and had this nagging feeling that we wouldn't be lucky come morning when it came to the weather.

I was driving the first tent stake into the frozen ground with a rock when a distant crack echoed from the rim above us. I jumped to my feet as one of our horses screamed in pain, lunging forward on its hind legs. I dropped the rock and pulled my pistol free as Sam's gelding fell over on its side, whickering, legs thrashing in the snow. Sam was running for his horse when another shot rang out. Moses let out this awful bray, sinking down in the snow and I knew our mule had been hit. I took off in a run for the closest tree to get out of the line of fire.

I heard Sam's Winchester explode. The rifle shot echoed among the oaks around me and died away, leaving only the sound of the mule honking. For now, the sharpshooter on the rim had stopped firing at us.

I hoped Sam's answering shot had been enough to scare him off.

WILLIAM W. JOHNSTONE
THE ASHES SERIES

Available wherever paperbacks are sold, or order direct from the Publisher. Send cover price plus 50¢ per copy for mailing and handling to Penguin USA, P.O. Box 999, c/o Dept. 17109, Bergenfield, NJ 07621. Residents of New York and Tennessee must include sales tax. DO NOT SEND CASH.

LONE WOLF

Frederic Bean

Pinnacle Books
Kensington Publishing Corp.
http://www.pinnaclebooks.com

PINNACLE BOOKS are published by

Kensington Publishing Corp.
850 Third Avenue
New York, NY 10022

Pinnacle and the P logo Reg. U.S. Pat. & TM Off.

First Printing: February, 1997
10 9 8 7 6 5 4 3 2 1

Printed in the United States of America

Introduction

Georgina Cooper thought she heard a noise. She looked up, wondering, setting her knitting aside. It was easy to imagine strange noises in this savage wilderness—some were not imagined, she knew. Darkness surrounded their small dugout. Light from a firepit in the center of the room danced across dried-mud walls, creating shadows that moved unnaturally, like demonic spirits of netherworlds that she'd read about in mythology while she was in school back in Boston. Her rocking chair gave a squeak when she got up to peer through a blanket hanging over the door. Nathaniel had not found time to fashion planks for a door quite yet, busy with more important things before winter set in, gathering enough food so they wouldn't starve. Nathaniel's gentle snoring from a pile of quilts nearby was comforting now as Georgina crept through the blanket curtain up a steep slope leading from their dugout to ground level to see what was making that strange sound.

She paused at the top to allow her eyes to adjust to total darkness, although the sky above her was sprinkled with stars. She cocked her head and listened for the noise again, hearing only silence, Nathaniel's snoring, the crackle of flames from a fire inside a dugout belonging to their friends Dave and Myra Collins less than twenty yards away.

She passed a roaming glance around her, to the river, then the pole corrals where Dave and Nathaniel kept their horses and mules. Once, Georgina thought she saw a shadow moving among the animals, but when she tried to find it again

it was gone. She was imagining things, she told herself. However, there had been that strange howling. . . .

Quite suddenly, a barking noise came from the riverbanks,
the call of a wolf. The cry startled her so badly she had begun
to wheel for the safety of their dugout before she recognized
it as a sound made by an animal. Her heart fluttered momentarily until she calmed herself.

"I'd better wake Nathaniel," she whispered, for she feared
a wolf might attack one of the horses or a mule. On another
night not too long ago, a lobo wolf had circled their camp,
sniffing the wind like it might be considering a meal. Sighting
that wolf had seriously frightened both girls—their daughters
were not fully accustomed to the sights and sounds of the
wilderness yet. Dave and his son had driven the creature off
with a single rifle shot fired over its head, she remembered.

Georgina watched the river until a night chill on a breath
of wind from the west made her shiver. The wolf did not
bark again, and she wondered if it would be better to let poor
Nathaniel sleep. He'd been gone hunting all day and she
knew he was exceedingly weary tonight. Perhaps it would
be best to ignore the wolf, unless it came closer.

A soft sound on the slope behind her brought a smile to
her face, for she knew it would be Nathaniel, aroused from
his slumber by the wolf's call. She turned to speak to him.

Something struck her breastbone with tremendous force.
Air rushed from her lungs all at once. She heard a cracking
noise in her chest, like splintering kindling wood, followed
by a blinding flash of white-hot pain. Her eyes bulged wide
and her mouth flew open to scream, but a ham-sized hand
clamped her jaw shut. She felt something tearing inside her,
a sharp object moving down the middle of her belly accom-
panied by fiery pain so intense that her knees gave way. Her
mind could not comprehend what was happening to her, so
swiftly had the violence begun.

She was slammed to the ground on her back, stunned,
unable to speak or breathe. Waves of pain raced through her,

paralyzing her limbs, her tongue. A giant shadow stood over her, that of a man holding a long-bladed bowie knife. She stared up at him when she found she could not scream to warn the others, nor could she make a move to stop him, whoever he was. Despite agony so deep it rendered her almost senseless, there was something about the man's shadow she found vaguely familiar. Then quickly, the dark form whirled and went out of sight without uttering a word.

For a few seconds all was still, quiet, until a bloodcurdling scream came from inside the dugout. Georgina tried to lift her head. Sheer desperation forced her to make an attempt to get to her feet, for she knew that scream—it was her daughter's tiny voice, and the terror in it now gave Georgina strength to rise in spite of a knife's deep passage through her midsection. She got her elbows planted and somehow sat up shakily, blinking away wave after wave of excruciating pain in order to make some effort to rescue her eldest child.

The scream ended abruptly, before Georgina could steady her arms in a sitting position. Another voice, Nathaniel's, gave a muffled shout. A thud, then a groan, and total silence afterward sent Georgina rocking forward to her knees in a desperate attempt to help her husband and daughters before it was too late, even as she told herself there was little or nothing she could do. All that mattered was reaching them, being there.

Something warm and wet spilled down the front of her dress. When she looked down, it appeared that dozens of black snakes had begun to crawl from her stomach—she knew she must be imagining this, for it was not possible that she bore snakes the way she carried children inside her. Swaying back and forth on her knees, she saw dark snakes wriggle to the ground, glistening wetly in light from pale stars above. They were squirming and crawling around her in the most awful way. More of them slithered from her belly, inky serpents from hell that surely could not have dwelled inside her body without her knowledge. This truly had to be some sort of evil apparition, the work of the devil.

She reached for the snakes with both hands, meaning to cast them aside or prove they were only figments of her imagination, but when her fingers closed around them she experienced another wave of raw pain so intense it almost rendered her unconscious. She heard herself cry out feebly, weakly, like a newborn calf in search of its mother. And at the same time she knew the snakes were real, for she felt them squirm, felt their slimy coating as they wriggled between her fingers.

Georgina fell forward, her head awash with dizziness, across the snakes. She lay there a moment gasping for air, enveloped by a haze of red pain too overpowering to allow her even the slightest movement. From far away she heard another cry, a shout—or was it a scream? She had the vague sense that it came from the direction of Dave and Myra's, yet she could not trust her senses now—hadn't she seen serpents crawling from her stomach? Only an addled person saw snakes where none could exist. . . .

A piercing shriek echoed from somewhere close by, from their dugout, and suddenly Georgina remembered her family. Summoning all her strength, she began to crawl forward, clawing dirt with her fingernails, inching down the dark slope toward Nathaniel, Sara, and Denise, dragging snakes behind her. The shriek became a wail, thinning, until Georgina recognized it. Denise, their youngest daughter, was begging for her life until, like Sara and Nathaniel, her voice was stilled suddenly, completely.

Tears flooded Georgina's eyes, not from physical pain, but for the sake of her husband and children. An inner voice told her they were dying and that she would also die from the wound to her stomach unless someone came to help them. The shadowy figure with the knife meant to slay them all; and it seemed incomprehensible that he would do this without warning, for no reason. What had they done to him?

She managed to crawl a few feet more to the blanket, sobbing quietly, ignoring her terrible pain and the snakes she dragged behind her, aware that blood was also pouring from her belly, for she could feel its wetness with her bare feet when she crawled to the doorway. Her arms trembled violently now, all her strength ebbing away. She pulled herself into the room, a room that would serve as their basement when Nathaniel began a cabin above it in the spring.

There, in light from the fire, Georgina raised her head to see what fate had befallen her family. What she saw was beyond her ability to comprehend, far worse than anything her blackest nightmares could have prepared her for. She stopped breathing altogether, frozen to the spot by stark terror as though she'd been captured in a block of ice.

A muscular giant stood over Sara with his fist knotted into a lock of her golden hair. He looked down at Georgina, pausing with the blade of his huge knife against Sara's forehead. In a glimmer of firelight, it appeared the giant's eyes were glowing red, a demon's orbs, like a monster from some storybook about creatures inhabiting the bowels of the earth. The monster held Sara by her tresses, her head twisted at an unnatural angle so she seemed to be watching the roof, then there was a deep grunt and in the same instant, a flash of steel.

Georgina collapsed on the hard dirt floor when she saw her daughter's scalp torn from her skull. It was too much for her to witness without going into shock. She lay on her stomach in a spreading pool of blood, shutting the scene from her mind as if she closed a door to her thoughts. Instead, she dreamed of their trip westward from Boston that spring, the pretty flowers spread across countless empty plains west of the Missouri. She loved all flowers, especially the wild varieties since they came in so many vivid colors.

Her eyelids fluttered and closed. Nathaniel had promised he would dig flower beds around their new cabin next spring. He was a man of his word and he would do this, for her. He had said not to worry about all the dangers they faced in the wilderness, for they would face them together, as a family, along with Dave and Myra. Life would be good out West. Not to worry about tales of wild Indians there, for they were at peace with the white man now that an important treaty had been signed.

Georgina's unbearable pain grew less. She imagined she saw beds of colorful flowers blooming around a new cabin. She felt sleepy.

One

I was sweeping out the office on a brisk fall morning while trying to get a fire going in our potbelly stove to take a chill out of the place. That little building had so many cracks in the walls that when a wind blew up it sounded like a dozen cowpokes stood outside playing harmonicas out of tune. Wind came whistling through those cracks so fierce our Wanted circulars did a little dance where we'd nailed them on the walls. A time or two I'd offered to chink the cracks with mud and flour sacking, but Sam would always say we were in the peacekeeping business and weren't paid carpenters by trade. In the dead of winter we sat around in our coats listening to wind screech through the cracks, shivering like half-drowned tomcats even though our stove turned red from a blaze we kept in it. I wasn't inclined to argue with Marshal Ault over a small thing like the chance we'd freeze to death in our own office. I was only a deputy and he seldom ever let me forget that he made the important decisions for the United States Marshals Service in the western district of Indian Territory. When I brought it to his attention that we were sure to freeze solid before the spring thaw, he would say, "Put more wood in that damn stove, Mr. Dudley. That's why they make 'em with a door in the side." Sam's temperament wasn't as bad as all that, usually, but when I made mention of fixing the cracks from time to time, like on a particularly cold day when a wind howled down from the north, it put a burr under his saddle blanket. Fixing things around our office wasn't a notion he'd seriously entertain, even if I offered to do all the work. As a result we had desk drawers that wouldn't close, a door with one rawhide hinge where an iron hinge busted in half, and plenty of other things that were only half fixed. Our big potbelly worked right and so did our coffeepot, which was nearly all Sam cared about in that office other than his hide-bottom chair. We had an office close to Fort Sill at Cache, which could hardly be called a town—just a general store and a blacksmith's shop sitting across a dusty wagon road from the marshal's office. We had a jail cell in the back but Sam rarely ever used it. If we had prisoners, which we did from time to time, we took them out to the army stockade for transfer back to Fort Smith where they stood trial. I sometimes felt that if we locked a few of our prisoners in that jail in the wintertime, there'd be a hell of a lot less crime in our district. A man who's froze ain't nearly so likely to break the law again, facing a jail term at Cache if he got caught the next time. I told Sam once about this drifter who called himself Tooter Blake, who swore he'd rather be hung than spend one more night in our jail last winter. Sam hardly batted an eye when he said that was the reason he didn't want me wasting time fixing cracks in our wall, that he meant for them to be a deterrent to dishonest men.

I got the sweeping done early and a fire coaxed to a blaze in the stove by the time I heard Sam's horse. Sam kept a home and a wife close to Fort Sill, making a two-mile ride every day to the office when we weren't out in the Territory looking for lawbreakers. Sam and Clara had been married for better than twenty years by the time I signed on with the marshals service. When I first heard Sam talk about his wife, I'd have sworn they couldn't stand the sight of each other. But it wasn't long until I learned this was just Sam's way, to complain about how Clara fussed over him and gripe about women in general. He loved her deeply, but he would rather be horsewhipped than admit it to anybody. And the truth was, even though she was a tiny woman and he was better than six feet of lean muscle and meanness, she had the upper hand when they were together. Sam had no fear of the worst bad hombres in the Territory; but when he faced Clara, he got meek as a lamb until he was out of the house and well out of earshot.

The coffee was just about ready when Sam got his horse put away in a shed behind the office. His boots clumped across the front porch and the door banged open. I could tell by the look on his face he wasn't in the best of moods.

"Colder'n blue blazes out there, Leon," he said, slamming our thin plank door so loudly it hurt my ears. "I've never been plumb to the north pole, but I'd nearly swear there ain't nothin' but a barbed-wire fence or two between here'n there." He stamped over to the stove and pulled off his leather gloves, warming his hands.

"Coffee's nearly ready," I said, standing my broom in a rear corner. A gust of icy wind fluttered Wanted posters on the north wall of the office. "If I was to fix those cracks, it wouldn't be quite so breezy in here."

Sam gave me one of his looks. "If you hanker to find work in the carpentry profession, then why the hell'd you sign on to be a marshal, Leon? It's high time you made up your mind which you aim to be, a carpenter or a lawman. I reckon you could hang a claw hammer in that holster you're wearin'—put nails in those cartridge loops instead of bullets."

I grinned. It was just Sam's way of funning me. "Did Clara give you a bad time this morning?" I asked, taking down two clean tin cups from the washstand.

Sam adopted a look of indignation. "She has given me a bad time every single day since I was fool enough to marry her, son. If I've got any advice you'll listen to, Mr. Dudley, don't ever let marryin' cross your mind. Women were put on this earth for the sole purpose of makin' a man's life miserable, like a skunk or a rattlesnake. There's no reasonable explanation for the existence of skunks or rattlesnakes, 'cept to hand out grief for the poor bastard who happens to run across either one. Same can be said for women. If it wasn't for the fact that they can be soft and sweet once in a blue moon so a man loses his senses over females when he's young an' foolish, there'd be no such thing as matrimony unless a man was plumb out of his head."

"I take it Clara was mad about something," I said, pouring coffee, shivering even though I was wearing a wool coat and my longjohns under my denims, with two pairs of socks.

"Hardly a day goes by when she ain't mad about somethin'," Sam remarked, taking the cup I offered, blowing steam from the rim.

A particularly vigorous gust of wind screeched through a big crack below the front door. Even though our potbelly had begun to glow red, I was freezing. I took a sip of scalding liquid and winced when it burned my lips and tongue. "I'm sure glad we got back before this norther hit," I said. We'd been up north on the Cimarron River until a few days ago, putting a stop to a gang of gunrunners trading rifles to Kiowa renegades. We'd rounded up an old adversary of ours, a troublemaker named Jack Tatum who made a regular habit out of selling guns and whiskey to Kiowas and Comanches when he wasn't putting his brand on somebody else's cattle. Me and Sam had a run-in with Tatum back when we went to Palo Duro Canyon down in Texas looking for a white girl taken captive by Quannah Parker's band of Kwahadie Comanches. We got Tatum and two of his associates hauled down to Fort Sill just in time to escape the first bad winter storm blowing down from the high plains. By the look of the sky this morning, I wouldn't have been surprised to see the first snowflake fall before dark.

"We could find ourselves out in this miserable weather if Major Donaldson gets confirmation on those scalpings at Antelope Hill on the Canadian," Sam reminded me. Yesterday the post commander informed Sam that eleven settlers had been found scalped and badly mutilated near the western boundary of the Territory at a place called Antelope Hill. That was still renegade Comanche country, close to the Texas panhandle, as wild a place as any I'd ever seen. A wire had come to Fort Sill asking for routine patrols in that region. The army was sent out, but it was our experience that cavalry patrols rarely ever came up with much after a trail got cold. Sam maintained that most cavalry scouts couldn't find their own asses with two free hands. He had a low opinion of men in uniform, with only a rare exception.

"I'd hate to think of spending much time out in this wind," I said. "Looks like it could snow before nightfall."

Sam walked to a window. Wind rattled a loose pane of glass. "This ain't no job for a sissie, Mr. Dudley. Maybe you oughta give serious thought to followin' the carpentry profession in a place where it's warmer."

This was Sam's regular habit, testing me to see how badly I wanted to be a U.S. Marshal, only he did it in a joking way. At first I'll admit it got under my skin a little, until I learned how to take it. Sam's manner was usually gruff and to the point, but underneath he was patient with the beginner's mistakes I made and spent a lot of time showing me things I needed to know. We had become good friends in the two years I'd spent as his deputy. In tight spots he'd gotten to where he trusted me. A few times he actually paid me a compliment, especially when it came to my shooting and the way I handled myself in a pinch. I'd proven I was a good shot with a rifle on more than one occasion and Sam respected me for that, even if I was still a little short when it came to nerve once in a while. "I'll admit I like it warmer than this," I said. "I grew up in Mississippi. Never saw snow before until I got here."

"It'll be a hell of a lot colder'n this up at Antelope Hill if we have to go," he said, squinting out the window at nothing in particular, watching dust blow across the road in front of the office. "Probably snowin' there by now. Sleetin' too, which is worse. Harder on horses."

"Do you figure it was Comanches who done it?"

Sam grunted, nodding once. "Comanches leave a mark on

their enemies that's hard to forget after you've seen it. By the sound of that wire, I'd say it's Comanche handiwork all right. Up in that neck of the woods it's liable to be Bull Bear's bunch. I'd sorta hoped the Kotsotekas had settled down some. But when a new bunch of white settlers shows up on Kotsoteka hunting ground, it's only natural that it'll piss 'em off considerable. A Comanche don't understand what a treaty is. To them it's just a piece of paper. Most Indians don't understand how anybody can own a piece of land. To them, the land belongs to whoever happens to be on it at the time and only if he's tough enough to keep anybody else from takin' it away in a fight. When a white man builds a cabin on a piece of land, it's an open invitation for an Indian to make him fight to hang on to it. That's been Indian custom since the beginning of time. Hard to change their way of thinkin' with a piece of paper."

"I reckon not. But it won't change government policy when it comes to treaties even if the Indians don't understand what they're signing, will it?"

Sam scowled out the window thoughtfully. "Not in the least, Leon. We'll keep pushin' 'em off their traditional hunting lands until they've got no place left to go. Army brass would like to exterminate every last one of 'em, if they could. An Indian's nothing but a damn nuisance to men in Washington. Can't say as I agree with what we're doin' all that much, squeezin' them onto tiny reservations that ain't fit for a billy goat nor hardly big enough for 'em to turn around in. It's no wonder they get pissed off once in awhile."

"But they can't get away with scalping settlers like they did up at Antelope Hill," I argued. "The telegram said some of those people were women and children. The army has to stop them from pulling more of those kinds of raids."

"That's the part that don't fit, Leon. It sounds like the work of Comanches, until you think about it. Comanches prize a white woman. They make slaves out of 'em or, if they're young and pretty enough, they turn 'em into whores for their young men or they trade 'em to the Kiowas or the Crows. It don't make any sense that Bull Bear would slaughter women like that."

I turned my back to the stove to warm it. "So what's the explanation? The wire said the bodies were mutilated. That's the trademark of a ritual Comanche killing, ain't it?"

"Usually. To tell the truth I haven't got it figured out myself. Now toss some more wood in that damn stove. That's why they hung a door on the side of it, in case nobody informed you."

I put on a glove and opened the stove, tossing more sticks of split oak inside. Wind howled around an eave so strongly it shook rafters above our heads. "Gonna be one hell of a storm," I observed, peeking out a window. "I sure hope we don't have to go for a ride in it."

Sam palmed his cup for its warmth, staring out another pane of rattling glass like he hadn't heard what I'd said. "It just don't make any sense that a Comanche raidin' party would gut an' scalp women an' kids like that wire claimed. Comanches put a signature on their dead enemies, but they don't make war on any women or children no matter what color they are."

"Maybe whoever sent the wire made a mistake."

"Maybe," Sam muttered, like his mind was someplace else.

Looking north, I saw this big bank of black clouds building along the horizon. I didn't need to be reminded what it would be like to ride a horse through a storm like the one headed toward us—me and Sam had been out in winter weather up in the Nations plenty of times. "Maybe the army will find out what happened up there and track down whoever was responsible."

Sam turned from the window, looking disgusted with my logic. "There's about as much likelihood of that as there is a snowball freezin' to the ground in hell," he said.

I turned my front to the stove so I didn't have to look at

Sam. I reckon it was wishful thinking on my part, mainly because I didn't want to think about what it would be like to be huddled on the back of a horse in a blizzard. But something deep inside me warned that we'd be out in a storm before this was settled. It was a pretty sure bet Sam wouldn't wait 'til spring to find out what happened to those settlers at Antelope Hill.

Two

Babcock Woodley liked to be called Babs. He was as salty as most of the range-bred horses he rode and could cuss a blue streak when he was riled. He drank an inordinate amount of whiskey most of the time and took baths only in the spring and summer when the weather was warm. But when it got cold, Babs avoided contact with bathwater like the plague; and as winter lengthened, he developed a smell that rivaled a polecat's perfume. It had been chilly for a few weeks when Babs stopped by the office that same windy day the storm blew in, and Sam told me he could smell Babs before he rode his horse up to our hitchrail, seeing as how Babs was traveling with the wind at his back.

Babs stamped his boots on the porch, a common cowboy custom just in case fresh cattle droppings happened to adorn a cowboy's feet, then he burst into our office with a half-wild look in his eyes. "Howdy, Sam. Howdy, Leon." He slammed the door and made for that stove like it was the only reason he'd bothered to stop by. "Worst goddamn thing I ever saw, Sam," he said, tearing off his gloves to warm his hands, eyeing an empty coffee cup on a peg above our washtub, although he didn't ask for coffee right then.

"What was that, Babs?" Sam asked, moving away from the stove since heat would worsen Babs' smell.

"Them settlers up yonder," he said, like we should know what he was talking about.

I remembered that sometimes Babs scouted for the army. He knew parts of the Territory like the back of his hand from years driving cow herds up cattle trails to Kansas.

"You saw 'em?" Sam asked, keeping more than a polite space between himself and our visitor.

"Sure did. It was colder'n a well-digger's ass by the time we got there. Them bodies was froze stiff, what wasn't et up by wolves an' coyotes. Eleven of 'em, scalped an' gutted with their intestines scattered all over the place like busted ropes. Worst sight a man ever cared to see. The men had their peckers cut off an' stuffed in their mouths like they was eatin' sausages afore they died." He eyed the cup again. "Mind if I had me a little squirt of that sweet-smellin' Arbuckles?"

"Tell me about the women and children," Sam said, nodding to me that I should pour a cup for Babs.

Babs scowled, like he was trying to remember. "There was at least four womenfolk, best I recall. They was sliced open same as them others. How come you to ask, Sam?"

"Were the women scalped?" Sam ignored Babs' question, asking for the details he wanted.

"Sure was. There was this one real cute little blond gal, I remember. What was left of her scalp that wasn't bloody was real light blond. They cut her teats off, too. There was so goddamn much blood on the ground it looked like it'd rained red raindrops all over the place. Wasn't hardly a patch of ground nowhere in sight that wasn't covered with blood."

While I was pouring coffee for Babs I blanched a little at the thought of the scene he described. A girl with her teats cut off was a bit much to contemplate before my breakfast. . . . I handed Babs the cup and shook my head.

"It don't figure," Sam remarked, watching Babs take a pint of whiskey from an inside pocket of his tattered wool mackinaw to add a splash to his coffee, even though it wasn't much past eight in the morning yet.

I knew what Sam was getting at, but Babs apparently didn't.

"What don't figure?" Babs asked, adding redeye to his cup in a generous amount. "Any fool could see it was the work of them goddamn northern Comanch', Sam. A blind man woulda knowed it was Comanch' who done it by the way them poor folks was cut up like a mess of catfish bait."

"Comanches wouldn't have scalped pretty young women. Even a bunch of young bucks drunk on Boisah Pah would've kept the young girls alive to use 'em in other ways." Sam made a face, like he suddenly caught a whiff of Babs' ripe smell when the stove began to warm him up. He moved closer to a front window. "It may have looked like something a Comanche would do, but my money says it was somebody else."

Babs seemed dumbfounded. "Who the hell'd be crazy enough to slaughter eleven settlers like that, take the time to cut 'em up so bad? You figurin' maybe it was Apaches that far north?"

"Hard to say," Sam replied, turning to that window like it helped him think. "But I'd nearly gamble a month's pay it wasn't Comanches who done it." He took a deep breath, and then I knew it was fresh air blowing through the cracks he wanted.

"You ain't makin' no sense," Babs declared, corking his pint and returning it to his pocket. He slurped whiskeyed coffee and let out a contented sigh. "If a white man wanted to steal all of their livestock or rob those folks, he'd shoot 'em down an' take what he was after. Apaches would scalp 'em, but they wouldn't be wastin' all that time cuttin' off them dead men's peckers or cut them bodies open so their entrails fell out. That's strictly the way a goddamn Comanch' leaves his enemies, so everybody knows it was the Comanch' who killed 'em. Hell, Sam, you know more about them damn Comanch' than any white man this side of creation. How come you got any doubts about it?"

"Because of the women. Comanche bucks value yellow-haired women almost as much as they do good horses. They wouldn't kill pretty young girls like that. They'd keep 'em, and that's the part that don't make any sense. Somebody wanted Comanches to get the blame for what happened up there. I'd nearly stake my life on it."

"But who?" I asked before Babs could ask the same question.

"I haven't got that part figured out yet." Sam turned away from the window to Babs—I could have sworn he wrinkled his nose. "Who buried those settlers?"

Babs aimed a thumb at himself. "We did. Ground was damn near froze, but we got shallow holes dug. I was scoutin' the way fer a train of empty supply wagons down from Dodge City. We'd no more'n crossed the South Canadian when we found 'em. We sent a rider to the telegraph office at Elk whilst the rest of us dug them holes. Nobody knew there was a settlement at Antelope Hill until we found what was left of it. Wired Major Donaldson about it, an' we passed the patrol he sent on our way back here."

"How long has it been since you found the bodies?" Sam asked offhandedly, still keeping his distance from our guest.

Babs rolled up his eyes. "Five, make it six days now. We wasn't but a few days ahead of this big storm that's headed our way."

Sam emptied his coffee cup. "Too long," he remarked. "Too long for any sign to be there in all this wind." He gave me one lone shrug and faced the window again. "The army won't find out anything, that's for sure. They don't know what to look for, and if they did, they'd never find it."

"The ground was too hard an' too dry for tracks," Babs said with authority. "I looked all 'round an' didn't see much, 'cept fer where they drove off all the livestock, a few cow tracks an' a handful of shod horses an' mules."

Sam grunted, although he didn't bother to turn around when he remarked, "There's more proof it wasn't Comanches. The very first thing a Comanche does is pull the iron off stolen horses because they know a shoe makes 'em a hell of a lot easier for a white man to track. Everything you've told me convinces me that raid wasn't done by Comanches."

Babs seemed perplexed, and so was I. "Who the heck would go to all that trouble making it look like Comanches?" I asked.

Sam's clear-blue eyes became thoughtful slits a moment. "I reckon somebody who wants trouble between Comanches and the white man, Mr. Dudley. Somebody who wants the army to push Bull Bear's bunch farther east, closer to this reservation. That could mean cattle ranchers who want the grazing or some investor who wants to build a town close to Antelope Hill. Blaming the Kotsotekas for slaughtering eleven white settlers would bring the army down on Bull Bear—start another big war between soldiers an' northern Comanches. General Crook hears about this, an' he'll order a big sweep up yonder to drive the Kotsotekas out. Somebody wants that land free of Indians, and this is one way to get it done."

Babs looked doubtful. "I've seen more'n my fair share when it comes to Comanch' killings. Those folks was gutted like they was hogs at butcherin' time, same way Buffalo Hump's Kwahadies do white men over in the Texas panhandle. I've traveled all over the Caprock, an' I've seen jus' about every kind of torture there is done to a white man by the Comanch'. For my money, I say it was northern Comanch' who cut those folks to pieces. I don't lay no claim to knowin' as much about the red bastards as you do, Sam Ault; but if you'd been there, you'd have swore it was Comanch' who wiped out those sodbusters."

Sam sighed without taking his eyes from the window. "That's what somebody wanted you to think."

I recalled those cowboys from the Goodnight Ranch that Quannah Parker tortured and killed down at Palo Duro. They were staked out on the prairie with their eyelids cut off and their bellies sliced open, left alive to suffer unimaginable pain until loss of blood claimed them. But Quannah had spared the little white girl we were looking for, even though she had suffered unspeakable acts at the hands of several young Kwahadie warriors. When we finally arranged a trade for her, she was pregnant—only fourteen years old and showing signs of having been beaten and starved. The Kwahadies kept a leather collar around her neck afixed to a rope like she was a stray dog. "What Sam says is true," I said with the memory of the Grumann girl fresh in my mind. "They do think a lot of young white women, insofar as they don't seem to want to kill them. I can't say all that much for the treatment they give white-women captives, but they leave them alive—so they can use them."

Babs slurped down more of his drink. "Four of them we did find was women," he remembered. "Cut to ribbons, same as the men we found. I still say only a goddamn Comanch' is bloodthirsty enough to carve up bodies like that. There ain't no other race of people on this earth who git more pleasure out of whittlin' on human flesh. Makes a man's belly churn to see how they use a knife. . . ."

I had to agree. I still dreamed about finding those men on the prairie the next morning down in Palo Duro, after listening to them scream all night. Quannah's warriors hooted and called to each other until just before dawn imitating coyotes. Sam was the one who told me it wasn't coyotes we were hearing. A coyote barks four times and then it howls. Comanches signal each other with five barks before they howl, telling the others where they are in the dark.

"Comanches didn't invent cutting up their victims," Sam said quietly, looking out our window at the building storm. "Learned it from Mexican scalp hunters a long time ago. The government in Mexico City was offerin' gold for Indian scalps to help clear out tribes claimin' land Mexico wanted. Old Chief Nocona told me it was Mexicans who showed Comanches how they treated enemies, so it didn't take the Comanches long to return the favor. Only Comanches did 'em one better—they started leavin' victims alive after they cut them up, so they died real slow."

Babs drained his cup and smacked his lips. His teeth were yellow from tobacco use and one at the front was broken off. He hooked his thumb in a worn cartridge belt around his waist with an old Mason Colt .44 hanging from it. "I'll agree Meskins are inclined to use knives a lot, Sam, but there ain't no Meskins to speak of up here in Injun Territory, so I'm stickin' with my idea that it was Comanch' who killed them folks up yonder. Too cold in these parts fer a Meskin. Meskins like hot weather." He did a quarter turn and tossed his cup in our washtub. "Much obliged fer the Arbuckles, boys. Time I got back on that hoss an' made the ride out to see Major Donaldson. Army owes me money fer some work I done in the spring, an' I aim to collect it today so I got enough money to see me through 'til it thaws. I'll tell him what you said, 'bout it not bein' Comanch' up at Antelope Hill. He'll most likely have his doubts, too, same as me." Babs buttoned his coat and put on his gloves, tugging a badly sweat-stained Stetson down close to his ears. "Be seein' you next spring," he said, as he made for the door, boots clumping hollowly across floorboards when he went out into a mighty blast of cold wind.

Sam watched Babs through the windowpane while he mounted his red roan gelding. "Some things have a natural bad odor, Leon," he said as soon as Babs reined away from the building. "A skunk has got an excuse for the way he smells because the Almighty saw fit to make him that way. But a man don't come naturally with a foul smell—he has to work at it. If it wasn't so damn cold, I'd open that door so this place could air out some."

"Some gents don't take to bathing real regular," I agreed. The wind carried the sound of Babs' horse moving away. I thought back to what Sam said about the massacre at Antelope Hill. "Who could have killed those settlers to make it look like Indians?"

"I've been wonderin' myself," Sam replied, carrying his cup over to the stove now that Babs wasn't in the vicinity.

"Only way to find out is to ride up there, I reckon. We sure as hell ain't gonna solve no puzzles sittin' around here."

"It's so cold," I protested, thinking about making a ride in this weather. "By the look of those clouds, it'll be snowing here by dark. We'll freeze."

Sam cast a meaningful glance my way. "It's our job to look into it."

"But the army sent a patrol up there . . ."

"Same as sendin' a fox to watch chickens, Mr. Dudley. They won't find a thing and they'll make a mess of the ground so there won't be a track left no place. If we got there before it came a big snow, we might find the direction those tracks went."

I sensed there was no talking Sam out of the notion that we ought to go. He was getting a dose of wanderlust after being around the office for a few days. I hung my head, considering what it would be like to ride straight into a freezing north wind for more than a hundred tough miles through rugged country. We were sure to suffer. I'd need to pack my spare longjohns and all the socks I owned, my wool greatcoat. That room I rented at the back of Miller's General Store would be darn near empty if I took everything I needed. "It sounds like you've made up your mind," I said, listening to wind howl outside.

"You don't sound all that keen on it," Sam observed dryly. "I've got a notion it has to do with that freckle-faced girl of Dave Miller's."

"That isn't it," I said quickly, too quickly perhaps. "I don't give a hoot about Bonnie Sue. Not in that way I don't."

Sam mocked me with a stare. "A young man has got urges. I was young once, an' that's the reason I'm livin' in misery with a woman who complains from sunup 'til I go to sleep. If you've got a lick of sense, you'll close your mind to women entirely. It may be hard while you're younger, but you'll enjoy peace in your old age, unlike some of us."

"I'd never marry Bonnie Sue."

Sam made a sour face. "I said the same thing once about a woman named Clara Higgins, but I was weak when it came to sins of the flesh. In the Garden of Eden, everything was quiet an' mighty peaceful until Eve showed up. It was Eve who told Adam about the apples, how sweet they tasted. One bite of that apple, an' poor ol' Adam got tossed out of Eden forever. All on account of how a woman beguiled him with her charms. Clara is a direct descendant of Eve, Mr. Dudley, and so is Bonnie Sue Miller. Clara makes me apple pies all the time."

I figured I'd better not say that Bonnie Sue made me apple pies. Sam already had all the ammunition he needed. "Clara makes real good pies," I said, my mouth watering when I recalled the last pie Clara baked for the two of us. "It was peach pie, if I remember right."

"Every now an' then she runs out of dried apples," Sam told me, sounding disgusted. He cast an eye to the front window. "I reckon we oughta go up on the South Canadian to have a look-see at Antelope Hill for ourselves. Only way we'll ever know who killed those settlers. I'll ride home an' pack a few things. Lock up the office and meet me there. Remember to dress warm, an' bring plenty of extra cartridges for our rifles, just in case we find ourselves in a tight spot."

I could almost guarantee we'd find ourselves in a tight spot before we got back to Cache. "I'll have Mr. Miller sack up some corn for our horses and enough staples to last us two weeks."

Sam nodded, downing his coffee. "Bring our pack mule an' that tent, so we'll have a windbreak. Don't forget to remind Dave to put some whiskey in with our food. Whiskey takes a chill out of a stiff wind."

I hated the taste of the stuff, but I nodded my head in quiet agreement. I was shivering just thinking about riding into that storm.

"We'll stop by the fort an' find out what Major Donaldson knows about it," Sam said. "Not that he'll know anything might be a help to us." He buttoned his coat and took his Winchester from the wall rack. "Don't forget those extra shells," he said on his way to the door.

I gave our potbelly stove a longing look before I started over to Miller's store. It would be awhile before I enjoyed the comfort of a warm room again, even a room with big cracks in the walls.

As though it needed to remind me of the weather, a rush of chilly wind whistled under the front door. I shivered and fastened the front of my coat.

Three

Bonnie Sue Miller might have been called pretty if it hadn't been for so many freckles. She had red hair like her father and her mother's green eyes. When I told her that Sam and I were on the way north to Antelope Hill, she insisted on frying me up some eggs and bacon before I left so I'd have a bellyful of warm food for the first part of our ride. Bonnie Sue was just eighteen, and that's a bit on the young side for me. I was twenty-three back in the summer. After two whole years being Sam's deputy, I felt a lot older than twenty-three. The western end of Indian Territory ages a man faster than what he's accustomed to and Sam makes a habit of putting his deputies to the test on a regular basis, so there's hardly any time to age slow.

"How long will you be gone, Leon?" Bonnie asked, stirring my bacon in a skillet atop her ma's wood stove.

We were alone in their kitchen off the back of the store so we were able to talk without anybody listening. "A couple of weeks, I guess. That's up to Marshal Ault, and our circumstances."

"Will it be dangerous?"

She was beginning to sound more and more like Clara, like a wife. "It's always dangerous in the Territory, but we know how to handle ourselves. Don't worry yourself none."

She looked over her shoulder. "I will worry some."

"You shouldn't."

"It'll be cold as the dickens. You could catch your death."

"I'll dress real warm. Stop fussing over me."

She went back to her frying pan. She was wearing a pair of men's denim pants that were a bit too tight, showing off some of her curves, and a green-flannel work shirt. Bonnie Sue wore her hair in pigtails most of the time, which made her look like she was much younger. But she had one feature that erased any doubts about her age, an oversized bosom like her mother's that made me stare too often. When cowboys or soldiers came in the store, they peeked at her bosom when she was where she wouldn't notice. Men stared at her ma's chest when Dave wasn't looking. Alice Miller was still a pretty woman. Bonnie Sue would be real pretty if she could have washed off all those big red freckles. I'd kissed her once, back in the summer. It was a real dark night, and I'd been out for a walk underneath the stars when I saw Bonnie Sue fetching water from their well behind the store. I sauntered over real casual-like and struck up a conversation. One thing led to another, and before I knowed it, I bent down and gave her a kiss. She didn't act flustered and she even asked me to do it again. I hadn't really wanted to, but I did, maybe because it was so dark I didn't notice all her freckles so much. Remembering how she beguiled me that night, I thought about what Sam said happened to Adam in the Garden of Eden one time, how Eve told Adam he should taste those sweet forbidden apples that got him tossed right out of the garden on his ear.

"I can worry if I want to," she said, teasing me, giving me a playful smile.

I didn't like the way she was trying to work me, telling me that she could worry when she wanted. Could Sam be right that Bonnie Sue was a direct descendant of Eve? "I hope you didn't bake any apple pies yesterday," I said matter-of-factly, like I was talking to myself.

"It just so happens I did. I baked two pies. One is wild plum; the other is apple."

"Don't feed me any apples today."

Bonnie Sue turned at the waist so she could see me. "You always did like apple best. What's wrong with apple pie?"

I didn't want to have to explain it. "I just ain't in the mood for apples, that's all. Wild plum is practically my favorite kind anyway."

I gazed out her kitchen window. Wind was blowing so hard it bent the tops of red oaks behind the store. Off to the north I saw that bank of clouds getting darker. And closer. "It could snow before sundown," I told her, passing time. "We'll be riding directly into a north wind for three or four days. I'll be lucky not to get frostbit on the end of my nose." I tasted hot coffee sweetened with a lump of brown sugar she had poured me in a china cup while I waited for my eggs. "Marshal Ault got this itch to take a look at that settlement at Antelope Hill. He don't think it was Comanches who killed those folks."

Bonnie Sue put my eggs and bacon on a plate like she hadn't been listening. When she carried it over to the table, she was wearing a great big smile. "I'll cut you a slice of plum pie for dessert."

I picked up my fork and didn't look at her. "Just make sure it ain't apple. To tell the truth I'm sick and tired of apples lately."

She let me eat in silence, but she was watching me and that made me a little uncomfortable. I cleaned my plate and took the piece of plum pie she offered. "It's mighty good," I told her as I shoveled the last bite in my mouth. "Better'n apple pie, for sure."

She came around the table as I was standing up. "I'd better see if your pa has our supplies ready," I said. I noticed she had a different look in her eye.

I was about to leave when she put her arms around my neck so I couldn't. I felt my cheeks turn hot.

"Nobody'll see if you kiss me," she whispered.

"C'mon, Bonnie Sue. I ain't exactly in a kissing mood, what with facing a hard ride into freezing cold wind. Besides

that, we hadn't oughta do it in broad daylight. Your ma might
walk in on us."

"Ma wouldn't care. She told me she likes you."

"Your pa wouldn't like it, I'm nearly sure. . . ."

She stood on her tiptoes and kissed me anyway, before I
was able to think. She planted her lips on my mouth and left
them there, tightening her arms around my neck so I couldn't
back off like I wanted.

I finally put my arms around her waist and kissed her back
so she wouldn't get her feelings hurt. The whole time I knew
my face was red as beet juice. When she let go of me, I
nearly ran out of the kitchen to see about our supplies, thinking how right Sam was to say that Bonnie Sue Miller was
close kin to the woman who fed Adam those apples up in
Eden.

Our old brown mule was a kicker, mean as dirt to put a
pack saddle on when it came to the britching harness, but
he was as good a trail mule as any I'd ever handled otherwise.
Sam named him Moses because he was getting a little long
in the tooth, a twelve-year-old. As mules go, Moses had a
calm disposition if you stayed clear of his back legs. He led
without setting back on the halter rope and he could hold a
steady trot all day if he got plenty of grass and water. Leading
Moses out to Sam's house at Fort Sill, I pondered how close
I'd come to getting my skull broke when I forgot and walked
behind him to fasten the britching. To that mule's credit, he
warned me by flattening his ears just before he swung his
right-rear hoof, giving me just enough time to dodge out of
the way before I would have gotten my skullbone or my left
knee crushed. It paid to be careful around a mule all the
time, a fact I knew from having grown up in the Mississippi
Delta where we plowed cotton fields with teams of mules.
More than one old-timer around Possumbelly Flats had a

dent in his head or in his ribs from forgetting to honor a mule's hind end while hitching up the harness.

Sam's house sat just to the west of Fort Sill behind a low hill covered with oak trees. I rode down the lane with my coat collar turned up. My hands were already freezing in spite of my gloves. Smoke curled from Sam's chimney, bending sharply in the wind. Now I had an idea just how miserable we would be when we headed north to Antelope Hill. Making sure of things I knew Sam would investigate, I checked the diamond hitch tied over our camping gear and supplies on the mule's back. The rope was in place where it oughta be. I had five extra boxes of Winchester .44 cartridges in my saddlebags, enough to fight a war if that's what we found ourselves in on the South Canadian. I had this bad feeling down in my gut that a war was what we were headed for up north. Whoever slaughtered and butchered those settlers meant business. We weren't likely to just ride up there and have an easy time finding out who did it.

I tied off my bay and the mule to a porch post and climbed the steps, checking my boots to make sure they were clean before I knocked. Clara kept a neat house, floors mopped and swept 'til they had a shine. Sam complained all the time about her mopping and sweeping, I remembered.

As soon as I knocked, the door came open. Sam had impatience on his face.

"Took you long enough," he grumbled. "I reckon it was that Miller girl's doing."

He showed me inside when I didn't say anything. "Clara's got a fresh apple pie just out of the oven," he said, with a tone in his voice that said I should have expected to have apples at his house. "She wanted you to have a piece before we leave."

I noticed he said it real softly. "I had this big slice of wild plum pie at Bonnie Sue's," I told him quietly.

Sam looked over at me. "You'll eat some of Clara's pie

so I can leave here in peace, Mr. Dudley. Make room for it somehow."

I nodded and followed him to the kitchen, taking off my hat when I remembered my manners. Sam claimed that Clara took a real strong stance on proper manners in her house, making him take off his hat and clean his boots outside, besides never uttering even a single cussword under her roof if he wanted to sleep there—on account of cussing belonged down at the barn.

"Good morning, Leon," Clara said warmly, smiling as she took a saucer down from her cabinet to cut me a piece of pie. "You're just in time for warm apple pie with whipped cream. I took it out of the oven a little while ago."

"Apple's my all-time favorite," I said, glancing sideways at Sam when I said it. "And yours is the absolute best."

Clara smiled. For a tiny woman, less than five feet even when she was wearing shoes, she cast a long shadow when Sam was around; and I could tell by the way he hung back near the kitchen door things hadn't gone well when he told her we were leaving for the north. "You always say peach pie is your favorite, Leon," she said. "I suppose a man can have two favorites, just so long as they aren't women." She gave Sam a look and handed me a plate piled high with steaming apple pie covered in whipped cream. I was so full of Bonnie Sue's cooking that I nearly choked looking at that piece of pie, but I sat down at the table to eat it with Sam looking over my shoulder.

Clara brought me a cup of coffee. "There now," she said in a satisfied way. "A young man has to eat in order to grow."

I couldn't say that I'd be growing in the wrong direction if I ate much more pie. "It's delicious," I told her around a big mouthful.

She smiled. "I'll finish packing Sam's things." Her smile faded quickly when she looked at Sam. "Of all the fool notions, to set out on a trip in weather like this. Sometimes I wonder if my husband has taken leave of his senses." She left the kitchen for their bedroom.

"Women," Sam muttered unhappily. "Now Clara's taken to the idea she can forecast weather. She says this will be the worst blizzard we've had in ten years, all because our milk cow put on an early coat of winter hair."

"I sure hope she's wrong," I said, staring helplessly at the rest of my pie. I worried my belly would burst if I ate one more bite, yet I knew I had to finish it. I dug in with my spoon and prayed for a miracle.

"She'd never admit it," Sam whispered hoarsely, with a trace of bitterness. "She has never admitted to bein' wrong in almost twenty years."

We heard Clara's footsteps. She came into the kitchen with Sam's warbag and a pair of red mittens. She dropped his bag on the floor. "I knitted these for you this fall," she said, as she offered Sam her mittens. "They'll come in handy with this awful blizzard coming."

Sam eyed those mittens like he'd seen a rattler. "I can't wear something like that!" he exclaimed.

Clara stood a little taller with a stern look in her eyes. "And pray tell why not?"

Sam lost some of his color. "Because folks would laugh at me. A full-growed man don't wear no red mittens. Besides that, I couldn't use my guns because there's no place for my damn trigger finger!"

"I will not tolerate profanity in this house, Samuel David Ault!" she snapped.

They glared at each other a moment until Sam meekly bowed his head.

"Give me the mittens," he said quietly. "I'll wear 'em when nobody's lookin'."

Major Harold Donaldson didn't appear to be all that happy to see us when a soldier showed us into his office. He looked up at us over his wire-rimmed spectacles and pursed his lips. "Good to see you, gentlemen," he said, and by the sound of it not meaning a word. There was occasional conflict between the army and U.S. Marshals over who had jurisdiction in the Territory. Sam made it quite clear from the beginning he aimed to do his job any way he saw fit without regard for the army's wishes.

We shook hands with Major Donaldson and took chairs opposite his desk. It was warm in the room. I noticed that mud chinked its walls in places where cracks would have been. A fire crackled in the fireplace.

"We're headed up to Antelope Hill," Sam began. "I talked to Babs Woodley about what they found up there. From what he told me, I don't think it was Comanches who killed those folks. Me and my deputy aim to take a look around. Before we left I thought I'd find out what you knew about it . . . if you'd heard any more."

"No word yet from Captain Ross, but it's utter nonsense to make the statement that Comanches didn't do it. Didn't Woodley tell you how badly the bodies were mutilated?"

"That's one reason I don't think it was Comanches. He told me four women were cut up and scalped. Comanches keep women they take from their enemies. Women have value, like money or a good horse. They wouldn't kill women any more than you would set fire to money the army pays you. Babs said one of the women was young and pretty, what was left of her. A Comanche would keep a woman like that. Last thing he'd do is gut an' scalp her."

Major Donaldson straightened in his chair. "Come now, Sam. I've seen women killed by Comanches before. If you'll remember, the entire Baker clan was wiped out by Quannah's bunch over at Buffalo Gap three years ago."

"I remember it," Sam agreed. "Two of the women were found dead with rifles in their hands, but they died when their cabin burned down with them inside. Comanches don't fight women unless the women are warriors themselves. If a woman fights, she becomes a warrior in their eyes. Some Comanche women are warriors. They undergo the same training as a young Comanche boy, an' I can tell you from experience they make one hell of a bad enemy to have to fight."

The major didn't put much stock in what Sam told him, and I could tell by the look on his face. "It would be pointless for me to argue the matter with you," he said. "You've already made up your mind. I still say the raiders were Comanches and that's what I'll put in my report to General Crook. Unless Captain Ross convinces me otherwise."

"If you send a report like that to Crook, he'll order a big military campaign against Bull Bear's Kotsotekas," Sam declared tonelessly. "Bull Bear's people are probably innocent. If you hold off sending your report to General Crook, I may be able to find out who's responsible."

Major Donaldson gave Sam a mirthless grin. "I am already satisfied as to who is responsible, Marshal. As soon as Captain Ross gets back, I'm sending my conclusions to my superior officer. By the way, the citizens up at Elk are arming themselves for more conflicts with Comanche raiders. I instructed Captain Ross to give them whatever assistance he could fortifying the settlement in the event those Indians show up again. I fully expect to hear of more raids by Comanche renegades. Less than half the Comanches are honoring the treaty we made with them. They won't stay on this reservation like they agreed they would. Some are always running off to start trouble somewhere."

Sam looked down at his boots a moment. "Maybe they're only gettin' hungry, Major. If you had to eat the kind of shit this army gives 'em, you'd run off, too. A starvin' man is a hell of a lot more likely to cause problems."

Major Donaldson spread his palms in a helpless gesture, only I knew he didn't really have much sympathy for his Indian charges here at the fort. "I give them what the quartermaster sends me," he remarked. "It's not my fault if some of it gets spoiled from time to time."

Sam got up and I followed him out of my chair.

"Wish you'd hold off on that report to Crook," Sam asked for the second time, then he wheeled away from Donaldson's desk with his mouth set in a grim line.

Four

A cold gray rain began from the northwest driven by gales of chill wind. Those first few raindrops stung our cheeks like ice. I delved into my warbag for my slicker and Sam did likewise as we tilted our hat brims to keep rain from our eyes while we sleeved into our oilskins. Our horses lowered their heads with ears flat against their necks. My bay plodded forward, but Moses pulled back a little on the halter rope, as if to say he wanted no part of traveling into this storm. I got my slicker fastened and took a look at the horizon. Blue-black clouds boiled above low hills in front of us. Farther north lay the Wichita Mountains, peaks shrouded with storm clouds. We followed a seldom-traveled road to Elk across open range through some of the emptiest country in the Territory. Elk was roughly sixty miles to the northwest as a crow flies, but the road climbed and twisted through the Wichita range, requiring at least two days of hard riding. Antelope Hill was in a bend near the south fork of the Canadian River, two more difficult days in the saddle. I knew we'd be real lucky to make those foothills below the Wichitas by dark today, and by then rain could turn to snow and sleet. Snow is a sight more tolerable than rain for a man aboard a horse. I was looking forward to seeing raindrops turn to snowflakes.

We crested a hilltop where the road made a bend westward in a forest of post oaks. Leaves dropped from trees with every big gust of wind, swirling, becoming whirling dervishes full of fall colors: bright reds and yellows, every shade of brown. As it was the first winter storm, trees were shedding quickly, but with rain drenching those leaves they fell soddenly to earth when the drops came down harder and thicker. Pretty soon my hat was soaked and the brim drooped low to form a spout in front of my face and down my back. Just as I predicted, we were miserable traveling into a fast-moving storm, but Sam would never have admitted he was just as miserable as me since it was his idea to ride in it.

Where trees were thickest on either side of the two-rut road we got out of the wind a little, enough so Sam could talk in his regular voice without shouting to make himself heard.

"It ain't too far from being cold enough to freeze. If this turns to sleet, we best start lookin' for a place out of the wind to pitch our tent. We'll wait for the ice to turn to snow before we strike this trail again. It don't make much sense to use our animals so hard. If we can keep movin', there's the tradin' post at Beaver Falls where we can get dry for a short spell. These horses will need the rest."

I felt like saying he didn't mind the hard use of his deputy right then, but I wisely kept my mouth shut. Even when Sam was wrong, he didn't like to be reminded of it. We rode around that bend and met a blast of wind-driven rain worse than anything we'd encountered so far. I tipped my hat into it and let the bay find its own way, with me riding blind as a bat.

Indian Territory can be a brutal place for more reasons than just its weather. Since the western part was supposed to be land set aside for Kiowas and Comanches by the Medicine Lodge Treaty, it had more than its share of troubles. The eastern part was put back for more peaceful tribes like Cherokees, Chickasaws, and a few smaller bunches. But the western half, what we were in now, contained the most warlike Indians on earth, parts of the five Comanche bands, and plenty of hostile Kiowas. A Kiowa chief by the name of Ten Bears agreed to a peace treaty in exchange for a big hunk of the western half of the Territory. The army policed Indian matters and kept an eye on the reservations. Trouble was, there weren't enough soldiers to go around and because the land was empty, law-breakers from other states and territories made it a gathering place. Thus, we had all manner of tough characters in our jurisdiction—cattle and horse thieves, robbers and killers, be-sides a collection of undesirable types who made a dishonest living off trading with the Indians themselves. It was a good bet that when we spotted men we didn't know in open country, a Wanted circular was out on them some place or another. Not that there weren't a few honest men crossing this region, but it was my experience they were in the minority. I'd made a practice of keeping my gun handy whenever we saw strangers. I carried a .44 Colt revolver and a Winchester rifle, both cham-bered for the same ammunition, a trick I learned from Sam real early in our association. Sam explained that when a man is in a hurry to reload his guns there isn't time to make a leisurely selection of the proper caliber.

To be honest, I still wasn't much shakes when it came to the use of a pistol. I could draw reasonable fast and hit what I was aiming at most of the time. But when a rifle was needed, I didn't have to take a back seat to nobody. I grew up shooting squirrels with a rifle out of treetops in a Mis-sissippi riverbottom. Even Sam, who was mighty reluctant to hand out compliments, said I was one of the best shots with a long gun he had ever seen. Since I came to work for Sam, I'd had to prove my marksmanship a number of times. Deep inside, I still regretted having to shoot so many men even if it was in the line of duty. I'd killed more than ten Indians and three white men. I didn't count the ones I wounded in pitched battles we fought with Kiowa renegades, or that time down in Texas when we tangled with Quannah's band. I was never cut out to be a mankiller; however, some-times it was a necessity that came with my job as a deputy marshal. The western district we were assigned to was full to the brim of hard cases and wild Indians who sometimes needed a reminder that me and Sam knew how to shoot.

We rode down a steep grade following ruts that were ankle deep in rivers of mud, making footing treacherous for our mule and the horses. Sam's big black gelding didn't cotton much to any bad weather, and there were times when his horse refused a request to cross a swollen stream or swim a river. My bay was a decent river horse and Moses would swim when it was forced upon him, yet Sam was fond of his black despite its faults and he was real knowledgeable when it came to horseflesh.

When we reached the bottom of the hill, I raised my hat brim just enough to see what lay in store for us. Across a windy flat, more tree-studded hills awaited our arrival. Sheets of rain fell before my eyes, making for a mighty sorry sight to a traveler who was nearly frozen to death. I judged the temperature wasn't much above freezing by now. Every once in a while, a big chunk of ice struck my slicker or my hat, and the sound made me wince a little.

"It's getting colder!" I cried above the hiss of rain and wind blowing through treetops around us.

"Don't take many brains to figure that one out, Mr. Dudley. A man whose ass is froze to his horse knows it's real cold. If I didn't have any more'n that to say, I wouldn't waste my breath. I already knew it was gettin' a mite chilly."

Sam's mood had turned as foul as this weather. I hunkered down inside my oilskin and kept quiet while we rode across a mud flat to the next stand of trees, vowing not to say another word to Sam until springtime, not unless he spoke first.

A dark sky made it impossible to guess time and I wouldn't risk getting my new pocket watch wet to look at it in the rain. I'd bought myself a watch down in Fort Worth as a birthday gift to me. Sam and Clara gave me a barlow knife, which surprised me since I hadn't expected anything from anybody. What family I had was scattered, a brother in Alabama who didn't answer any letters I sent and a married sister in Illinois who hardly ever wrote back. My folks were dead, my pa from a drowning while he crossed a rain-swollen river on a mule, my ma from grief shortly after pa died. So when Sam and Clara gave me that pocketknife it was like they were family. Clara baked me a cake with burnt sugar frosting, just about the best cake I ever had. And I owned a pocket watch now, only I feared getting it wet if I took it out in this downpour, thus I could only judge it was late in the afternoon. We were still miles from the trading post at Beaver Falls, if I remembered this country correctly. Besides, I had a feeling we'd find ourselves unwelcome there. Beaver Falls was often a hangout for men of low breeding and an occasional man on the run from the law someplace else. It had a saloon, which is known to attract undesirable types from time to time. What with the weather being so bad, I figured we could wager on finding just about every no-account owl-hoot there who happened to be in riding distance of whiskey and a place with a roof and a stove. Wearing our badges, we'd be as welcome as two skunks showed up at a barn dance.

After more than an hour of hard riding pelted by raindrops the size of goose eggs, we crossed a ridge above Beaver Creek that I recognized. Down below, in a winding valley obscured by a wall of gray rain, I could see the outline of a log building sitting on the creek bank. A shed out back was crowded with horses and mules, which was my prediction all along. The saloon would be full of visitors coming in from the storm.

"Looks like a busy place," Sam observed, guiding his black down a slippery slope where the road took us to Beaver Falls. "I imagine it's that drinking parlor. I reckon I can use a drink or two myself to take the chill out of my bones."

I hadn't said a word for the last hour; but now that Sam had spoken his mind, I said, "They won't be any too glad to see a pair of lawmen, if I'm any judge of the characters we'll find inside. We'll need to watch our backsides real close."

Sam's expression was hidden by his water-soaked hat brim. "I never go anyplace where I don't keep an eye on what's behind me," he remarked, like I should have known this. "If you aim to stay alive with a badge pinned to your shirt, you'll do the same. Only a tinhorn would do otherwise."

Our horses slogged into the valley at a jog trot, sensing fodder and shelter from the rain down below. Somewhere near the log building a dog began to bark at our arrival, warning whoever was inside that strangers were coming. I started counting mules and horses in corrals behind the trading post, reaching a figure of more than twenty. I was sure there would be some among the owners of those animals who wouldn't take kindly to a visit by a pair of U.S. Marshals.

We rode up to an empty hitchrail in front of the place and swung down without being greeted by anyone from inside, although I kept a sharp eye on the front door just in case some gent came out with a gun. As soon as I'd tied off my horse and the mule, I opened my slicker so I could reach my pistol in a hurry if a need arose. I saw Sam climb a set of sagging steps to a covered porch running across the front of the place. I fell in behind him and got set for trouble the minute we went through the front door. Our boots sounded heavily on those porch planks, announcing us in much the same way as the barking dog was. It was then I noticed someone peeking through a curtain covering a window next to the door.

"Somebody just spotted us," I said, aiming my thumb at the parted curtain. "If they recognize either one of us, we could be in for a gunpowder howdy-do, should some be wrong-minded men in there."

Sam saw the curtain move yet he continued to walk up to the door without slowing strides. He opened his slicker and swept it back so it rested behind the butt of his Colt. "This ain't no occupation for a fearful man, Leon," he muttered, reaching for a latch string dangling through a hole in weathered planks covering the entrance.

I was about to say I wasn't afraid, just being cautious, but right about then we heard a commotion coming from behind the building. Somebody shouted, "Run fer them hosses!" Sam wheeled when he heard a voice.

I took off in a run for the end of the porch while clawing my pistol free of leather. I got to a corner of the trading post just as three men made a dash for pole corrals off the back. In driving rain it was impossible to see who they were; however, the fact they were running from the arrival of U.S. Marshals was all the proof I needed that we had to stop them from riding off.

I cocked my .44 and fired over their heads in the same split second they made the wall of a shed covering the north side of a corral. The explosion from my gun got trapped under the roof of the porch, doubling the sound of it, making my ears ring. "Hold it there, boys!" I cried.

They were out of sight by the time Sam got there. His gun was drawn. He peered around the corner real careful, and then he gave me one of his looks.

"Who the hell were you shootin' at?" he demanded.

"Three gents ran to that shed yonder trying to get away."

"Why'd you shoot? Were they carryin' guns?"

"I couldn't really tell. It was raining too hard. I fired over their heads, but they kept on running. . . ." I heard the front door swing open on squeaky hinges. A man came out cradling this big double-barreled shotgun, and I had to choose between turning my pistol on him or covering the shed where the three men were in hiding.

Sam squared himself in front of the gent carrying a scatter gun. But instead of raising his Colt, he aimed a finger. "Put that shotgun down, Billy, or I'll be forced to ram it up your ass sideways," Sam growled.

My heart was hammering and my mouth was dry. The next move was up to this bearded owlhoot carrying a shotgun—I'd heard Sam call him Billy.

A tense moment passed. Billy made no effort to lower those twin shotgun barrels aimed at us. He stared at Sam with a dull-eyed expression. I could smell stale whiskey.

Billy was drunk, making for a dangerous mix with his finger resting on triggers that could send loads of buckshot at close range, cutting both me and Sam to ribbons.

Five

"You got no call to come ridin' up to a place shootin' at my friends like that," Billy snarled, little drops of spittle flying from his lips when he said it, sounding drunk, slurring his words a bit. He showed no inclination to lower his shotgun.

"If you don't get that damn gun out of my face, I'll have to bust your skull, Billy," Sam warned, taking a step closer like he wasn't afraid Billy would shoot him. Sam hadn't raised his Colt or shown any sign of being worried, coming straight at Billy with his gun dangling beside his leg. He towered over Billy by half a foot or more.

Billy saw Sam coming—he took a wobbly short step backward. I wanted to keep an eye on the shed out back, but not while some drunk was covering us with a twelve-gauge. I aimed my pistol at Billy and hoped for the best without glancing over my shoulder to see what was going on behind us at the corrals.

Cat-quick, Sam grabbed the barrels of Billy's shotgun with his empty hand, at the same time swinging his Colt in a looping arc that struck Billy's left cheek so hard it sent him spinning off the porch. I watched Billy sail through the air and land in watery mud flat on his face near our horses. My bay snorted and almost sat back on the reins.

Another commotion came from the corrals. Three mounted men galloped through an open gate behind the shed, leaning over their horses' necks, spurring hard to make a stand of oak and cedar on a sloping bank leading down to Beaver Creek.

"Those men are getting away!" I shouted, raising my .44 even though it was an impossible shot at this distance when my targets were almost obscured by a curtain of heavy rain.

"Let 'em go," Sam said.

I questioned Sam with a look before I spoke. "They took off like scalded tomcats when they saw us, Marshal. It's even money they're running from a warrant someplace. . . ."

"Let 'em run," Sam ordered, watching Billy lift his face out of a mud puddle. Blood ran from a gash across his cheek. "Damn near every son of a bitch in this Territory has broken the law a time or two. Until we find out who they are, there's no need to work ourselves into a sweat. When Billy gets done with his mud bath, I'll ask him who his friends were."

Lowering my revolver, I turned around to watch those riders push their horses across a flooded creek. Sometimes it didn't make much sense, the way Sam saw fit to enforce the law. I was convinced we were letting some dangerous men get a big jump on us. The way it was raining, their tracks would be washed out in half an hour or less.

"Get up, Billy," Sam said, balancing the shotgun in the palm of his left hand. "Next time I tell you to put down a gun, you'll be more inclined to cooperate. I've never asked a man twice to do anything. I hope you'll remember that."

Billy came slowly to his hands and knees in muddy ooze, his limbs shaking with effort. He spat a mouthful of blood. When he looked up at Sam, there was murder in his eyes.

"I shoulda killed you when I had the chance, Ault," he said, raindrops pelting his face helping to wash off some of the blood and mud clinging to his dark beard.

Sam took a deep breath. "Plenty of men have tried, Billy; and as you can see, I'm none the worse for it. Another thing you need to remember is that I'm a hard man to kill. If you happen to take the notion again, be quicker about it. Now tell me about your friends who just lit out of here. Who are they, an' why'd they take off in such a hurry?"

Billy rocked back on his haunches and touched the cut on his face gingerly with muddy fingertips. "I'm bleedin'," he said, a trickle of blood seeping from his lips when he spoke. His tongue worked the inside of his cheek briefly. "You knocked out one of my goddamn teeth!"

"I'll knock the rest of 'em out if you don't tell me who it was ran out the back door," Sam said evenly, inching a little closer to the edge of the porch where a sheet of rain washed down from a slanted roof. "You said they were friends of yours."

Billy's face became a mask of hatred. "Can't recall their names right off." He knelt in the downpour, glaring up at Sam, looking mighty silly resting on his knees out in such terrible bad weather.

Sam's face was changing color, turning red. "Maybe if I was to bend this scatter gun over your head it'll help you with your memory. If I don't hear you jabberin' some names real quick, I'm gonna be forced to smack you with these heavy gun barrels. Now don't make me do that, Billy. Your head's gonna hurt an' my arms will be plumb wore out from bashing on your empty skullbone. It makes a hell of a lot more sense to tell me those names. It'll be easier on both of us." As if to make his point with more clarity, Sam holstered his Colt and gripped that shotgun stock with both hands, wielding it like a giant club. Glancing up at a curtain of water cascading from the roof, he stepped off the porch, making a splash where his boots landed beside Billy.

"Don't hit me!" Billy cried, cringing, shielding his face with muddy hands.

I knew Sam was mad as hell to be standing out in the rain getting his feet wet. He raised the shotgun high over his head and made like he meant to swing it down.

"They's just three pore ol' cowboys who got in some trouble up in Kansas," Billy said, cowering away from those two ugly iron barrels poised above the top of his skull. He walled the whites of his eyes and swallowed real hard. "One goes by the name Tom Burke. Another's called Shorty, only I never did know his last name. The skinny feller is Bob Starnes. I swear I'm tellin' you the truth, Marshal. They didn't hardly do nothin' at all—it was trouble over a woman."

"What kind of trouble?" Water poured off Sam's hat and he was getting madder by the minute because of it.

"There was this whore by the name of Molly. All three of 'em held her down, on account of they drank up all their money. All they took was a buck-jump apiece, a free one. They lit out of Abilene headed this way an' got caught in the storm, until I heard horses an' looked out the window. I told 'em I saw a U.S. Marshal outside."

I watched Sam lower his club. He broke open the shotgun to pull both shells out, then he tossed it in the mud beside Billy and wagged his head, pocketing the loads. "I'll remember those names you gave me. If it turns out they're wanted for something else up in Kansas, I'll come lookin' for you, Billy; and when I find you, I swear I'll haul your lyin' ass to jail. I'm gonna be real unhappy if I learn your friends are wanted for cattle rustling."

I was still covering Billy with my .44 while Sam climbed to the porch again. Sam looked at me before he stomped mud off his boots. I judged he was mad as a nest of hornets so I thought I'd better explain. "I saw them running. I fired up in the air."

Sam glanced over his shoulder when he heard Billy getting to his feet. "Let's go inside," was all he said, reaching for the latch string again.

I holstered my pistol to follow Sam through the door wondering what he was so riled up about. When I'd seen those men race out the back door, my instincts told me they were running from us. I did what any lawman would be expected to do in a situation like that, only Sam found something wrong with the way I handled it. I knew one thing for sure—

at the first opportunity he would tell me in plain English what I'd done that didn't suit him.

We walked into a lamplit room smelling of stale cigar smoke and whiskey vapors. Off to the left more than a dozen men sat on empty shipping crates or makeshift benches against a wall of mud-chinked logs. A plank resting atop two big wood kegs served as a bar. The right side of the building held rows of shelves lined with trade goods and foodstuffs. I noticed right off that every man in the place watched us come in. An old man standing behind the bar nodded and spoke to Sam. I remembered him from some of our earlier visits as owner of the trading post, but right then I couldn't recall his name.

"Howdy, Marshal. Always glad to see you an' your deputy out this way," the bartender said.

Sam returned his greeting with a silent nod of his own, all the while examining faces scattered around us for men he recognized, men who might give us problems of the kind Billy presented the moment we got here. When he was satisfied, he said, "I never saw so many friendly folks in one place before, Roy. Damn near every customer you got is wearin' a great big smile. Ol' Billy Cooper sure acted happy to see us just now, runnin' outside with a shotgun like he'd been appointed to a committee in charge of makin' us feel welcome here."

The gent Sam called Roy picked up a rag to wipe off his bar with a careless swipe or two. "I'm real sorry 'bout that, Sam," he said. "Every now an' then Billy has a little too much whiskey for his own good, but he sure as hell ain't no official welcoming committee representin' Beaver Falls Trading Company. You're as welcome here as the president of these United States or the king of England would be. Same goes for your deputy. By way of an apology for what Billy done, I'll buy both of you a drink of my best whiskey, imported all the way from Kentucky. That oughta show how sorry I am for that little inconvenience outside caused by one of my drunk customers. Ain't no law against a feller who finds hisself drunk, is there, Sam?"

For reasons I didn't understand quite yet Sam hesitated to cross the room to take up Roy's offer. I examined some of those customers again, looking for men I might recognize from a Wanted-poster description. To a man they were hard characters, unwashed and unshaven, typical of the types we usually had problems with.

"No law against bein' drunk so long as he ain't an Indian," Sam replied, passing a second glance over mostly bearded faces staring back at us. "Knowin' you like I do, Roy Weeks, I'd take an oath on my own mother's grave you wouldn't sell no whiskey to any Indians."

Roy busied himself with his rag again. "You've got that right," he agreed quickly. "Only white men get served whiskey here." He knew Sam was being sarcastic about it, but there was nothing else he could say.

For a time we listened to rain drumming on the roof and log walls, until Sam was finished looking at Roy's patrons. "Pour us those free drinks you offered," Sam said. "If you got no objections, my deputy will put our animals in your barn out back until this storm lets up."

"You aim to stay that long?" Roy asked, noting that some of his customers appeared edgy about having marshals there. Not a word had been said by anyone else until now.

Before Sam could answer, two men dressed in greasy buckskins got up slowly from one of the benches. One with a matted brown beard adorning his chin spoke to Roy. "We'd better be movin' on, Mr. Weeks. Sounds like that rain won't never quit, an' we got a long ride ahead of us."

Sam held up his hand. "Before you boys leave, I need to ask everybody some questions. Eleven settlers were killed up on the Canadian a few days back. They were scalped an' cut to pieces. I need to know if any of you have seen Indian activity lately, any big bunches of warriors, or Indian sign. Just to put all your worries to rest, that's why me an' my deputy are headed up this way. We intend to find out who killed those settlers if we can. Anything you might recall could be a help."

When the sound of Sam's deep voice ended, there was only the splatter of raindrops outside. Nobody was going to volunteer a scrap of information to lawmen, apparently.

Roy put two glasses on his bar, then he uncorked a bottle of whiskey and poured. "It's been real quiet 'round here, but we've heard there was trouble up north. Comanches on the prowl again, that's what I been hearin' from some trail hands comin' back from Abilene an' Dodge." He looked around the place. "Any of you see somethin' unusual these past couple of weeks?"

A few heads wagged. Others were still. The two men standing up made no comment at all, staring back at Sam and me with no friendliness.

Roy corked his bottle. "Like I told you, Marshal, it's been real quiet 'round here."

"So it would seem," Sam remarked, thumbing his hat back. "I reckon maybe it wasn't Indians, since nobody has seen any. Could be it was white men who scalped those folks, maybe to make it so everybody thinks it was Indians who done it."

The bearded gent who had spoken to Roy turned to Sam. "Why that's plumb crazy. Not even the sorriest white man this side of the Mississippi would stoop to scalpin' his own breed. No white man would ever do such a thing as that. Got no reason."

I could tell Sam's temper hadn't cooled down all that much when he said, "Are you callin' yourself an expert on sorry white men, mister? Because if you are, I'll challenge that statement with my own observations on the subject. When it comes to sorry white men, there's nothing too lowdown for some I've known who frequent this end of the Territory. They'd scalp their own race or anybody else, if there was a profit in it. The color of a man's skin has got mighty little to do with his nature; so unless you've got proof that Indians

killed those folks at Antelope Hill, I'll come to my own conclusions as to who took their scalps."

The man in buckskins was getting set to offer more argument on the side of white men when I heard a sound behind
us. Those squeaky front-door hinges let out a yelp and I went
diving into my holster for my gun. I had my Colt fisted and
aimed for the door when I saw who it was coming inside.
Billy Cooper, looking like a drowned rat soaked in mud,
slipped quietly into the room with his empty shotgun. He was
shivering something awful when he closed the door behind
him, until he noticed the muzzle of my .44 aimed for his belly.

"It's real cold out there," he explained, suddenly bending
down to put his shotgun on the floor so I wouldn't think he
had any intentions of using it.

I lowered my gun as soon as I saw how pitiful he looked,
all soaked to the skin like he was. "Just being on the safe
side," I said, putting my pistol away.

Somebody across the room chuckled. "You look worse'n
my Aunt Maude's sick pig, Billy."

Several men laughed. "C'mon over to this stove, Billy, so
you don't freeze up around your joints."

More laughter helped to ease some tension in Roy's saloon. Billy crept over to a potbelly in a corner of the place
and held his hands close to the fire while the laughter died
down. I saw Sam head over to the bar. There were a few
whispers when I went over to join him for those drinks Roy
gave us, but for now it did not appear we'd have any more
problems with patrons.

The pair dressed in buckskins decided to wait out the rain
after all, settling back down on one end of an empty bench
close to the stove, paying no attention to me and Sam.

"Much obliged for the whiskey," Sam told Roy, toasting
him with his shot glass before he tossed his drink back.

I took a small sip of mine, not liking the taste but needing
to feel warmer inside. Roy acknowledged Sam's thanks, although he was making it plain he wished we hadn't come,

turning his back on us to dust off a row of glasses on a shelf behind him.

I kept an eye on that room despite my observation every-one was ignoring us now. They were a collection of rough-looking men if I'd ever seen any. A little voice inside my head told me that we could expect more trouble at any time if there was a shift in the general mood.

Outside, the storm continued to drench Roy's trading post with a torrent of water. I listened to rain pelt those wet logs a moment longer, then I downed what was left of my whiskey and went out to put our animals in the barn, shivering when a blast of icy wind swept around a corner of the building, making me real thankful we weren't out in this weather. One thing I knew for sure . . . we wouldn't find any tracks to follow up at Antelope Hill after a downpour like this. A mis-erable ride of a hundred miles would probably turn out to be a waste.

Six

"You remembered Billy Cooper from some place before," I said as we rode our horses into a veil of swirling snow-flakes. It was a couple of hours before the rain stopped and turned into a snowstorm at Beaver Creek, allowing us to leave. My pocket watch had pointed to five o'clock when we left Roy's establishment. By now the temperature was well below freezing, somewhere in the middle twenties, if I was any judge of cold.

"Billy has graced the insides of my jail a few times," Sam recalled, bending into a stiff wind thick with falling snow. "He used to have a problem with his lariat rope. Seems his loop was always landing around the neck of cows that didn't belong to him. Some of his neighbors down in Texas started to complain that he drove their cattle across the Red River into Indian Territory now an' then without their permission. I arrested him an' took him to Texas to stand trial. Hadn't seen him lately. I reckon his term as a guest in a Texas prison ran out. Time has a tendency to fly by before you know it."

"I wonder if he'll go back to his old habits."

"A skunk don't hardly ever lose its stripes, Mr. Dudley. A man who steals livestock generally stays in the same profession until somebody decides to hang him. A rope is probably the only way to keep Billy from becomin' a cow thief again. We can expect to meet up with him before too long, if I'm right about his lack of character, most likely with that

same kind of difficulty when it comes to proving ownership
of his cattle."

"I've never seen a hanging," I said, never having wanted
to.

"It ain't a very pretty sight. When a gallows platform
drops out from under a doomed man's boots, he starts to
dance a jig with his tongue stickin' out, makin' a terrible
racket while he starts to choke. No reason I can think of why
anybody would care to see a hangin' more'n once."

I didn't want to think about anybody choking to death so
I let the subject drop. "It sure got cold in a hurry. Maybe
your wife was right when she predicted the worst winter in
ten years."

"I'd hate to think she was right about it. She claims to be
right about damn near everything as it is. If she starts be-
lievin' she can predict weather, I'll be in for mighty sore ears
until my dyin' day. She'd never stop remindin' me that she
was the one who told me."

Our horses' hooves whispered softly through deepening
drifts accumulating where wind deposited piles of flakes.
Moses plodded along behind us, flopping his big ears back
and forth. Dark skies above the Wichitas blackened with the
coming of night. Pretty soon we would need to find a campsite, a place for our tent close to water so our animals could
drink. So far, Sam hadn't mentioned anything about the shot
I fired at Beaver Creek when those cowboys ran away. It
wasn't like him to forget about something I'd done when it
didn't quite suit him. Summoning my courage, I decided to
ask him why he gave me that stern look. "I got the impression you weren't real happy when I fired over the heads of
those men leaving the trading post."

He let a moment of silence pass. "Once in awhile you've
shown a tendency to be too quick to use a gun. A gun is the
last thing a United States Marshal ought to use in the line of
duty. We didn't know who those men were or why they were
runnin' from us, but you took it upon yourself to shoot at 'em

anyway. I was meanin' to talk to you about it after supper. Don't be so quick to reach for your gun or you may wind up shootin' the wrong man one of these days. You need to learn to ask questions before you get so all-fired trigger-happy."

"I wasn't trying to hit them, Marshal. I aimed high, hoping they'd stop when they heard my gun go off."

Sam wagged his head like he didn't agree. "When a man hears gunfire, stopping is just about the last thing he's inclined to do if he's got other choices. A gun should be your last resort when nothing else works. Otherwise, you handled yourself right well back yonder. A little too trigger-happy at first, but you kept a cool head after we got inside. You'll learn. It don't come all at once."

That was like Sam. Along with a gentle scolding he'd given me an offhanded compliment. "I'll be more careful," I promised. There was no point in saying any more.

We crossed a snow-covered ridge where mud from the previous rains was already turning to ice beneath our horses' hooves. My nose and ears were numb from the cold, and my hands were tingling inside my gloves. At least my feet were warm enough, I told myself. When my feet got a chill in them, I was about as miserable as a man can get.

By the time we had trouble seeing our way in the dark, it was so cold my teeth were chattering. I'd been wishing for a fire so I could bake some of the frost off my face. Sam was determined we should keep moving, I suppose making up for lost time we spent at Beaver Creek waiting for the rain to end. We were entering a range of foothills leading into the Wichitas. Directly in front of us, I could see snow covering mountains when there was a letup in gusts of wind driving snowflakes into our faces. It was beginning to look like Clara was right, that we were headed into one hell of a winter coming early to this country. But I knew better than to say such a thing in front of Sam. He had enough sand in his craw anyhow. Instead, I decided to ask about making a fire. "I could use a cup of coffee," I said, trying to keep my teeth from rattling.

Sam was studying the trail ahead and didn't answer me. He swung his head back and forth a time or two before he said, "I smell smoke. Somebody else has got a fire out yonder someplace and we'd better hope they're friendly. It'll be smart to pay closer attention to things from here on. We wouldn't want to ride up on the wrong bunch in the dark."

"You figure it's Indians?" Suddenly I wasn't noticing the cold quite as much, sniffing the wind myself for smoke smell.

Once again, he didn't answer me, standing in his stirrups for a better look at the darkening land around us. Snow drifted across the tops of silent hills, washing down from steep slopes less than a mile away to the north and west. Trees had begun to accumulate a covering of snowflakes where limbs grew thick. A lessening of wind seemed to occur all at once after we started up one side of a bald knob. We'd shed our oilskins right after it stopped raining and I was glad of it now. Oilskins can make more noise than a tin can full of rocks when a man is trying to keep quiet.

Near the top of the hill Sam slowed his horse and reined to a halt. I stopped my bay and the mule, trying to guess what it was Sam was worried about. No matter how hard I tried, I couldn't get a trace of smoke scent from the air; but ever since I'd met Sam, I learned early that his senses were much keener than mine. He could find unshod pony tracks on a slab of marble or a sheet of ice, and I'd never seen anyone with a better sense of smell.

It was hard to see anything in all that snow falling from a sky the color of ink, but we sat there for quite a while before Sam was willing to ride. He heeled his horse over the crest and kept to dim wagon ruts that were now even harder to see covered with a couple of inches of snow. Here and there, tufts of dry bunchgrass sprouted from a blanket of white in openings between dense stands of trees. In this region, oak and cedar forests grew so close together they became an impenetrable wall that a horseman couldn't navigate without difficulty. Slopes in front of us were covered with trees, providing a thousand hiding places for anyone who might have dishonest intentions for travelers like us crossing through the Wichitas. A bushwhacker would have an easy time of it with so many places to lay an ambush, and I suppose that was why Sam was being so careful now.

I listened to our horses plod through powdery snow while I watched the lay of things. Frost curled from my bay's muzzle in little white clouds, reminding me of the cold; however, right then my thoughts were elsewhere, on whatever it was making Sam so cautious all of a sudden. Just a whiff of wood smoke and he was edgy as a cat under a rocking chair. I told myself this was the reason he was still alive in a dangerous occupation, being extra careful when his senses warned him that someone else was in the vicinity.

We crossed a heavily wooded switchback running up the first big mountain in our path where ruts followed the gentlest grade for wagon teams. Big freight wagons made passage this way up to Elk and then Dodge City, but they usually had escorts of cavalry from Fort Sill to protect valuable cargo. Since last year, there hadn't been any mishaps to wagon trains because the Kiowas and Comanches were keeping an uneasy peace with white men across the Territory. This was the reason Sam was surprised to learn about the scalpings at Antelope Hill. For almost a year there hadn't been a single report of Indian troubles in our district, until a handful of Kiowa renegades led by Pale Eye started raiding up on the Cimarron during the summer. We'd put a stop to that and Sam figured it would be the end of Indian problems for quite a spell. The wire describing what happened on the Canadian caught us both by surprise.

Easing our horses along that switchback, Sam kept turning his head back and forth, seeking a source for the smoke he smelled or the flicker of a distant fire. I still couldn't detect any smoke when I drew in a breath, but I was sure it wasn't Sam's imagination. He didn't make mistakes of that kind.

Suddenly Sam jerked his black to a stop at the edge of some snow-laden oaks. Beyond the trees lay an open meadow running to the bottom of a shallow ravine. About a quarter mile down the arroyo, we saw the faint glimmer of a campfire.

"It ain't Indians," Sam whispered.

I wondered how he could tell so far off, before we could see anybody around the flames.

By way of explanation Sam said, "Whoever it is, they aren't smart enough to shield their fire with rocks. A blind man could see it for miles. I reckon they might be travelers who got lost heading West. On the other hand, we may have run across another breed of varmint who don't belong out here in a protected Indian hunting ground." He pulled off one glove and reached behind him into his saddlebags, intending to have a look with field glasses. "Stay with our horses," he added quietly, swinging down from his saddle, handing me his reins. "I'll work my way down through these trees for a closer look. Try not to make any noise before I get back. Keep a tight rein on our horses."

He was walking among the oak trunks before I could ask what he wanted me to do if there was any trouble. Sam wouldn't figure there'd be any kind of trouble he couldn't handle, I suppose. I watched him until he disappeared into the shadows, listening to the quiet rustle of his boots in fresh snow.

To satisfy my own curiosity I took out my pair of binoculars and aimed lenses at the fire, adjusting the focus until I found a flicker of light. I saw several shapes huddled around the flames looking like men wrapped in blankets. I studied them for a spell and found one with a peculiar shadow. It appeared he was wearing a woman's hat, the kind with a wide brim and a cone-shaped crown. Seated directly across from him I saw a man resembling an Indian with a blanket hooded over his head, firelight reflected off his face. I counted five more men warming themselves around that campfire. And farther down the arroyo I saw tethered horses on a picket rope.

I swung my glasses back to the strange hat. The man who wore it appeared larger than the others. I couldn't recall ever seeing a man in a woman's hat before, until something in the back of my brain told me a woman's hat wasn't what it was. It was a Mexican sombrero. A ring of little silver conchos decorated the crown. Babs Woodley told us this country was too cold for there to be any Mexicans so far north. I could prove he was wrong if I had the chance to show Babs who was camped down below.

I was examining things real close when Moses decided he was lonely. He lifted his muzzle and brayed as loud as he knew how, announcing the fact that someone was hidden in the forest. A mule can bray louder than a big steam locomotive's whistle, especially when its owner doesn't care to draw attention to himself. I dove off my bay's back to grab that old mule's nose, knowing I was too late—the damage was already done. By the time I got Moses quiet I could hear Sam's footsteps running toward me.

I turned to look at the ravine. Shadows were moving all at once, darting this way and that. Sam was gonna be fit to be tied when he got back because I'd neglected to think about keeping our mule quiet. He would give me a good chewing-out and I knew I had it coming. Holding my hand over Moses' muzzle, I silently cursed my carelessness.

Seven

Sam raced up to his horse out of breath. Even in the dark I could tell his jaw was set on account of what I'd done. He made his saddle seat in a hurry and grabbed the reins.

"Of all times for that goddamn mule to sing," he snapped as he wheeled his black around, heading away from the ravine.

I understood his anger was directed at me. I jumped my bay in behind his gelding, dragging Moses by his halter rope. When I looked back to the arroyo I couldn't see any firelight. Those men doused it to keep from making targets of themselves and after I thought about it, that was the logical thing to do as soon as they heard a noise. I was wondering why Sam was in such a hellbent hurry. Had he seen something or someone down there making him think we'd get ourselves in a scrape? There shouldn't be anything to worry about unless Sam knew who they were or had some reason to believe they were up to wrongful activities.

We rode deeper into the trees at a trot, half blind in inky darkness and falling snow, moving higher up the switchback to get away from that spot where Moses brayed. We were making a hell of a lot of noise traveling so fast, a fact I'm sure hadn't escaped Sam's notice. I wanted to ask what it was he saw that made him so jittery. Was it the Mexican? Did Sam know who he was? It didn't seem sensible for this to be the only reason we took off so sudden-like. I recalled seeing one of them who looked like an Indian; Sam was especially cautious around Comanches, causing me to wonder if this was the reason we were making fast tracks away from there.

An answer to all my questions came mighty quick. Off to our left I could hear the drumbeats of galloping horses. By sighting between trees while we kept pushing through deep forest, I spied a group of riders heading up a slope toward the place where we'd been watching their fire. I counted four men riding hard for the oaks through sheets of windblown snow-flakes; these weren't the actions of friendly cowboys coming home from a cattle drive. By accident we'd stumbled onto something else, owlhoots who didn't take kindly to strangers traveling in the dark. It was only a guess but I figured it had something to do with the big Mexican wearing a sombrero.

It wasn't long until we struck a stretch of open ground. I kicked to a lope when Sam hurried his horse to a gallop. Moses didn't much like being forced to run with loaded packs but he did consent to hurry some after his lead rope was dallied around my saddlehorn. With snow flying from our animals' hooves we rode up the side of a white-blanketed mountain to a pile of big rocks we could use for cover. Sam reined around behind those boulders and jumped down be-fore his black bounded to a halt, jerking his .44 Winchester from a rifle boot hanging below a stirrup leather.

I led Moses to the same spot and got down from my saddle as quickly as I could, glancing back to see if they were fol-lowing us. At first I couldn't see anything because snow was drifting down so heavily, until I heard more pounding hooves coming from someplace below our rocky fortress, announc-ing the fact they'd found our tracks.

I pulled my rifle, levering a shell into the firing chamber while I crept over to a break in the rocks giving me a clear view of barren ground between us and the trees.

Suddenly, three horsemen burst from a thicket to our right at breakneck speed, charging in our direction. I saw Sam shoulder his rifle.

"Who are they?" I asked, loud enough for him to hear

despite thumping hoofbeats and our horses gasping for wind behind us.

"Never got the chance to find out," Sam growled, "thanks to that infernal mule. Whoever they are, they ain't real sociable."

The riders closed distance; less than two hundred yards were between us and now I could see they carried rifles. "It doesn't make sense they'd come after us like this if they aren't up to something, unless they've got us figured for Indians or robbers."

When a hundred yards separated us from the four riders, they drew to a halt. I'm sure they saw our prints in the snow leading to cover and thought better of charging straight at us. I could make out that sombrero on one of them. Another one appeared to be the Indian I'd seen across the fire. For a moment they sat their mounts quietly while clouds of steam blasted from their horses' muzzles. I was expecting one of them to shout something at our hiding place, a warning, but it was Sam who spoke to them first.

"Don't ride any closer!" he yelled. "We're U.S. Marshals from Fort Sill and we've got you in our gun sights!"

I saw one of them turn to the others. He said something we couldn't hear. He wore a flat-brim hat pulled low in front and it was hard to see his face in bad light. The big Mexican sat his horse staring up the mountain like he wanted to tangle with us anyway, resting the stock of his rifle on his thigh. But he turned his horse as soon as the rest did. Without saying a word, three of them wheeled their mounts and started back downslope at a walk. The gent who ordered the others away booted his rifle and sat still in the saddle, his face tilted up to see where we were. He rested one elbow on his saddlehorn like he felt real comfortable being there.

"Wonder what this is all about?" I asked, relaxing my grip on my rifle stock. "One of 'em is staying behind. Maybe he aims to talk to us."

"Maybe," Sam agreed, lowering his gun sights, although

I'd heard him use that tone of voice before when he doubted things. "Watch real close those others don't try to slip up behind us. Two more are around here someplace. I counted six before that damn mule sounded."

I saw the lone cowboy raise his hands to show us they were empty. "Sorry, Marshal!" he cried. "We heard somebody and just naturally assumed it was Injuns! Our Injun scout warned us this was Comanche country!"

Sam straightened behind a rock. "Ride up where we can see you!" he shouted.

It seemed the stranger hesitated a moment, then he lowered his arms and urged his horse forward. The closer he got to us, the harder I tried to make out his face. We waited until he was twenty feet away before me and Sam came out from behind the pile of boulders; and when we did, the cowboy stopped his brown gelding abruptly. I carried my Winchester beside my leg, keeping an eye on him just in case he made a move for a gun. We'd seen him boot his rifle, but there was no way of telling if he had a belly gun inside his coat.

"We weren't expectin' to find any federal marshals way out here," the stranger said. "Sorry we chased you off. We've been a mite jumpy since we crossed the Red a few days back. We hired an Osage scout to show us the way to Dodge. We was warned down in Fort Worth this country was thick with Comanches."

"Wrong time of year to be headed to Dodge, ain't it?" Sam asked.

It took awhile for an answer. "We talked about goin' all the way up to Montana. Thought maybe we'd winter in Dodge, then ride north in the spring. Heard tell there's all sorts of good grassland up on the Yellowstone. Plenty of work for a cowhand, too."

For reasons I couldn't quite figure, Sam wasn't buying the cowboy's story yet. "Don't hardly make much sense to be ridin' through this snowstorm. Makes me wonder why you'd wait for bad weather to make such a long ride clear to Kansas."

"No law against it, is there? The storm sorta snuck up on us. Caught us out in the open."

Sam took a look around before he replied, making sure the others weren't behind us. "No law against crossin' the Territory so long as nobody breaks the law while they're here. This land belongs to Indian tribes an' unless a white man pays for grazing rights on it, he don't belong here. But ridin' through ain't no crime, so if you boys are of a mind to ride to Dodge in a blizzard you're entitled to do it." Sam walked closer to the cowboy to get a better look at him. Falling snow and darkness made him difficult to see. "Maybe we'll meet again on the trail. We're headed to a place called Antelope Hill where some settlers met up with scalping knives. That's not far from the road to Dodge City."

"We heard there was aplenty of Injuns on the warpath north of the Wichitas. Maybe now the army will put a stop to it, if enough innocent people keep losin' their lives. Too bad 'bout them folks at Antelope Hill. I reckon I'll head back to camp, if you ain't got no more questions. Sorry we took out after you like we did, but a man can't be too careful where there's Injuns runnin' loose."

I was half expecting Sam to say he wasn't convinced it was Indians we were after, but instead he said, "There's a cavalry patrol from Fort Sill combing that area along the Canadian. If there are any Indians causing problems, we'll find 'em. If your Osage scout knows his business, he'll keep you wide of Comanche hunting ground. That's about the quickest way to lose your hair in these parts, chasing off their buffalo."

"We'll make it a point to remember that, Marshal." He gave us a nod and reined his horse around.

I moved nearer to Sam as the cowboy rode off. "You don't sound like you're convinced those boys are on the level," I told him when our visitor was out of earshot.

Sam waited before he answered me, squinting into the dark. "They aren't ordinary trail hands, and that story about goin' up to Dodge City and Montana don't ring true. Dodge is damn

near a ghost town in the winter—nothin' for a cowpoke to do
to earn any money. I've got my suspicions there's another
reason why they're here, but offhand I can't figure what it is."

"If they were gunrunners like Jack Tatum and his bunch,
we'd find rifles at their camp. We could wait for daylight
and have a look-see. What makes you so sure they aren't
trail hands like he claimed?"

"Little things. First off, his saddle ain't a double rig, so he
can't do much ropin' with a single cinch. One cinch-strap is all
that's keepin' his saddle on his horse's withers. A cowboy who
makes a living off the back of a horse would never ride that
kind of a three-quarter rigged saddle. A busted cinch could get
him killed. Another thing is his saddlehorn. It ain't rawhide
wrapped. If he was to dally a rope around it, the dally wouldn't
hold and he'd be shy two or three fingers when his rope jerked
his hand through. He ain't any more a range cowboy than I'm
a Methodist preacher. What he told us is a pack of lies, but
what I don't know yet is what they're really up to."

Everything Sam said made sense; however, they were
things I would never have noticed. "I wasn't paying any attention to his saddle," I admitted.

Sam turned to me. "Payin' attention to small things can
be the difference between dyin' and stayin' alive, Mr. Dudley.
If you keep your eyes an' ears open, you'll live a lot longer
if you aim to keep wearin' that badge."

I looked downhill. The stranger had disappeared into
snowfall and tree trunks. "I'll learn. I suppose I was too busy
watching him to see if he had a gun hidden in his coat."

"He did. That was another thing didn't add up to him bein'
a cowpoke. He was wearin' a gun in a cross-pull holster.
Only a gunslick or a cardsharp carries a pistol like that. Most
cowboys can't hit the side of a barn with a pistol, an' they
sure as hell ain't worried about a quick draw."

"I hadn't noticed that either."

"The bulge of his gun butt was turned the wrong way. Pay
a little more attention to things like that, the way a man

carries his sidearm, for instance. It'll tell you a lot about who he is an' what he does for a living."

I was glad for the dark just then, knowing my face was red. It embarrassed me when obvious things escaped my notice. "I know I've got a lot to learn," I said, shouldering my Winchester for the walk back to our horses.

"Like I told you before, it don't come all at once. Let's move north a ways and find a spot out of this wind so we can get a pot of coffee boiled. I'm damn near froze to the bone."

We rounded the rocks and booted our rifles. I hadn't quite gotten over feeling foolish for missing things Sam had seen when we talked to the stranger. I made myself a promise that I'd pay closer attention the next time.

After we got mounted Sam led us along one side of that big mountain to a drop where we could see a trace of the wagon road to Elk again. I kept looking over my shoulder, wondering if we'd ever know what those men were doing here.

Settling back against the cantle of my saddle, I discovered how cold I was. My feet had turned to ice standing in all that snow, and a chill ran up my spine. The land around us was black as pitch. If it hadn't been for a blanket of white covering the ground, it would be mighty hard for us to find our way without a star in the sky to guide us and no moon.

I turned up my coat collar and stuck my hands in my pockets with my reins wrapped around the saddlehorn and the mule's rope. My bay would follow Sam's gelding without any guidance from me. I started to shiver from head to toe. At times like these I pondered just what it was about being Sam's deputy that made me want the job. The pay was low and most of the time we lived in our saddles. But along with a good-sized measure of hardship came a hell of a lot of satisfaction, those times when we put lawbreakers behind bars where they rightfully belonged. I could never have explained it any better than that to a stranger. I liked what we were doing, even at times like this when I considered the risks.

Eight

By the time Sam found a campsite that suited him I was so cold I couldn't feel anything at the end of my nose and my toes hurt like they had a thousand needles in them. When I got down from the saddle I had to stifle a yelp because my feet stung so badly touching ground. Sam selected a pocket in some rocks cut into the side of a mountain to build a fire where we were out of the wind, but I was pretty sure he picked this tiny canyon so we'd have protection on three sides from a bullet, just in case we had any uninvited company. It was so dark I couldn't see how anyone could find us, but Sam never was inclined to leave much of anything to chance.

"Loosen your cinch, but don't strip your saddle," he said, tying his horse to a low tree limb. "We might need to ride out of here in a hurry."

I tied my bay to another limb and tethered Moses. "Do you think those men are following us?" I couldn't imagine why they would in a storm like this, nor could I guess why Sam was so uneasy.

Sam was walking kind of stiff, picking up fallen branches where he could find them under all that snow so we could get a fire started. "I take extra precautions when a feller lies to me," he said after he got a small armload of sticks. "That fanciful tale we heard about Dodge City an' Montana don't make a lick of sense. Those boys haven't got me fooled, so we're bein' real careful until we know what they're up to.

Maybe they're just passin' through, but I'm not ready to get my head shot off turnin' my back on 'em. If they've been trailin' us in this storm, they've got more to hide than I first suspected. Bein' on the safe side is what we're doin' now. One mistake is all it takes around desperate men."

I loosened the cinch on Moses and my bay before I took one of our small bags of corn from the packs, pouring a few kernels in the snow so the animals could eat. I understood why Sam was suspicious of those characters, but I also figured they'd have to be crazy to tangle with Federal Marshals unless they were really looking for trouble. "They'd have to be mighty dumb to try to ambush us," I said, giving Sam's black a handful of corn. "It wouldn't make much sense even if they are on the run from the law someplace else. They'll probably keep moving in another direction if you're right about them being gunslicks like that feller who did all the talking awhile ago. The one wearing the big sombrero acted real peculiar. Seemed he wanted to ride up close and trade gunshots with us."

Sam knelt to clear a place in the snow for our fire. "You were payin' attention when you begin to notice little things of that nature. The Osage was hangin' back in case there was any shootin', but the Mexican wasn't afraid of us. Him and the gent wearin' the cross-pull rig were the ones to watch. I'm glad to know you're beginnin' to notice small details. They can make the difference between stayin' alive or windin' up dead."

I cast a look around us. Sheer rock walls fifty feet high rose above treetops in the canyon. Snowflakes swirled over the rim where wind passed across the face of the mountain, making it harder to see what was up there. Sam didn't seem worried that a sharpshooter might climb up to take potshots at us, so I didn't give it much thought when I began walking around looking for more firewood. I heard him strike a match. It would feel mighty good to get warm again. With hot coffee in my belly I might be able to survive the rest of the night without turning into a block of ice.

I gathered downed limbs and twigs, whatever I could find in the snow without walking too far from our animals, trying hard not to shiver or let my teeth rattle too much. Sam was blowing on a tiny flame, begging his fire to life by the time I got back with more wood. I noticed that our horses were gobbling up corn as fast as they could, but old Moses appeared to hear something, pricking his long ears toward the rim like he was about to bray again. I wondered how a mule could see anything up there with it being so dark and snow falling. I dropped the firewood and gave the direction Moses was looking a close inspection. "I think our mule sees something up yonder," I said, slitting my eyes when a few snowflakes struck my face.

Sam looked up, first at the mule, then to the rim. He gave things a lingering stare, eyes wandering across snow-clad rocks, pausing when he came to trees or brush. I wondered if I needed to fetch my rifle.

It was when Moses returned to nibbling corn that Sam went back to tending our fire. "Probably just a varmint," he muttered softly, adding more sticks to the flames.

I wasn't quite so sure. Even as cold as I was, I offered to climb up. "I can take a look around if you want."

"No need," he said, like he knew we were alone.

I went looking for more wood, but I kept glancing up now and then to see if anyone was watching us.

Our fire was sheltered by a circle of stones we dug from a thickening layer of snow blanketing the canyon floor. Snow kept falling, settling over treetops, making conditions about as bad as they could get for men and animals. I was hoping Sam wouldn't want to keep riding tonight, because that fire felt mighty warm and the coffee we drank sure tasted good. But if Sam got an itch to move on we'd be in our saddles again.

Sometimes I had a hard time figuring what it was that made him think the way he did. I didn't need to be reminded we had a job to do, but after all this snow and rain there wouldn't be any tracks to follow at Antelope Hill. Without a trail to follow, I didn't see how we'd be any closer to finding out who killed those settlers when we got up there, only I didn't dare say anything like that to Sam unless he brought it up first.

We sat close to the flames, listening to wind howl over the canyon and the much closer hiss of snowflakes falling among trees around us. Sam took a pint of whiskey from his coat pocket to add a splash to his coffee. He offered me some and I declined it by wagging my head.

"Hell of a storm, Mr. Dudley," he said, corking his bottle.

I decided to take a chance. "It'll be next to impossible to find any sign of those raiders on account of this snow. What'll we do?"

"Nose around a little. Ask questions if we happen across a traveler or two. We'll ride over to Bull Bear's camp soon as the storm lets up. I 'spect the Kotsotekas will deny they took part in it, but we'll ask anyway. Maybe they've seen somebody hereabouts lately who don't belong."

"Seems like we're looking for a needle in a haystack. This is wide open country. It could take all winter for us to comb every inch of it; and if your wife is right about this being a bad year for weather, we'll be miserable cold. I ain't complaining, Marshal, but this looks like a mighty tough job for two men."

Sam gave me the eye. "Sounded like you was complainin'," he observed.

"I wasn't. Honest. But we've got our hands full, what with it snowing and all."

"You're wonderin' why we don't head back. It's real simple. We've got a duty to protect the citizens in this end of Indian Territory. Hell of a job for just two men, but it's ours anyway. When somebody kills eleven people in our jurisdiction, we have no choice but to investigate the circumstances.

Find out who's responsible if we can. We can't get that done sittin' on our ass in the office back at Cache. The army couldn't find out who did it if we gave 'em all winter an' summer to look. That don't give us but two choices: Forget about it or investigate ourselves. I took this job because I believe in what we're doin', protectin' decent folks from dishonest men. If you don't feel the same way about bein' a marshal, then you oughta quit."

The weather was playing hell with Sam's mood. "I never said I didn't feel that way, only that it looked nearly impossible to find the men who did it on account of this storm. It's weather I was worried about, not our duty."

Dancing firelight etched deeper lines into Sam's leathery face while he continued to stare at me. He palmed his tin cup and didn't say anything for a spell.

"I swear I wasn't complaining," I told him when it appeared he didn't intend to discuss it further. "I was trying to figure out what we'd do after we got there." I added more wood to the fire. "I believe in what we're doing out here . . . most of the time I do. Once in awhile I get to feeling sorry for some of those Indians, the peaceful ones. That reservation at Fort Sill isn't fit for keeping dogs. It's no wonder some of them run off from time to time, just to catch a breath of fresh air away from the stink."

Sam's expression softened. "I tend to agree sometimes, only I keep such opinions to myself, mostly. The way they keep them penned up, feedin' em rotten food, takes away their pride. An Indian is usually a prideful man because pride is about all he's got. When you rob him of that, it don't leave much. But on the other hand, we can't let them take what they want by use of force or nobody's safe. Somewhere in the middle there has to be a way for Indians and white men to live together. That's what Indian Territory was intended to be, a place where the tribes could have hunting ground an' a little bit of freedom. Little by little, we started takin' back what freedom we gave 'em by allowing a few cattle-grazin' permits. Now the cows have crowded out all the buffalo so there's nothing left for an Indian to hunt. The white men start losin' cows and they blame Indians for it, which brings the army down on 'em. It don't seem fair to an Indian, but it's the way it is because that's the law. It's our job to enforce those laws, even though we don't always agree with 'em. I never complain about it anymore to our bosses up at Fort Smith because nothin' is gonna change. I used to argue that it was us breakin' the treaty most of the time, only nobody wanted to hear it."

A sap knot hissed in the fire. I thought about what Sam was saying, that white men were responsible for many of the treaty violations. Sam had a soft spot in his heart for Indians, most especially Comanches. There was something about Comanches he respected even though he showed a genuine fear of them when we were near their villages. Sam knew Comanches better than just about any white man in the Territory, and if he felt there was a good reason to be afraid of them, I didn't need any coaxing to be of the same mind. "It's hard to find many white folks who have any sympathy for what the army does to them," I said, thinking out loud. "After so many years of fighting them, I suppose it's only natural to have some hard feelings."

"I reckon," Sam sighed, like he hadn't been listening very close, thinking about other things. He watched the sky a moment. "Let's pitch our tent. No sense pushin' through this snow in the dark if we don't have to. By mornin' we'll be able to see a little better—won't be ridin' plumb blind. If we're lucky, this storm will break before sunrise."

I got up to fetch our tent from the mule's back, dusting off the seat of my pants where snow stuck to me like cold glue. I had this nagging feeling that we wouldn't be lucky come morning when it came to the weather.

I was driving the first tent stake into frozen ground with a rock when a distant crack echoed from the rim above us. When I heard the noise, I jumped to my feet. In that same instant one of our horses screamed with pain, lunging forward on its hind legs. I dropped the rock and jerked my pistol free just as Sam's black gelding fell over on its side, whickering, legs thrashing in the snow kicking up a small whirlwind of white flakes around the spot where it collapsed. Sam was running for his horse when another gunshot rang out. My bay broke its reins and whirled around in the other direction. Moses let out this awful bray, sinking down in the snow, and I knew our mule had been hit. I realized I was just standing there dumbfounded after the second shot sounded—I took off in a run for the closest tree trunk to get out of the line of fire from above.

"Grab your rifle!" Sam yelled, dodging back and forth among the trees to present a moving target.

I wheeled around to look for my bay, hearing hoofbeats off to my left. My horse had broken its reins and I'd have to chase it down to get my hands on my rifle. Breaking to a run, I almost fell over a rotten log and barely caught my balance in time when a third shot popped behind me. A speeding lead slug whacked into a tree close by. My feet thumped across fresh snowfall making a muffled noise while I ran. Pretty soon I was out of breath and I still couldn't find my horse in the darkness.

I heard old Moses bray, and in spite of the danger we were in, the sound broke my heart. Even though that mule tried to kick me every time I walked behind him, I'd grown attached to him. It was knowing a bullet caused the animal's pain that made me feel worse about it. And by the way Sam's horse fell, the gelding was likely dead, or dying. My breath came in short bursts the longer I ran, and before long I was too tired to continue. Gasping, I stopped and turned around just in time to hear Sam's Winchester explode. A stabbing finger of light flashed from behind a faraway tree to mark Sam's position. The rifle shot echoed among the oaks around me and died away, leaving the only sound that of Moses honking so pitifully near our campfire.

Then I heard my bay snort near the mouth of the canyon. I clutched my pistol and took off in a trot toward the noise with my heart laboring. Something had frightened the horse, forcing it to a halt. I hurried forward, crouching down, staying to shadows wherever I could even though my boots were making a racket that would announce my arrival if anyone happened to be waiting for me near the canyon entrance. For now, the sharpshooter on the rim had stopped firing at us. I hoped Sam's answering shot had been enough to scare him off.

LONE WOLF

Nine

I glimpsed a shadow moving in front of me, the outline of a horse backgrounded by a wall of rock where the canyon narrowed to only a few yards. I was sure it was my bay—I broke into a run even though my lungs were about to burst, trying to head it off. I wasn't thinking about finding someone else so close to camp and stumbled blindly among thick tree trunks until all at once I saw a rider aboard the horse I'd seen, a man wearing a long duster coat with his collar turned up. I staggered to a halt and drew a bead on him with my Colt, forcing my hands steady in spite of the cold chills gripping my arms and legs. I waited just a fraction until I was sure of my shot, then I squeezed off a round aimed at the rider's chest.

My pistol roared, butt slamming into my palm. A brief flash of light winked from my gun barrel, accompanying the explosion. I blinked because of the light, not quite sure I'd hit what I aimed at. I heard a cry just as the roar from my gun faded. The man toppled sideways out of his saddle and landed in a snowdrift as his horse bolted away from the bang of the gun. Snowflakes burst into the air around the spot where he landed, and for a time I was unable to tell if he moved again. His chestnut horse raced out of the canyon trailing its reins. I watched the downed rider a few seconds more before I risked getting any closer. A wounded man is subject to lie still for a while, stunned by a bullet. I meant to make sure he wasn't going to wake up while I was out in the open.

I listened to the drum of running hooves in the snow. I was surprised to find our bushwhacker so soon after he fired down on us from above . . . or was this another man guarding our escape route if we tried to make a run for it? I hunkered down behind a tree as soon as I considered that possibility, peering around at the forest shadows, places where a man could hide. My hands shook so badly I had trouble keeping my gun steady covering my surroundings—it wasn't only the cold making me tremble, for I was scared to death right then. Things got real quiet all of a sudden, when I couldn't hear his horse running any longer. I calmed myself as best I could and took a deep breath, glancing over to the spot where the rider lay. He hadn't stirred, nor had he made a sound since I knocked him off his horse.

Now I knew those men had been trailing us, waiting for the right opportunity to shoot us down. It puzzled me a little that Sam's horse and our mule had been their targets. There had been plenty of chances for a sharpshooter to drop either me or Sam, if he was a good shot with a rifle. Was the bush-whacker's aim bad? Or had he been trying to leave us afoot in this awful blizzard?

I became aware that Sam wasn't shooting at anything. It was so quiet I could hear the whisper of falling snow landing around me. Moses wasn't braying any longer, and I assumed our mule was dead. We were in one hell of a fix without horses or a mule in the middle of these rugged mountains. Unless I found my bay or got lucky enough to catch that runaway chestnut, we'd have to walk to Elk or all the way back to Beaver Creek. And Sam would be steaming over what happened, mad as a cornered bull because we'd let these bushwhackers slip up on us.

When it was clear nobody else was close by, I straightened up and crept toward the body, still being cautious, with my gun aimed at him. I wanted to see if I recognized him from the bunch I saw when they chased us up that mountain. We hadn't gotten a good look at any of their faces in the dark, but I figured I would know if the man I shot was one of them.

I left the trees carefully and made my way over to the base of the cliff. Snowflakes dusted my hat and coat after I was out in the open. My boots made a soft crunching noise until I came to the spot where the body was sprawled in a snowdrift. A dark stain had spread around him, blood that was being covered by snow drifting into the canyon. I looked down at a face I'd never seen before. Sightless eyes stared up at the sky in a face frozen by sudden death. A sweat-stained hat with an eagle feather afixed to its hatband lay beside the body. The dead man appeared to be some sort of half-breed, although I couldn't begin to guess what type of mix he was. His skin was darker than most and his cheekbones were high, giving him a bit of an Indian look. But his hair was cut short the way white men wore hair, and I wasn't able to decide if he was really any part Indian. Indians were a topic I didn't know all that much about, being from Mississippi. I knew enough to know they could be mighty dangerous if they were men of intemperate disposition.

I noticed a Winchester rifle lying in the snow. After I had another look around, I walked over to pick up his gun. It was a model '73 like mine, showing signs of neglect, rust on the barrel and a few cracks in the stock. I cradled it and thought about my horse. Before I went searching for the bay I needed to tell Sam about the bushwhacker I dropped with a lucky bullet. Firing my pistol at that range I'd been fortunate to hit him.

I looked down at the body and that was when it truly struck me I had killed another man in the line of duty. I tried not to think about the lives I'd taken as a U.S. Marshal. Most of the time I could shut those memories out, but now and then I dreamed about how I felt when it happened or I saw their faces—the way they looked after I shot them. I didn't want to remember any of them now any more than I cared to see the man lying near my feet. I shook my head and turned away, trudging back toward camp with the dead man's rifle balanced in one hand, my Colt dangling from the other.

I'd only walked a short distance when I heard a horse, the soft rattle of membranes in a horse's muzzle when it experiences fear or an unfamiliar scent. The sound came from my right. I circled a stand of oaks and found my bay gelding in a clearing, broken reins dangling from its bridle bit.

"Whoa, boy," I said quietly so the gelding would recognize my voice. I approached slowly and holstered my pistol. The bay let me walk up without running away. I caught what was left of the reins and started back in the direction of camp, leading my horse. With Sam's gelding felled by a bullet and our mule dead, my bay was the only animal we had left to get us out of these mountains.

I came upon a grim sight when I got back to our fire. I saw Sam's black gelding lying on its side in a pool of blood, motionless now, dead from the first slug fired at us. Moses stood, hip-shot, underneath an oak tree with blood running down his rear leg from a deep gash across his croup. A bullet had sliced open his flesh clear to the bone, bone that looked flinty-white when I got close enough to see the damage.

Our little fire had died down to glowing embers, and right at first I couldn't find Sam among the shadows around me. I heard a footfall in the snow, then another, coming from the other side of the firepit.

"I heard a shot," Sam said, almost a whisper, staying clear of dim light from the coals.

"I killed a man," I explained. "Only there must have been two of them. The feller I dropped couldn't have gotten down off the rim quick as that. The first shot came from up yonder, from the east side. That was the slug that killed your horse. I was chasing my bay when I ran across this rider near the mouth of the canyon. He appears to be some sort of half-breed. His hair is cut short, but his face looks Indian to me.

He's wearing white-man's clothes. I found this rifle lying beside him."

"What happened to his horse?" Sam asked, peering past me in the direction I'd come.

"It ran away, but maybe we can find it. A little chestnut with a star in its face. It got spooked when my gun went off."

"We need another horse real bad." Sam lowered the muzzle of his rifle, glancing at Moses. "Our mule may be hamstrung. Can't tell until it gets light. Right now his ass is real sore an' I ain't inclined to risk taking a closer look at his backside until he settles some. Let's take a look at the bastard you shot an' see if we can locate his horse. If there was two of 'em, I 'spect the other one caught that chestnut an' took off with it. Those owlhoots turned out to be lousy shots with a rifle. Otherwise we would both be dead as fence posts."

"Maybe it was only a warning not to go any farther. I got this real strong feeling the bunch we found at that ravine may be some way connected to the massacre at Antelope Hill. It's only a hunch, but like you said, they didn't fit in with the usual types we see in this part of the Territory."

Sam walked past me, following the tracks I left in the snow. "Sometimes a hunch is all it takes," he said. "Bring your horse so one of us can ride circles lookin' for that chestnut. If we don't get our hands on another horse, it means one of us has to walk plumb to Elk. I'll let you figure out who that's gonna be, Mr. Dudley, seein' as how you're my deputy."

We wound our way through the woods to the place where I got that lucky shot. By the time we got there, a layer of fresh snow had begun to cover the body. Sam knelt down and dusted off the dead man's face with the brim of his hat while I stood guard. I didn't want another look at him, so I turned a different direction while Sam examined the corpse.

"You were right about him bein' a 'breed," Sam remarked. "He don't look familiar. Can't tell if he was with those boys we met up with before on account of I never got a good look at the rest of 'em, but it's a good bet he was. Nobody else figures to be of a mind to start shootin' at us way out here. He's sure to be one of them, only I can't think of a reason why they'd make targets of our animals. Looks like, if they wanted us out of the way, we would have been the ones duckin' lead. Maybe it's simpler than that—they couldn't shoot straight or see us in all this snow."

I couldn't figure it either. "It don't add up," I agreed, shivering from the cold, stamping my feet in the snow to warm up my frozen toes. "Could be they only wanted to scare us off."

Sam stood up, giving the canyon a sweeping gaze before he turned to me. "I'll ride around to see if I can find any tracks that horse left behind. Build up our fire a little. I don't look for more trouble tonight, but keep your eyes open." He gave me a one-sided grin. "That was some fancy shootin' with a handgun. Your slug caught him square in the middle of his chest. I couldn't have done better myself." He took my bay's reins and tied them together where they were broken, then he stepped in a stirrup and mounted.

Even cold as I was, I couldn't help but feel proud over the compliment he gave me. "I was lucky I guess."

Sam tugged his hat down low and rested the butt plate of his rifle on his thigh before he rode off. "A man usually makes his own luck, son. I never was much of a believer in the fates. If you're prepared for most any situation, you'll be in better shape than a man who ain't. To my way of thinkin', luck don't have all that much to do with it."

I watched Sam ride slowly out of the canyon, keeping my bay in a walk. Pretty soon I lost sight of him in the snow. With a dead man's rifle resting on my shoulder, I started back to camp, considering what Sam said about luck. Being prepared was better than being lucky according to him, and right then I was ready to agree. But that was before I remembered how badly my hands were shaking when I fired my Colt. Privately, I had to believe there had been a little pinch of luck in that shot.

When I got back to camp, I passed by Moses on the way to the fire. That poor mule was standing in a pool of blood the size of a saddle blanket. The deep gash across his rump was torn clear down to his left hock, one reason Sam worried about a hamstring. I knew Moses was in a lot of pain just then. There was nothing I could do for him, and the thought saddened me. Life was a harsh proposition for a mule in the first place, being a work animal. It was worse when one got hurt, because there was little anyone could do to lessen its suffering. I couldn't look at Sam's black gelding again because I'd liked that horse, even if it wasn't all that good crossing rivers.

Resting the rifle against a tree, I added wood to the coals to build up our fire. My hands and feet were freezing; my cheeks stung like I'd been slapped a few times. I reckoned I was about as miserable as I'd ever been, feeling as poorly as our injured mule. Stamping my feet to keep them warm until flames got going, I looked up at the sky, wondering if I'd made the right choice to become a deputy marshal. There sure as hell weren't any frills that came with this job. The pay wasn't much, twenty dollars a month and found. What was it about being Sam's deputy I liked? At that particular moment I wasn't real clear coming up with any answers.

Back in Mississippi, I'd had the chance to become a clerk at Fitsimmons General Store. I'd shunned the job for more exciting work as a sheriff's deputy in Natchez. But I'd always wanted to go out West, see open country, and when I saw an advertisement in the Natchez newspaper asking for apprentice United States Marshals at Fort Smith, Arkansas, I applied at once. Nobody told me I might wind up in the middle of Indian Territory working for one of the toughest men in the marshal's service. Nobody bothered to explain that I'd be spending most nights sleeping on hard ground in every kind of weather. There was a hell of a lot they didn't tell me at the beginning.

Snowflakes danced among black tree limbs while I was

thinking about my choice to become a marshal. If I'd elected to take that job at Fitsimmons Store, I'd be warm tonight, with a pillow for my head while sleeping in a cozy room. And I wouldn't have a single dead man on my conscience to interrupt pleasant dreams about gentler things. Instead, I'd chosen work that robbed me of sleep when ghosts entered my slumber, faces of men I'd killed in the two short years I'd been Sam's deputy.

Flames licked up the sides of limbs in the firepit. I bent down to warm my hands, pushing everything else from my mind. I'd picked a bad time to have second thoughts about my occupation. I was stuck in this blizzard for the time being, beginning a manhunt for killers who slaughtered eleven people, among them women and children. Until this assignment was over, I couldn't allow myself to think about alternatives.

After a bit I looked up at the top of the canyon. Hardly an hour ago, speeding bullets had come pouring down on us from above. I knew I should feel lucky, no matter how Sam felt about luck, to be alive just now.

Still edgy, I picked up the dead man's rifle and backed into the shadows so I could be prepared, just in case my luck ran out.

Ten

Sam didn't come back until the sky had begun to gray in the east. I'd been feeding our fire through the night, wondering if Sam met with any misfortune. I was mighty glad to hear him ride up when he did, although the sounds of a horse sent me scrambling for my rifle until I recognized him. He swung down, his coat and hat covered with snow he brushed off when he walked to the fire.

"There was three of 'em," he said. "They rode south soon as they picked up that loose horse belongin' to the feller you shot. I trailed 'em as far as I could, until the tracks disappeared in all this fresh snow." He pulled off his gloves to warm his hands above the flames. By the look on his face I could tell he was fuming over what happened, most likely the fact that he couldn't find the two who got away.

"I made more coffee," I told him, taking our pot from the edge of the coals so I could pour him a cup. I was bone tired from being up all night, but I wasn't going to let it show. "We can travel whenever you're ready. Most of the bleeding stopped where Moses got sliced open, and he's putting weight on that bad leg now. If we move slow, I think he'll make it okay."

Sam merely nodded until he got some coffee down. "A mule's a lot tougher'n a horse," he said. He looked at the carcass of his black gelding covered by a thin layer of snowflakes. "Hated to lose mine like this. Always figured that horse would drown, the way it hated crossin' rivers. Wish I could have gotten my hands on those others. I'd have made them sorry they shot down a good horse. Way they lit out, I don't figure they'll be back."

I thought about the body of the half-breed. "What'll we do with the man I killed? We can't carry him to the closest settlement on account of we're down to one horse and a lame mule." I was hoping Sam wouldn't want to bury him—the ground was frozen hard by now.

"Ordinarily I'd be inclined to dig a grave, but these ain't ordinary circumstances. I reckon we'll leave him to the wolves. He wasn't carryin' any papers to say who he was." Sam glanced up at the sky. "Let's have a look at the mule. If you put a twitch on his nose, maybe I can sew his flank with needle an' thread. If he ain't crippled too bad, we can travel slow to Elk. Without any more trouble, we oughta make it before nightfall."

I winced a little, thinking about what it would be like to walk all the way to Elk in this snow. I didn't need any reminder as to who would be doing the walking.

When we first caught sight of remains of the old army post in the distance, I felt like shouting. My feet were frozen solid and there was hardly any feeling in my hands or my face. Sam had given me those red mittens Clara made for him when I complained about how my fingers hurt in the cold. Right then I didn't mind wearing red mittens and I would have gladly worn another pair on my feet. I'd never been so cold in all my life after walking most of the thirty miles to Elk. Sam walked some, letting me on the bay for short spells, but he couldn't keep it up for long. Moses had a limp in his right hind leg, yet he managed to carry our gear without too much suffering after Sam stitched his torn flesh. My bay was done in, too; and by the time we could see a gate in the crumbling ruins of the fort, both animals were ready to collapse. It had stopped snowing in the morning, giving us the chance to make sure we weren't being followed. We saw smoke coming from fires inside the walls at Elk, and just thinking about how good it would feel to get warm, I was able to hurry leading our mule while Sam rode out front. We crossed a flat plain covered with half a foot of snow to reach the ruins. Trees had been cleared all around the walls, leaving a prairie dotted with stumps. A group of horsemen rode out to meet us, five uniformed troopers from the patrol led by Captain Ross.

A pink-faced soldier halted his squad a few yards in front of Sam, blocking our way. "Have you men seen any Indians?" the trooper asked.

Sam wasn't in the mood to be questioned right then. "Get out of my way, soldier boy, or I'll put you in irons! I'm the U.S. Marshal from Cache. Anybody asks any goddamn questions, it's gonna be me!" He reined around the cavalry troop and continued on toward Elk. I plodded along at the rear leading Moses, a bit embarrassed by Sam's gruff manner. All the soldier wanted was to know if we'd seen Indians.

The troopers swung in behind us for the half-mile ride up a gentle slope to the walls. The army abandoned its outpost at Elk a few years earlier after the Medicine Lodge Treaty, and now it served as a temporary settlement for cowmen and their families who held permits to graze government land along the far western boundary of Indian Territory. In truth, the grazing permits were a violation of the treaty, yet cattlemen were able to convince men in Washington that too much grass was being wasted. In order to give this hungry nation beef, federal lands should be grazed, they argued. Only no one thought about hungry Indians who had no more buffalo after cows and hunters pushed them elsewhere.

That last hundred yards to rotting timber walls encircling a few log cabins was the longest stretch of the day for me. I was able to smell smoke by then, making me think about how warm a fire would feel when we got there. I was stum-

bling now and then when we walked through the gate. I saw
a cluster of men standing around a big fire near a pole corral
and that's where I was going when I heard someone say,
"Hey cowboy! Them's sure pretty red mittens!"

I looked down at my hands, too numb from the cold to
take the mittens off. I pulled Moses toward that fire as hard
as I could without worrying about what I looked like. When
I got to the fire, I sort of slumped over on my rump, too
tired to stand any longer. I started feeling dizzy. Then it was
like someone blew out a candle—suddenly everything went
dark as pitch.

I woke up in a warm room lying on a bed. A woman was
there trying to feed me hot soup, only I couldn't swallow.
My throat was stuck shut for some reason; and even when
I tried, I couldn't get any soup to go down.

"You're awake now," the lady said, smiling. She was a
plain-looking woman, her skin hardened by too many hours
in the sun. I did my best to return her smile, and that's when
I swallowed some of the broth.

"Yes, ma'am," I said, remembering how things went black
after I got Moses to that fire. "Sorry to be so much trouble.
I must have passed out. It was awful cold today. We walked
all day to get here. Some bushwhackers shot one of our
horses and wounded our mule." I pushed up on my elbows,
feeling a little shaky at first. "Where's Marshal Ault?" I
asked, looking around a sparsely furnished room made of
logs. A rock fireplace in one wall gave off the most wonderful heat.

"He's with my husband and Captain Ross," she replied as
she offered me more broth. "They're talking about the Comanche raid up on the Canadian. Those poor people were
all killed in a most dreadful way, butchered like they were
livestock. We're all scared to death the Comanches will strike
here this winter. The captain is trying to persuade us to leave
until those Comanches are driven back to their reservation."

"But this *is* their reservation, ma'am. This is a part of

Indian Territory that was set aside for Comanches and Kiowas by the treaty."

She gave me a stern look, like she didn't agree. "We have permits for our cattle and that gives us the right to live here. We aren't squatters, if that's what you mean to imply. We were told we could stay at this abandoned fort while we saw after our cow herds. We all got a letter from Washington approving the use of these old buildings for our living quarters. The Indians are supposed to be peaceful here. We were given assurances that the army would protect us."

I saw no sense in arguing it with her, for in point of fact she was right. The government allowed them to stay here and to graze their cattle even though it broke the spirit of the treaty signed by the tribes at Medicine Lodge. It was politics, which wasn't my line of work. "Marshal Ault doesn't believe it was Indians who killed those folks, ma'am. He thinks it was made to look like Comanches done it."

The woman stared at me real hard. "Why would he believe it was anyone else? Who else would do such an awful thing to women and children?"

"That's just it," I started to explain. "Comanches wouldn't slaughter women or female children. They'd take them prisoner or something, but they wouldn't kill them, according to the marshal. Ask anybody in these parts and they'll tell you that Marshal Ault knows Comanches better'n most any white man around. He claims it couldn't have been Comanches at Antelope Hill or the women would not have gotten scalped like they did."

I noticed the lady's face changing color, turning pale when she put the bowl of soup down on a table beside me. "I can't let myself think about it," she said, turning away, her hands clasped in her apron. "There are six women here including our daughters. We have two, Tom and me. I won't think about the possibility it could happen to us. I simply can't. . . ."

I was immediately sorry for what I said about the women and children being scalped. "I shouldn't have mentioned it.

I know you folks must be scared it might happen here; but now that me and Marshal Ault and the army is here, we'll get to the bottom of it. Don't worry. Whoever was responsible will be real sorry to find Sam Ault on their trail."

Something I said made her grin, only there wasn't much good humor behind it. "You sound very brave, young man. Perhaps we'll all feel better knowing you are here."

I sat up and tossed an old quilt and a moth-eaten blanket to one side so I could swing my legs off the bed. Strips of rawhide in the bed frame creaked when I got up. My boots were near the fireplace drying out, along with Sam's red mittens. I recalled someone poking fun at me for wearing those mittens when we came to Elk, but that was about the last thing I remembered before I blacked out. My gun belt and hat were hanging from wood pegs on the wall. Reminded of my manners, I said, "Thanks for the soup and letting me rest here, ma'am."

She smiled. "I'm Alice Anderson."

"I'm Leon Dudley, Deputy United States Marshal," I told her, thinking I didn't look much like a deputy marshal in my stocking feet without my hat and gun. "Like I said, no need for you to be worried about things now. You and the others here will be safe."

There was a little twinkle in her eye when she said, "That's good to know, Mr. Dudley."

I crept over an earthen floor to pull on my boots. Standing next to the fire, I noticed several tintype likenesses on a hand-hewn plank mantel. One was of a blond girl. She was so pretty I couldn't stop looking at her while I stepped into my boots.

"That's our daughter Anna," the woman said.

I heard the pride in her voice. "She's real pretty, ma'am. Maybe just about the prettiest girl I've ever seen."

Mrs. Anderson's tone changed when she said, "Anna is engaged to be married in the spring."

I understood that the message was meant to discourage

me. I nodded and looked the other way. "Whoever she's gonna marry, he's a lucky man. Now if you'll show me where Marshal Ault and your husband are talking to Captain Ross, I'd best get there myself or I'll have to face the music from Sam."

She pointed to a doorway leading into another room. "Go out the front. You'll find them in the cabin across from ours."

I shouldered into my coat and put on my hat, strapping on my gun before I left. "Thanks again, Mrs. Anderson. Sorry I was so much trouble, but it was awful cold walking through all that snow today. I reckon I nearly got froze to death."

I walked into the other room and that's when I saw Anna. I almost swallowed my tongue after I got a look at her in light from a lantern on the table where she was sitting sewing patches to the elbows of a man's shirt. A younger girl sat across from her, threading a needle. They both looked at me and smiled. My heart gave a little flutter while I reached for my hat brim so I could tip my hat the way a gentleman should. "I'm Leon Dudley," I stammered, nodding to them, feeling Anna's eyes on me.

"Hello," she said quietly. "I'm Anna, and this is my sister Carrie."

I put my hat back on my head right quick when I remembered my hair wasn't combed. "Pleased to meet you both," I told them, in a hurry to get out of the room.

I went over to a sagging plank door lined with deerskin and let myself out, feeling downright foolish for the way I acted in front of Anna. As soon as the door was closed behind me, I took a deep breath and let it out slowly. Anna Anderson was indeed one of the most beautiful girls I'd ever set eyes on. My belly did a little flip-flop, remembering her blue eyes and the way she had been looking at me.

Across a snowy compound I saw a larger log building with a plume of smoke twisting from a rock chimney into skies darkening with dusk. Hundreds of footprints in the snow showed where men had gone inside. I tugged down my hat when a breath of cold wind blew across the compound, then I stepped away from the Anderson cabin with my shoulders rounded inside my coat. I'd only gone a few feet when the door opened behind me.

"Mr. Dudley!" It was Anna's voice. "You forgot this pair of red mittens."

I wanted to crawl into a hole and hide rather than admit I had red mittens. "Those aren't mine," I said weakly, turning so I could take them in spite of my terrible embarrassment. "They belong to Marshal Ault. His wife made them for him."

Anna was grinning when I came over to take the mittens. She said, "You were wearing them when my dad and the others carried you inside so I assumed they were yours."

"My hands were cold," I said, stuffing them into a pocket of my coat hurriedly. I was so embarrassed I wanted to die. I made ready to leave, muttering, "Thanks," before I walked away. I'd been unable to look her in the eye when I took them. I took long strides away from there, cursing my bad luck. Anna would think I was part loco for wearing red mittens, but the damage was already done.

Eleven

Bearded faces watched me enter the cabin. Six men wearing a cowboy's work clothes and heavy mackinaws sat on stools or leaned against log walls. A bearded soldier dressed in a dark-blue coat and riding boots stood beside Sam near a fireplace at one end of a long room. Everyone got quiet as soon as I came in.

"Yonder's the kid with them fancy red mittens," a cowboy in buckskin leggings joked. "Appears he ain't dead after all."

I wanted to hunker down inside my coat again on account of those mittens, but it was what Sam said that kept me from being embarrassed.

"He's no kid," Sam declared in his booming voice, capturing everyone's attention. "This here's my deputy, Leon Dudley. He's one of the deadliest men with a gun I've ever run across. Don't let his youthful appearance fool you, boys. Just last night he killed a half-breed who tried to ambush us in the dark. Leon got him with a pistol shot at fifty yards. Put a bullet through that 'breed's heart when there wasn't any moon, snowin' to beat sixty, too. I can't make that kind of shot in broad daylight. And on top of that, he's a better shot with a rifle. Don't offer to get in no kind of shootin' contest with him or you'll lose a wager."

Sam was saving me from more teasing over the mittens, and I was grateful. "Howdy men," I said, glancing around. "Marshal Ault tells a mighty good story. It was more like thirty yards. I'd call it a lucky shot. Sorry I was delayed. I reckon I got a mite too cold today."

Sam motioned me over to the fireplace. "This here's Captain Dan Ross."

I shook hands with the captain, not liking him at once for the way he wouldn't look me eye to eye.

"And this here's Tom Anderson," Sam continued, inclining his head toward a rawboned cowboy slouched against the wall next to Captain Ross.

I took Anderson's handshake, noticing how he seemed to be an agreeable type with a friendly expression. "I'm obliged for the hospitality your wife showed me," I told him.

Anderson chuckled. "You took a chill. Alice didn't mind looking after you. That's one hell of a long walk from where you camped last night. The marshal was tellin' us about the troubles you had. None of us ever saw no bunch of gunmen like the men he described. They ain't from around here, that's fer sure."

"One was a Mexican in a big sombrero. He wouldn't be hard to remember if you'd seen him before."

"Maybe just outlaws passin' through," Tom opined, giving the appearance of being thoughtful. "This stretch of country can be full of hardcases now an' then, men driftin' from place to place lookin' for easy pickings."

"And troublesome Indians," Ross added. "We've had a time of it keeping the Comanches and Kiowas settled down. This last bit of business at Antelope Hill could be the match setting another big Indian campaign ablaze in Washington." He scowled at Sam for a moment. "The marshal says he doesn't think it was the work of Comanches because women were massacred. But that won't be enough to satisfy my superiors. Major Donaldson won't believe it either, and he'll be the one to send a report to General Crook."

"George likes killing Indians," Sam observed. He said it without feeling, but I knew he had low regard for General Crook.

"The warlike bands should be exterminated," Captain Ross was quick to say. "If they refuse to honor the peace treaty, then we have no other choice."

Sam wasn't in the mood to debate the issue with anyone. He shrugged and turned to Tom Anderson. "I need to buy a spare mule and a horse. I can give you a voucher for the money you can send to the paymaster at Fort Sill. We're headed up to the site where those folks were killed. We'll leave our crippled mule until his leg heals up an' I'll pay for boarding, if you've got no objections."

"You will be wasting your time," Ross said flatly. "We gave the entire area a close inspection. There is nothing to see, no trace of those redskins who did it, not so much as a hoofprint anywhere. And now this snow completely covers the ground, so I don't know what you hope to find up there. That region along the Canadian is entirely uninhabited. We covered every inch of it."

Sam gave Ross a disinterested glance. "We'll nose around to see what we can find, Captain, just in case there's somethin' you may have missed."

"Suit yourself, Marshal. In my opinion, it's a waste of the taxpayer's money."

It was the wrong thing to say to Sam, and I knew it before he exploded. "The biggest goddamn waste of taxpayer's money is when the army sends incompetent fools to handle a job like this," Sam growled, setting his jaw, cords standing out in his neck. "If Major Donaldson had any sense, he'd have asked us to come up here to investigate. Only Harry's too goddamn bullheaded to admit he don't know a damn thing about Indians."

Sam's outburst, and the fact that he was a head taller than Captain Ross, prevented the argument from continuing. Ross took a moment to collect himself. "I only meant to say that we combed the area thoroughly. . . ."

"That wasn't all you said," Sam recalled. "You said we'd

be wasting taxpayer's money. If there ever was a waste of tax money, it's hirin' fools to run the United States Army."

Everyone was watching Sam like they expected more trouble to come from him before it was settled. But when Ross didn't have anything else to say, Sam relaxed a bit. I took the opportunity to smooth things over by telling the captain, "Sometimes it's easy to overlook barefoot pony tracks. There've been plenty of times when Marshal Ault found horse sign where I couldn't see a thing. He's got a keen eye for it, and plenty of practice."

Ross averted his eyes. "We looked real hard. I sent out patrols in every direction. It was like those Comanches up and disappeared into thin air. There were tracks all around where those folks were massacred, but the only prints we could find were wagon tracks leading down here to Elk. I'm sure they were made by the empty supply wagons coming down from Dodge. It was one of their scouts who found the bodies."

"Babs Woodley," I said. "We talked to him before we headed up here. He told us about the mutilations, how the women were scalped. That's why the marshal doesn't believe it was the work of Comanches. They'd have spared young women, according to Marshal Ault, because they're too valuable to kill, 'specially the pretty ones with blond hair like those Babs found. . . ." I was suddenly aware of Tom Anderson's discomfort when I talked about pretty blond women. That's when I remembered what his daughter Anna looked like. I looked at Tom and mumbled, "Sorry. I know this ain't easy to hear for a man with two daughters and a wife."

"It's okay," Tom said quietly. "I'm not blind to the kind of dangers we face here. Alice and I have talked about leavin' if this trouble doesn't stop." He looked at Sam. "We've been losin' a few cows lately. We figured it was Comanches thinnin' our herds to take the profit out of ranchin' for us so we'd leave on our own. That was before they struck at Antelope Hill like they did . . . if it was Comanches who done it. It only makes sense the two are connected, our missing beeves an' that attack last week."

Sam screwed his face into a frown. "Who else grazes cows in this country?" he asked.

Tom answered promptly, "Grant Haskell over in Texas has a few head runnin' along the Canadian in warm weather. He tried to get more permits from the gov'ment, only they told him there were too many already, that the Injuns were complainin' about how cows were crowdin' out their buffalo. Haskell's a decent feller. His son aims to marry our oldest daughter next spring."

"I never heard of Haskell," Sam said. "Where can we find his ranch?"

"Follow the Canadian west into the Texas panhandle. It's a few miles across the border. Place sits right beside the river. Why would you take a notion to ride over to Haskell's?"

Sam gave me a sideways glance before he replied. "If this Haskell wanted grazing permits in the Territory, one way to get 'em is to get rid of some folks who already own 'em. I know it sounds like a long shot, but it's worth looking at."

"You'd be dead wrong," Tom declared, "figurin' Grant could be behind those murders. Hell, he's a cowman. He sure ain't no kind of killer."

Sam wasn't about to be swayed by argument. "If he isn't, he won't mind answering a few questions. An innocent man's got no reason to worry if me an' Leon ride over to have a talk with him. We'll also question Bull Bear about his activities. I intend to get to the bottom of this, one way or another."

A cowboy behind Sam cleared his throat. "You'll be barkin' up an empty tree if you blame Grant Haskell, Marshal. He's one hell of a fine man, in my opinion. The rest of us ain't all that convinced it wasn't Comanches. It's your idea they won't kill no young women, but I say there's plenty of evidence it was redskins who done that bloody deed up on the Canadian."

Captain Ross wasn't going to let an opportunity pass to say what was on his mind. "Major Donaldson says you're something of an Indian-lover, Marshal Ault. He has said before that you have a fondness for those heathen savages. You can blame whoever you want for what happened, but I intend to follow my orders and see to it that Bull Bear's tribe is honoring the treaty. Because if they aren't, General Crook will order a punitive expedition down to handle them. Armed force is one thing Comanches understand."

Sam had been too long without sleep to take a remark like that without bristling. "Ordinarily, I'd take offense when somebody calls me somethin' I ain't. But in this case I've only got to consider the source. Harry Donaldson is an incompetent fool, a man with cow shit for brains who couldn't tell the difference between an Indian massacre an' a prairie fire after it was over. What he thinks about me is of no consequence, but what he puts in his report could bring about the slaughter of a lot of innocent Indians who haven't broken the peace treaty. Until there's some proof that Comanches caused those deaths at Antelope Hill, I won't blame them for it."

Ross didn't quite know what to say and I could tell he was reluctant to push Sam any further, so he kept quiet. It was Tom Anderson who wasn't entirely convinced.

"Nobody else would be crazy enough to cut up those people like that, Marshal. Who besides a Comanche would take the time to chop up a dead body?"

Sam hardly hesitated giving his answer. "Somebody who wants us to think it was Comanches, someone with somethin' to gain by havin' them blamed for it. Maybe a cowman who needed more grazin' land . . ."

"You're talkin' about Haskell," Tom said. "You're wrong to figure it was him, dead wrong."

"Grant ain't made that way," another cowboy argued from one side of the room. "We all know him. He's honest as the day is long. I ain't sayin' he wouldn't fight to keep what's his, but he sure as hell wouldn't have nobody killed so's he could graze more cows. It ain't in him. Soon as you talk to him, you'll see how wrong you are. Grant's a God-fearin' man. Right's right an' wrong's wrong in his book."

"I'm not blamin' anybody just yet," Sam declared, gazing at the other faces around him. "Until I know for sure who done it, I won't point a finger. In the meantime, I suggest you men ride your herds in pairs, an' be extra watchful around strangers. If you see anyone you don't recognize, send word to me an' my deputy as soon as you can. We'll be up on the Canadian pokin' around at Bull Bear's camp or over in Texas talkin' to Haskell." He gave Captain Ross a nod. "As a last resort, I suppose you could send a rider to Fort Sill if you can't locate us."

For a time nobody said a word. A couple of the cowmen were exchanging looks. When it was clear no one meant to say any more, Sam spoke to Tom again. "We'd be obliged for the use of a stable for our horses tonight an' a place where we could bed down until sunrise."

"There's an empty cabin," Tom said. "The roof leaks some, but it'll keep you warm. It belonged to the Greeleys afore they gave up an' moved off."

"It'll do," Sam told him. "We'll turn in for the night, if it's all the same to you."

Tom made a half turn for the door until one of the other cowboys said something.

"I still say you're dead wrong about Grant Haskell, Marshal. He's the salt of the earth. Soon as you make his acquaintance, I know you'll take back them suspicions you've got."

"I don't suspect anybody right now, mister," Sam said after he gave the man a look.

Another cowboy muttered, "He don't even suspect it was them Injuns."

I was glad Sam ignored that remark when he went over to the cabin door. We hadn't made very many friends among these cowmen at Elk. They were of a mind to believe Comanches were responsible for what happened up on the Canadian River; and until somebody could prove otherwise, they'd keep the same opinion on it.

I followed Sam and Tom out into the night, wondering if I was able to believe the murders had been committed by someone other than Indians. I trusted Sam's instincts when it came to this sort of thing, but he was having a hard time convincing anyone else around here. If I had any doubts, I knew I'd better not mention them for a spell.

Tom pointed us toward a small log cabin off by itself in the snow. "There'll be some wood in the fireplace, enough to keep you warm tonight," he promised. "I'll see to your bay an' the mule. Come daylight, you can pick out another horse from my own saddle string."

"We're mighty grateful," I said when it appeared Sam wasn't going to say anything, like he was thinking about something else. He stopped all of a sudden and stared off at the horizon when we heard the lonesome cry of a wolf in the distance. It was a real eerie sound echoing through the darkness, making me feel uncomfortable right then. And maybe a little bit edgy, too.

Twelve

Early that morning Sam bought a red roan gelding from Tom Anderson for forty dollars and a sorrel mule, writing out government vouchers for both animals just as the sun came up on a cold, clear day with hardly a trace of wind. We'd spent a reasonably comfortable night in that abandoned cabin, sleeping close to the fireplace wrapped in our blankets. Sam didn't have much to say before we went to sleep, I imagine because he was as bone tired as I was after a long day getting to Elk in the snow. One thing Sam did mention before we turned in was how he was surprised the men who shot at us hadn't followed to see which way we went or come back to try their luck again. I half expected them to trail us, too, if it was the same bunch we ran across in that ravine. Maybe we gave 'em enough answering fire to take the fight out of their dispositions.

Tom and another cowboy who introduced himself as Bob Sims watched us saddle our horses. Mrs. Anderson was preparing us a big breakfast and I could hardly wait to set eyes on Anna again. Before I dropped off to sleep I thought about her, wishing for all I was worth I hadn't been in possession of Sam's red mittens yesterday.

"Some of us have been talkin'," Tom said, casting an eye to the soldiers' camp where neat rows of tents sat next to a place in the wall around Elk where some timbers were rotted away. "I reckon we ain't all that convinced it wasn't Comanches who killed those folks. Your argument that a Comanche wouldn't scalp young women ain't enough to satisfy most of us, Marshal. An' there's another thing that don't set well with us, that you'd think Grant Haskell could be behind it. After what you said last night about ridin' over to have a talk with Grant, it damn near sounds like you've made up your mind he's guilty. My daughter is fixin' to marry his son Ward next spring. Cap'n Ross thinks you've got a soft spot for Comanches makin' you blind to the truth."

I was expecting Sam to blow his cork over that remark, only he didn't. "I haven't made up my mind about anything," Sam said as he tied off his cinch-strap. "I only said I'd planned to have a talk with Haskell. Maybe he's seen strangers lately or a bit of Indian activity, a few renegades. I never said I thought he was guilty of anything. As to Captain Ross, he can think whatever he wants about me. I've got damn little use for the average soldier like him, on account of I never met one who had a lick of common sense."

Bob Sims bit off a plug of chewing tobacco and wadded it in his cheek. He was a wiry little man in his early thirties who had the look of a good cowboy. "There's a big bunch of redskins camped maybe sixty or seventy miles east of here. Appears they mean to stay fer the winter. I seen 'em buildin' winter lodges in this big valley about a month ago. Me an' Charley happened to run across 'em lookin' fer strays. We lit out of there like our britches was afire, figurin' they'd scalp us sure if they found us."

Sam watched me finish tying a diamond hitch across packs on our new mule. "What you saw is even more proof the Kotsotekas aren't huntin' scalps. No white man ever slipped up on a Comanche village without bein' noticed. Comanches are probably the most cautious people on earth. They'd have no less than twenty warriors watchin' their camp on all sides. If you got within seein' distance of 'em, it was because they allowed you to get so close without losin' your hair." Now Sam turned to Tom. "If he wanted to, Bull Bear coulda wiped out this settlement in a single afternoon. A hundred warriors armed with rifles would overrun these walls in an hour or less. But they've settled in for the winter, which is all the more reason they wouldn't stir up any troubles. That's why the massacre up at Antelope Hill don't fit with what I know about Comanches. Bull Bear knows a strike like that would bring the cavalry down on him. His women and children would be hunted down an' captured or killed. If he was plannin' a war, he damn sure wouldn't let nobody find his winter camp."

Tom and Bob exchanged glances. "Maybe you're right," Tom said, "only it's mighty hard to think anybody else would cut up a human being like that. . . ." He was interrupted by a voice from the front door of his cabin calling us to breakfast.

I saw Anna beckoning to us, and my heart skipped a beat or two. Hungry as I was for something besides dry jerky, I wondered if I could eat with her in the same room. A pretty woman can be a powerful distraction even when a man's real hungry.

"Food's ready," Tom said, starting for the cabin.

I fell in behind him, forcing myself to think about table manners and chewing with my mouth closed. My ma taught that we should eat slowly in the presence of womenfolk. With all these things to remember, I trudged through the snow, determined to make a good impression. It didn't matter that Anna was going to marry a cowman's son in a few months. She was such a pretty girl that I could hardly think about anything else.

I cast a look toward the army camp while we were making for the cabin. Soldiers were out and about, adding wood to cooking fires. I counted about thirty cavalrymen and a dozen tents, not much of a fighting force if Bull Bear's Kotsotekas went on the warpath. The longer Sam argued against those Comanches being responsible for that massacre on the Canadian, the more it was making sense. If Bull Bear wanted a war with white men, he sure wouldn't have let a cowboy like Bob Sims ride up to his winter camp. But what still didn't make any sense at all was why those killers butchered their victims Comanche-style. Whoever they were, they didn't know enough about Comanches to realize that it gave them away when they cut up young girls.

We entered the Anderson's cabin after stomping snow off our boots and pulling off our hats. I'd combed my hair and shaved my chin whiskers soon as I got up so I'd look presentable when we ate at Anna's. She was standing beside her mother at the wood stove with her hair all done up and brushed. As soon as Tom got the door closed behind us, she turned around and smiled. I never saw such a pretty smile in all my life, the prettiest white teeth and dimples in her cheeks looking like she'd put them there with the tip of her finger. She was wearing a blue gingham dress and a sweater, on account of how cold it was inside even though that stove nearly glowed red as a poker. She spoke to me first, to say "Good morning, Mr. Dudley." Then she said, "Good morning, Marshal Ault," and took a pan of biscuits from the oven to put them on a table set with china plates.

I muttered, "Morning, ma'am," and took a seat beside Sam, feeling like my cheeks were turning the color of that cast-iron stove. I vowed to mind my manners no matter what, feeling Anna's eyes on me now and then. She was making me mighty nervous. But I wasn't going to come unglued over it. I took a biscuit she offered and put butter on it, wishing like the dickens she would stop staring at me so often. Beautiful women can have a powerful effect on a man's appetite sometimes. Even though I was hungry enough to eat everything in sight, I forced myself to take small bites and chew slowly. We ate wild turkey eggs and bacon, with all the biscuits anybody could want washed down with coffee. To tell the truth I was glad when breakfast was finally over so I wouldn't feel Anna's deep-blue eyes on me so regular.

We thanked everyone and walked out to our horses. Tom came with us to see us off. Sam mounted his roan and gave the horizon a study before we left. "You keep your eyes peeled," he said. "Don't any of you get very far from here alone. If Ross and his men intend to ride regular patrols, it'll help keep anything from happenin' here, I'd imagine. Leastways until they're gone. And there's one more thing—if five hombres happen to show up in the next few days, don't turn your back on 'em. One is an Indian, an Osage. One's a big Mexican wearin' a sombrero. The one who did all the talkin' is a tall, lanky feller who carries a pistol in a cross-pull holster. Wears a flat-brim hat pulled down in front, so it's kinda hard to see his face."

Tom's expression clouded. "That sounds a little bit like a new ramrod who went to work for Grant. Seems like Grant told me his name was Will, Will James. Grant said he was from Missouri, only he wouldn't be takin' shots at strangers like that. Grant wouldn't allow it."

Now it was Sam's face turning thoughtful. "I know that name from some place or 'nother. Will James sounds mighty familiar."

"Grant wouldn't hire nobody who wasn't on the level, Marshal. Will's his ranch foreman. Only thing about him is the way he wears a pistol backwards so he has to reach across his belly to pull it. But that don't make him the same feller who took a shot at you the other night. Grant wouldn't permit no behavior such as that from one of his men."

"Maybe," Sam said, sounding more than a little doubtful in my opinion. "We'll talk to Haskell after we nose around what's left of that settlement. Until you get word from us, be on the lookout for strangers."

"Or Injuns," Tom remarked, like he still wasn't convinced it wasn't the Comanches who were responsible.

I told Tom, "Thank your wife and daughters again for that delicious breakfast. Best eating we've had for quite a spell."

Tom gave me a nod. We reined our horses and struck a trot out of Elk, passing the army camp without so much as a word or a wave farewell. I was leading our new sorrel mule and didn't look back over my shoulder until we were nearly out of sight from the opening in the walls But when I did glance backward, I happened to notice Anna standing on her front porch, watching us ride off. I almost waved to her, until I remembered that she was due to be married to Ward Haskell in the spring. Waving goodbye to another man's sweetheart wouldn't have seemed proper.

We aimed northwest, riding snow-covered hills and canyons. The Wichitas lay behind us now and the country was a mite easier to travel. Sun warmed the land, and pretty soon snow began to melt. Usually the first storm of winter is like that, a helluva blow along with freezing cold, then it warms some for a few days before the next norther strikes. Granted, it was early in the year for a blizzard like the one we'd ridden into, but weather in the Territory can be as unpredictable as it wants to be, despite what Clara Ault had to say on the subject. I hadn't lived here all that long, but it was long enough to know that the weather could change faster than a jackrabbit's run.

On toward noon, while we followed that same wagon road that would take us to the Kansas line and on to Dodge City, we came upon the remains of a burned-out wagon. It was hardly more than a charred shell, and by the look of it, the misfortune had occurred some time back. A few yards away, underneath a particularly large oak tree that had shed all its leaves, we saw four grave markers with names carved into pieces of wood plank. Sam called a halt near the planks so we could read what was on them. One said it marked the grave of Ned Carter, then Dora, Sue, and Bobby were laid out in a row. It was a chilling sight, thinking that a family lay below the ground here; and by the looks of the wagon, I figured it must have been Indians who killed them. Reading the two women's names, I was curious.

"If Comanches done this, how come two women got killed?"

Sam seemed to ponder it a moment. "I reckon it could have been Kiowas, or maybe the women got burned in the fire. I never said Comanches didn't kill a few women from time to time. If a stray bullet or an arrow happened to find the wrong target, it wouldn't grieve the Comanches none. But as a regular practice, they don't slaughter women because they've got value, like good horses." He looked northward, frowning. "It's just a feelin', Mr. Dudley, but I've got a hunch those settlers at Antelope Hill met up with a white man who's got a dose of greed. That feller I described to Tom Anderson sounded a hell of a lot like Will James to him. I don't reckon we'll know for a spell, but somethin' down in my gut tells me this James had a hand in what happened."

"Tom Anderson and Sims swore by Grant Haskell's honesty," I reminded him. "Salt of the earth is what they said about him."

"We'll see," was all Sam said, reining away from the graves to strike a trot along wagon ruts filling with water from melted snow.

We made camp in the shelter of some cedars atop a knob that gave us a view of all sides. Sam was still behaving like we had somebody trailing us, looking over his shoulder from time to time when we rode high ground. But when I asked him if anyone was back there, he said he couldn't see a thing.

We built a fire inside the cedar grove and roasted salt pork on forked sticks while coffee was boiling. As dusk became dark it got mighty cold again, even though snow had been melting until sundown.

I hobbled our animals on short grass within eyesight of our fire and carried our bedrolls back to camp, along with my rifle. I wasn't going to be caught again without my Winchester if we had company tonight. Sam was adding a finger of whiskey to his cup when I got back.

"I'll take the first watch," he told me. "Can't hardly get rid of this uneasy feelin', like we're bein' followed. But for the life of me, I can't spot nobody behind us. Maybe it's my eyes goin' bad with old age. . . ."

I spread out my blankets near the fire. "Could be only your imagination, I suppose."

He grunted, like I should have known better. "I hardly ever imagine things out here in the Territory. Most times, there's enough real danger so a man's imagination don't get much chance to be overworked."

I lay down, hoping I could sleep until my turn came to stand watch.

Thirteen

We crossed the Washita River about noon that day and kept on pushing to make the South Canadian before nightfall. Sam's roan didn't suit him all that well even though it was soft-gaited and an easy traveler. I guessed, more than anything else, he missed his black gelding. A man can get used to a horse's ways after a spell.

We crossed much of the same hilly country under clear skies and sunshine, although it was still colder than blue blazes when the wind blew. Some of the snow was melting where the sun struck open patches, but for the most part things were blanketed in wet snow and I didn't see how we'd find anything when we got to the settlement.

Our red mule wasn't much of a trail animal, it being used to a harness rather than a packsaddle. Times, I'd have to drag it along, which only tired my bay that much more. I couldn't stop thinking about that 'breed I killed in the dark, another life to add to my growing tally of dead men since I'd become a Deputy U.S. Marshal. But when I could manage to forget about seeing him lying in that snow, I thought about pretty Anna Anderson. Of all the women I'd seen since I came out West, she was the prettiest. And the way she kept staring at me while we were eating made me wonder about her forthcoming marriage to Ward Haskell. Why would she look at me when her mind should have been on him?

Sam kept turning back in the saddle like he expected to

see someone following us. When I did likewise, I couldn't
see a thing back there, just more empty land and forested
hills. It's a bit of an odd feeling, finding yourself all alone
under a big sky in open country, like there wasn't nobody
else in the whole world.

Toward evening we sighted the South Canadian winding
across a shallow valley in front of us. The ruts we followed
turned to the west, sloping down toward the river. Off in the
distance I could make out the remains of a couple of pole
corrals and the shells of two wagons half covered with snow,
empty bows looking like ribs on an animal carcass; but there
were no houses or a dwelling of any kind anywhere.

I rode up beside Sam, squinting in the sun's glare off the
covering of snowflakes. "Is that Antelope Hill?" I asked when
I pointed to a little rise where the corrals and wagons sat.

"That's it," he said quietly, sweeping the valley with long
looks in every direction.

"There ain't any houses. No sign they got burned down
if there were any to begin with."

"Settlers from back East are inclined to dig holes in the
ground first so they'll have a cellar when they build a cabin
afterwards. Those folks hadn't been here long enough to get
a cabin started, it don't appear. I can see a couple of mounds
over yonder. That'll be where they fashioned dugouts."

I could see the mounds he was talking about, two humps
of snow near the corrals. "Maybe that's where we'll find some
clue to who did the killings if we look hard enough. Maybe
they left something behind those soldiers didn't notice."

"Most soldiers wouldn't notice a Conestoga wagon in a
broom closet, Mr. Dudley," Sam remarked. "Trouble is, Captain Ross an' his men already stomped all over the place so
we won't be able to tell what's what. Be the same as havin'
a buffalo stampede right where we aimed to look."

Our horses' hooves made a swishing noise through deeper
snow as we rode closer to the river. I found myself thinking
this was the spot where eleven people lost their lives, dying

in a terrible way. The river bottom looked so peaceful now, like nothing had happened here.

Sam pointed to a few scattered cottonwood trees lining the river. "Yonder's where Comanches would likely have slipped up on those folks, usin' those trees for cover. After we see what's at the settlement, we'll ride the river for a ways, just to make sure we don't miss anything."

"You said you didn't think it was Comanches. . . ."

"I ain't seen anything to change my mind, Mr. Dudley. I aim to look, that's all."

With the sun just above the horizon, we rode up on what there was of the settlement. Crudely fashioned pole corrals and three sides of a roofless shed lay between two dugouts. Fire-gutted wagons dusted with snow sat beside the corrals, charred so badly hardly a plank in the bottoms or sides was usable. My bay gave a snort when we got closer, and I wondered what he sensed that made him uneasy. Maybe he somehow understood what had happened here in a way only range-bred horses could.

Sam rode to one of the dugouts and swung down, testing his legs after so many hours in a saddle. "Let's have a look inside before we go any farther," he said, tossing me his reins. "Tie the horses off an' loosen their cinches. Maybe there's somethin' in one of 'em those tin soldiers missed."

I took Sam's reins and rode into an empty corral, making a quick survey of our surroundings before I got down, in particular examining our backtrail to see if we'd been followed, although I knew Sam had been doing the same thing all day. I got down when I was satisfied we were alone, tying off our animals to a corral post before I loosened cinch-straps so the horses could blow. I saw a row of wooden crosses made of tree limbs behind one of the corrals. I counted eleven markers above the graves before I put our mule a safe kicking distance from our horses.

Sam disappeared into a dugout, tossing some kind of animal skin out of the way serving as a door. I walked over on frozen feet to join him, taking note of how little light was spilling down through the opening.

"There's a hell of a lot of blood," Sam said, kneeling down to examine something on the dirt floor.

Blankets and quilts were scattered about and every one had a bloodstain on it. Bits of furniture and clothing lay everywhere, along with cooking utensils and articles of clothing. A pale blue dress the right size for a very young child rested near one of the sleeping pallets, and I'd never seen so much blood on any other garment my whole life.

"One of the girls was real small," I said, my voice sounding hollow down in the ground like we were. The roof above our heads was made of limbs and branches with a few larger tree trunks for support. I could imagine what it must have been like to be there when the women and children were killed. "They must have been screaming something awful when it happened," I added, walking to a big wood chest turned on its side. "Somebody went all through their personal effects like they was looking for something."

"Probably those soldiers," Sam said, lifting a quilt so he could see under it.

"I never saw so much blood, Marshal. It must have been one hell of a bad way to die for all of 'em."

Sam stood up, looking at the walls briefly. "To my way of thinkin', there ain't no such thing as a good way to die. When I go, I hope it's in my sleep."

I was pawing through a few items at the bottom of the trunk when I found a tiny silver locket. When I opened it, I found a likeness of a girl with blond hair tied in pigtails. Engraved on the locket's cover was the name *Sara*. "One of the girls was named Sara," I said, taking the locket over to Sam. "She was a pretty thing."

He grunted when he looked at it. "A damn shame she had to die. But with that headful of yellow hair, there's no way she was killed by Comanches. She'd be worth a dozen good ponies to any warrior who needed a tarches."

"What's a *tarches?*" I asked, wondering if it was the Comanche word for wife.

"A female slave. They help around camp, gatherin' wood an' such as that. A young buck uses 'em to learn how to poke a woman—if she's pretty enough. Warriors trade 'em back an' forth when they get tired of one. They're nearly the same as money. That's why no Comanche would kill somethin' so valuable as a yellow-hair woman. It'd be like settin' fire to a handful of bank notes."

What Sam said made sense to me, only he'd had a hard time of convincing Tom Anderson and the others back at Elk to his way of thinking, not to mention Major Donaldson or Captain Ross. "That only leaves two possibilities, Marshal. It was white men who did this, or another tribe of Indians." I put the locket in a pocket of my coat for no better reason than it didn't seem right to put it back in the abandoned trunk.

Sam took a breath and made a face. "It still stinks of old blood down here. I'm ready for some fresh air. We'll take a look in the other dugout, but I figure we'll only find more of the same."

Climbing a slanting pathway to level ground, Sam led over to the next dugout and went down a similar slope to a deer-skin on a framework of limbs, stepping over an assortment of boot prints in the snow left by the soldiers. When Sam opened this makeshift door, I saw something that resembled a black snake a few feet past the opening.

"Watch out for that snake!" I shouted, reaching for my gun.

"It ain't a snake, Mr. Dudley," Sam remarked, by his tone making it sound like I should have known. "It's what's left of a string of human intestines. Probably got chewed off by a wolf or a coyote before Babs an' his bunch found the bodies. You can put your gun away. . . . It ain't gonna bite you."

I holstered my pistol quickly, embarrassed to be covering an intestine with a gun. "The light was bad," I explained.

I entered the dugout, and right away my nostrils filled with the smell of decay. Sam was over at a far wall examining a pile of bedding.

"Here's somethin' I didn't expect to find," Sam said as he knelt down for a closer look at some object lying on the floor.

I couldn't tell what it was until he picked it up and handed it to me. "It's a diary," I said, opening a small green book bearing the legend *My Diary*.

On the very first page was a name. "It belonged to a woman by the name of Georgina Cooper. Says here she was born in Boston in the year 1847." I thumbed through more pages, finding they were full of writing. She wrote with a neat hand, only there was a place or two where it was hard to read.

Sam gave the room a final glance. "Maybe she left a note to say where we could write to her next of kin about what happened. The family would appreciate knowin' what came of them."

"I might just read the whole thing, Marshal. It'll be a way to pass some time and there may be a clue in here somewhere's as to who killed her and her family."

Sam scowled. "That don't make a whole lot of sense. I'd be real surprised if whoever killed her gave her time to write down his name."

"I was only thinking there could be a clue as to who did it, maybe somebody she saw beforehand who came back. It's possible she saw somebody suspicious and wrote it in here." I put it in my pocket when the marshal wouldn't quit scowling at me. I knew he didn't think much of my idea, but it was worth a try.

"Let's ride the river before it gets dark," Sam said. "If you won't be too busy readin'." He went around me and climbed out of the dugout.

I followed him to the horses, wondering what that little book might have to say about the families who died here. It would be sad to read something a dead woman wrote in her diary. Whoever Georgina Cooper was, I'd be reading about her life up until the time she died, sharing her secrets. But it was more than simple curiosity making me want to read it. There was a chance, a slim chance maybe, but a chance she'd seen someone and made a note of it that could help lead us to the killers.

Sam was mounted by the time I got to the corral. He gave a look toward the river. "Let's see if we can find a shallow spot to cross over. I'd hate like hell to get my longjohns wet before dark."

We rode out of the pens and made a turn for the south bank of the Canadian at sunset. Like Sam, I was sure hoping we'd be able to find a low water-crossing. The idea of spending a night in wet clothes was enough to give me the shivers.

We got lucky, finding a crossing just above the settlement so shallow our horses scarcely went to their knees in icy black water moving sluggishly between the banks. On the far side, Sam turned east, the direction we would ride to reach Bull Bear's camp if Sam was of a mind to talk to the Comanches first. I was convinced we needed to talk to that Texas rancher by the name of Grant Haskell, because it sounded for all the world like his new ramrod, Will James, was the gent who fired those shots at us in the dark.

"We won't find anything," Sam declared after he halted his roan beneath the first stand of cottonwoods. "This snow's had time to melt and that will wash away any sign, if there ever was any to find."

I saw tracks in the snow where columns of soldiers rode down the river, now merely faint impressions after sunlight melted the snow. "Like you said before, the cavalry probably rode over any sign the raiders left."

Sam swung his horse away from the trees. "Let's find a spot to make a fire downstream. I'm needin' a bit of coffee sweetened with whiskey to cure what's ailin' me."

"I could use a shot of whiskey myself," I said, finding that my teeth were chattering now as darkness brought a dip in temperatures to the river valley.

Later on, I'd read some of Georgina Cooper's diary by firelight. Something told me, maybe only a hunch, that I'd find some clue to what happened at Antelope Hill.

Fourteen

After an evening meal of fried fatback and coffee, we sat as close to the fire as we could inside a cottonwood grove near the river's edge. I added a splash of whiskey to my coffee since it did tend to make me feel warmer. I judged the temperature was below twenty degrees and getting colder by the time our supper dishes were washed. The river gurgled softly as it flowed by our camp; and if it hadn't been for visiting the scene where eleven people died, I'd have felt mighty peaceful under the stars, even as cold as it was. We had our fire sheltered with rocks and our animals tethered close by. Sam kept prowling around the edge of those trees with his rifle like he expected visitors, but that was his nature more than anything else—he was a careful man in almost any situation and tonight, with us in dangerous country, he wasn't inclined to relax his vigilance any.

Resting my back against a cottonwood trunk, I took out the diary, bending over so light from the flames lit up the pages. I didn't know what to expect, reading what Georgina Cooper wrote, but I kind of got an eerie feeling reading a dead woman's words.

We set out from St. Louis in the spring, crossing over the wide Mississippi with high spirits and high hopes. Our wagon is a Studebaker, sturdy enough for the long journey we shall entertain, if God is willing. Sara spent her twelfth birthday in our wagon. Denise can't wait to be ten, she says. Nathaniel says he is happy with our new mules, although the horse he bought is not altogether trustworthy and it balks at even the smallest streams. But it isn't Nathaniel's sweet nature to whip an animal and thus we often wait what seems like forever at bodies of water, waiting for the bay, which Nathaniel has named Satan's Disciple because of its temperament, to make up its mind to cross. Dave has said the horse has learned to take advantage of Nathaniel's kindness at rivers, joking that it is smarter than its owner. But my dear Nathaniel will not be swayed into whipping the creature and I do sometimes wonder if Dave could be right about the bay's intelligence being quite high.

We are off for the far West, the land of boundless opportunity, a land-advertisement claimed, full of courage and a sense of high adventure. Poor Myra is having such a time in their wagon because of the five children, and it's only by the Will of God she can collect her senses. She is fortunate to have four boys, who will be such a help when we begin our new homes out West. They are strong, like their father, only still young. Myra's daughter hasn't taken well to the rough ride of a wagon, complaining of stomach distress for which we must make frequent stops so she can rush into the bushes. Dave is patient with her, as patient as my Nathaniel with his reluctant horse.

Our Studebaker is heavily loaded with supplies, and at night we must sleep on the ground; however, the weather is warm and not unpleasant. I'm so looking forward to seeing the western Territories where we plan to stake our claims. Nathaniel and Dave are most interested in the Texas panhandle, a funny name for a piece of a state. We've heard grassland is abundant there and there is rarely any difficulty with savage Indians. Sara says she can't wait to see her first wild Indian. The ones we've seen thus far seem quite tame and docile. We'll be traveling with a group of wagons across Missouri to Springfield, but from there on westward we'll be on our own since the wagonmaster says his group will be traveling further north than our planned destination. We should be passing well to the north of a terrible-sounding place known as Indian Territory, where Indians are allowed to roam freely as they hunt buffalo. We have yet to see our first buffalo, however our wagonmaster, Mr. Denkins, says we won't see any in Missouri and everyone is disappointed. We have seen drawings of these big hairy beasts, and I fear I'll be somewhat frightened of them if we happen to pass too closely. Dave believes they are mostly gentle animals unless they are provoked. Both girls are excited about seeing them, although Denise has asked her father to stay quite near to the wagon with her, should we encounter any.

Our first week has been uneventful, save for a mishap to my Aunt Elizabeth's dressing mirror, which has cracked despite many layers of quilts protecting it. A jar of pickles has also fallen victim to our Studebaker's rough ride; however, we ate them, being so careful to pick off bits of glass. One of our mules has begun to develop a sore spot on its withers, which I shall remedy with regular applications of bacon grease and a bit of padding I have sewn from cotton rags. Otherwise, our trip is going splendidly, although I'll admit to being somewhat weary of our wagon seat and Missouri scenery. It is chilly at night, but not uncomfortable. I've never seen Nathaniel so content with what he is doing. Out West, he will find his dream and his dream will be ours. We will have our own land and cattle. I've been planning our garden for months ahead of our departure, packaging seeds even though no one is sure what varieties of vegetables will grow in northern Texas.

The village of Springfield is a dreadful place, full of unwashed men who often stare at Sara and, sometimes, at me. It is as if they seldom see a woman here. Myra confided she noticed a man rubbing his crotch when their wagon passed

*and he was grinning at her the entire length of the episode.
She feared telling Dave about it, knowing Dave's short temper. The mule's sore is all but healed now, thanks to the
padding and grease. Sara and Denise entertain themselves
by braiding each other's hair when a road we travel is monotonous. We made the acquaintance of a nice family from
Ohio, the Cummings. Walter Cummings is a blacksmith
bound for California with his wife and three children. He
told Nathaniel about a place with bountiful grass near the
tip of Texas along a river known as the South Canadian. He
has given us a map showing where abundant antelope can
be found and rich soil good for growing a garden, although
he did warn Nathaniel and Dave about neighboring Indians
called Comanches. They do sound dreadful and Walter says
they can be easily provoked to a fight; however, a treaty of
peace has been signed with them and he believes they are
men of their word. Nathaniel has been so full of vigor since
hearing about this place. We have all agreed it is just the
sort of land we are seeking to homestead. Walter did caution
us to make inquiry as to boundaries, making sure we did not
settle on land conveyed to Indians by the treaty of peace. We
intend to make such inquiries upon our arrival there so to
be sure not to occupy land in Indian Territory.*

*We prepared a supper of rice and beans, of which my girls
have grown exceedingly weary. Nathaniel and Dave promised to go hunting this week after being told we are near
forests full of fat wild turkeys.*

*We have crossed some imaginary line into Kansas Terri-
tory at midday, passing a lone stake driven in the ground
telling us our location. Dave shot a turkey hen with his shotgun, and we will be feasting on the meat for days. Nathaniel
has seen a number of geese on scouting trips. We were told
by Mr. Denkins the rest of his party will be turning north
after crossing the Neosho River. Five weeks on the trail westward and soon we'll be on our own. I shall miss the company*

of other women and so shall Myra, and our children have enjoyed playing games with newfound friends we will no longer see. From what we have seen of Kansas, it is not at all a pretty place. There is a marked absence of trees.

We are alone for the first time in our travels and it is a somewhat disturbing feeling to be so isolated, with no one else to depend on. We stop often to repair damage to Dave's wagon as it has not fared as well as ours. Water can be quite scarce in this region. We stop at most every stream and river to fill our water kegs. Nathaniel's bay has shown some improvement in its temperament. All seems to be going well—other than the boredom we continually face. Denise is sometimes given over to crying fits when she feels particularly lonely. Neither Nathaniel nor Dave has been able to find any wild game and our diet has become very monotonous, as monotonous as this desolate land. I'm glad we are not settling in Kansas for it is a horrid place with no feature to redeem it.

Nathaniel has felled a deer with his rifle! It is a fat doe and everyone celebrates his marksmanship. He is quite proud of his accomplishment and has kept the skin to cure as a memento. While the children and I are in dreadfully low spirits following so many weeks of sameness, I've never seen Nathaniel so happy. I know we will all share his enthusiasm for our adventure as soon as we get where we are going. Myra has taken to sobbing at night when no one else is around. It is the monotony of this landscape which is driving her to the brink. We haven't seen a soul since we left Mr. Denkins's party. Surely no place on earth can be as empty and inhospitable as Kansas.

The weather is warm and pleasant; however, the land is so dry our wheels send up frightfully large clouds of dust. We have not seen anyone, and I confess to being lonely sometimes. Days pass while I sit on this wagon seat. We seldom engage in conversation now, save for the girls' squabbling. We have seen antelope from a distance, and while they are curious creatures, they do not come close to our wagons. Dave and Nathaniel have promised to hunt at the next opportunity to vary our routine diet. It is early in April. I have stopped marking days on our calendar since it does seem pointless.

We have encountered a major obstacle, a river not shown on our maps unless it can be the Cimarron, which will mean we are considerably off our course. Rains upstream have swollen the river and made it unnavigable, thus we must wait for the waters to recede. Antelope meat is lean and somewhat tougher than deer meat. Myra's son Oliver has come down with a case of the croup, and Denise is suffering from mild dysentery. It will soon be May and we seem no closer to our destination, slowed by frequent and unforeseen delays. Sara is quite homesick, wishing she had not come with us. Her skin is quite sunburned and she complains of even the slightest inconvenience.

We have found civilization! A small trading post operated by a whiskered man named Woods seems like New York City to us at a time when we were desperately needing contact with anyone. He is friendly and talkative, sharing his quarters with a pregnant Indian girl. He tells us we have strayed into the western tip of Indian Territory, but that the Indians have been peaceful until now. We bought badly needed provisions from Mr. Woods and were given directions to the South Canadian River which we so desperately seek so we may begin our homesteads. Everyone is weary of wagon travel, and we celebrate the nearness of its end. And we have sighted our first buffalos! These shaggy creatures are so fearsome we dared not approach the herd. They have short horns and fierce countenances, pawing the earth should we get too near with our wagons, snorting like hairy dragons. Denise

*believes she saw one breathing fire! We have camped at Mr.
Woods' trading post for the night, and all of us are so eager
to hear him tell his tales about this land. He seems very
knowledgeable when it comes to Indians and boundary lines.
It is truly a godsend that we happened upon his establishment
without having a road to take us there.*

*We now have sugar and wild plums. I am baking a wild
plum cobbler, and we've invited Mr. Woods to have some. He
has a milk cow and we will have cream to go with our plum
pie. Never have I valued such commonplace things, after
going so long without them.*

*We were all saddened to leave the trading post. Mr. Woods
was a coarse individual in his personal habits but a welcome
respite from our own company. Nathaniel seems cheered by
most of what Mr. Woods told us, although he did suggest we
use caution in our future travels, being this was Indian land.
We must cross a portion of Indian Territory to reach our
destination. Mr. Woods said the South Canadian area is a
fertile grassland and some of it is suitable for farming. We
have plowshares and digging tools to begin our new houses
and we hope to find plenty of good timber in the region.
Nathaniel and Dave plan to dig deep cellars first which will
serve as shelters until logs can be secured for solid walls.
Our spirits are soaring again and we all feel as we did in
the beginning of our journey, looking forward with great ex-
pectations to the commencement of our enterprise.*

*It is Thursday, the fifth day of May. We have encountered
a herd of wild cattle with long antlers. They seem unman-
ageable as domestic livestock, for when Nathaniel and Dave
rode toward them they took off like frightened deer. Dave
calls them longhorns, and they are that, indeed. Some of
them have horns at least six feet across, and I shouldn't care
to be close to one when it gets angry or provoked.*

Some of the landmarks Mr. Woods described are unclear,

and we hope we are not lost again. Mr. Woods cautioned us not to make a mistake by settling on Indian lands. We were told we would find a marker telling us where the boundary of Texas was. We are now following a river which we believe is the South Canadian, yet we cannot be sure. This is excellent grassland. We see more and more wild cattle in the distance and have hopes of locating their owners to get our bearings. No Indians have been sighted, and we take this as a positive sign we are finally in Texas at last.

I closed the diary when Sam summoned me to take my turn at watch. I felt like I'd come all the way from St. Louis in the wagon with Georgina and her family. There was nothing in her writing to tell us what might have happened. I still had a few pages left to read, and I promised myself I'd read them tomorrow.

I got up and carried my rifle to the edge of the trees with frosty breath curling from my nose. I knew what Georgina Cooper meant when she wrote about how empty this land can be. I leaned against a cottonwood, keeping a close eye on the snowy hills around us.

Fifteen

Dawn came clear and cold to the South Canadian valley. Just at sunrise a small herd of antelope came down to the river for a drink, wagging their long white tails, rubbery noses taking in our scent cautiously before they lowered their heads at water's edge where tall bulrushes glistened with a coating of frost. The snow caught early crimson sunlight, turning it pink in scattered low spots. The air was so still the smoke from our fire rose up as a column like it was meant to support the sky.

Sam watched our coffeepot absently, hardly noticing much of anything, as though his mind was a thousand miles away. He hadn't said a word since midnight.

"You appear distracted," I said, wondering what was eating on him so.

"I've been thinkin' about what we found yesterday, tryin' to figure who stood to gain from gettin' rid of those settlers. It just has to be a cowman somewheres. Bull Bear wouldn't bring a war party this far west so late in the year. Could be renegades, I reckon, only we ain't heard of no such activity lately. Kind of a puzzle, Mr. Dudley. It'd take a real desperate man to cut up womenfolk an' children like that, a man who ain't got a trace of a conscience or an Indian who believes there's nothin' wrong with cuttin' up his enemy. I still say it wasn't an Indian who did it. Only made to look that way, so Indians would be blamed."

"It has to be somebody who wants this grass, either for a cow or a buffalo," I agreed, adding sticks to our fire, thinking out loud. "It's kinda sad, reading what that woman wrote about how they got here. They sound like they were nice folks."

"Did she mention seein' anybody out of the ordinary after they got here?"

"Not yet. I ain't done with it," I said. "They got directions from a gent named Woods who runs a trading post up north a ways, only maybe they got lost. She wrote they figured they was settled in Texas."

Sam gave the river bottom a glance. "They wasn't. Too far east by thirty or forty miles, maybe. Hard to tell out here when there ain't no landmarks to speak of. Bad luck for them, if they met up with Comanches who knew this was Indian Territory."

"But you still don't think it was Comanches, do you?"

"Hadn't seen anythin' to change my mind on it. We'll ride the river east for a ways, maybe talk to that feller Woods at the tradin' post. I know ol' Barney Woods. He'll remember talkin' to those folks, but he's likely not to want to tell us much else if he suspects anybody who trades with him. Like if there's a bunch of renegades in these parts who buy guns an' ammunition at his place. He ain't gonna tell me he's doin' anything illegal."

"Renegades are another possibility, only I can't see where there's a profit in it, killing these homesteaders. Unless it was for their livestock."

Sam reached for our small cast-iron skillet "I'll fry up a mess of bacon before we pull out. Smells like that coffee's just about ready."

We poured ourselves cups. I settled down on my haunches and took out Georgina's diary. "I'll read a little more while you're cooking. Maybe there's something in here. . . ."

I turned to the page where I'd stopped reading last night, a funny feeling in the pit of my stomach. When I reached the last page with writing on it, I would have come to the

place where she died—a spooky notion, knowing I was reading a dead woman's last thoughts.

*On this eighth day of May we found our new home! It is
by far the most beautiful place we've seen so far, a smooth
hilltop which is high enough in case the river floods, with a
view of all sides. Dave and Myra have selected a homesite
west of ours and our men have already begun to dig! It is
such a grand feeling to be here where we will live out the
rest of our lives. The grass is so plentiful and the waters so
clear at the river. Surely no place on earth could be so in-
viting! Texas is a grand state, and we are pleased to be
counted among its new citizens!*

*The twelfth of May sees our garden newly plowed. We girls
planted everything imaginable—pumpkins, squash, cucum-
ber, corn, peas and beans, and so many tomato plants we
shall surely die of eating them all. Myra has made the most
wonderful scarecrow with Dave's old shirt and overalls, using a pillowcase for his face to make him as human as possible. Nathaniel went hunting, bringing back several ducks
for roasting, and he reports beaver in feeder creeks and turkey hens so fat they cannot fly. He found prints made by deer
in the mud and sighted a number of antelope upon a hilltop.
Our only disappointment is a shortage of good timber for
building; however, with the mules our men can drag logs for
a great distance. Things are going so splendidly we can't
believe our good fortune. This is truly paradise!*

*Dave and his son Tommy caught three catfish at the river
on grub worms. While they will be harmful for our garden,
we've put these dreadful worms to good use elsewhere. Our
meals are now a refreshing change from beans and dried
beef strips. Denise still has bouts with stomach ailment from
time to time. Nathaniel says it is merely that she isn't accustomed to wild game. We have no more plugs of blue mass to*

*give her, and I worry she may fall ill in a serious way. We
have no idea how far it is to the closest doctor, in that event,
and I can only pray she will get well on her own. The cellars
go well, although the digging is difficult work. We water our
garden every day from the river. Our mules and horses are
fattening on good grass. Dave has located a fine stand of
timber only a few miles to the south, which the men can
begin felling as soon as our cellars are dug.*

*Sara has periods of melancholy, missing life in a city with
so many distractions. But I'm quite confident she will adapt
to wilderness life in good time.*

*Our first seeds have begun to sprout! Bean plants have
come out first, along with our peas. Days are quite warm
while nights are still chilly. Good progress continues on our
cellars even as the men develop blisters from so much digging, yet hardly anyone complains. We are happy here. Content. All is as it should be.*

*By my best calculations, it is near the end of May. It has
not rained, nor shown any promise of it. Our garden grows
as if by magic. Corn plants are almost knee-high. We shall
have such a bountiful crop, some will be wasted. However,
in this heat our meat stores spoil quickly. Tommy was taken
ill and we suspect a deer backstrap was at fault. When our
cellars are covered, there will be a way to slow down spoil-
age, keeping things cool. If we salt deer and antelope, it may
keep much longer. I do so long for a taste of sweet butter
and cream, but a milk cow could not have survived an ar-
duous journey such as ours. We shall make do without milk
and butter for the present.*

*Nathaniel and Dave report seeing a number of longhorn
cattle to the west. They have brands, and we believe it is
proof someone owns them. It would be so welcome to have
visitors. Myra and I sorely miss having some company, and
the children could use a bit of cheering up.*

Dave returned with a number of stout timbers for roof beams over our cellars, and the trimming has begun. We all share great excitement planning our simple houses of logs. To our families they will seem like castles suitable for kings and queens.

July finds us living in our earthen dwellings at last, after many weeks of labor preparing a roof that will keep out most of the rain, if it ever rains here. I've been too tired to write my feelings down lately—tending to our garden, keeping varmints out at night while our days are full of other chores. Nathaniel says we will begin erecting cabin walls very soon. I'll be so grateful when, at last, we have a house. The men work tirelessly and I must not complain. Sara believes she spotted a wolf last evening at sunset, drinking from the river.

As I write this, my hands are trembling so badly I cannot be sure I won't spill my tiny bottle of ink. Three men came today, three of the most terrible-looking men I ever hope to see. One was a giant, a true Philistine Goliath with a face so dreadful he frightened the children beyond measure. They came from the west on horses, and one spoke so sharply to Nathaniel that Dave came to bear on them with his rifle. They said we were trespassers on grazing land belonging to them, and they ordered us away! They carried pistols and promised to use them if we did not do as they instructed. Nathaniel told them we fully intended to stay in accordance with provisions of the Homestead Act unless someone could show ownership, that we would prove-up our claims by right of preemption as set forth in the Act of 1862, and then file on them. The Goliath spoke harshly in broken English to Nathaniel after that, telling him his life would be in danger if we stayed. The giant is of another nationality, yet I have no idea what it might be. He is dark-skinned and bearded, wearing a large hat, and his voice is so deep it fairly shook the ground when he spoke to Nathaniel. Another said this land was grazing land for cattle

*and not farmland. He spoke softly, and yet I was more afraid
of him than the others. When he stared at Nathaniel, I knew
he meant to kill him unless we did as he asked. They rode
away, after warning us again to move off this spot. I am so
frightened of these men and I fear they will do us harm if we
do not leave. But Nathaniel will hear nothing of it unless proof
is given we are on someone else's deeded acres. My Nathaniel
knows the law, and he truly believes he is right to demand
proof of another's claim. I mean to speak to him about it again
tonight. What will it matter who has a deed to land if it costs
us our lives? My terror of those men will not go away. Our
tiny paradise has suddenly become a frightening place to be.
The children are so frightened, they have nightmares about
the giant.*

"Here's something," I said, standing up quickly, pointing
to the entry I'd read. "Three men showed up sometime in
July making the demand they move away. They claimed these
folks were trespassers on their land. One was a big feller—
Mrs. Cooper said he was a giant, like Goliath, and that he
was some other nationality. He spoke in broken English, she
says. All three men carried guns."

Sam stopped turning bacon with his fork. "What else does
it say about 'em?"

"Only that they'd use their guns if they had to. There's a
few pages more. . . ."

"Read the rest of it," Sam said, frowning. "Three men.
One was a giant. They ordered them off this land like they
owned it. Maybe she's about to tell us who killed them only
she didn't know it right then."

"A real big feller won't be that hard to find. She said he
wore a beard and his skin was dark. Wonder if she's describing that Mexican who was with those gents south of Elk."

"Maybe," Sam replied gravely, hooding his eyelids like
he was thinking real hard. "Tell me what else it says."

I went back to the diary. Only a few more lines had been written in it. I started to read out loud.

"Nathaniel is moody now, and he cannot sleep. At night he is restless, moving about with a gun. He hardly speaks to me or the children. He paces back and forth and his eyes are always on the horizon, as though he expects those men to return. We shall continue to build our houses; however, no one's heart is in the task. Whenever we go to the river for water, Nathaniel or Dave goes with us and always with a rifle or a pistol.

"Last night a wolf howled from across the river. A lone wolf makes a sound unlike no other animal, and we all shivered in our bedcovers when we heard it. My heart tells me the wolf is trying to warn us to leave, but Nathaniel has his mind made up to stay."

I took a deep breath. "That's the last entry. After that, all the pages are blank."

Sam was staring into the flames. "Three men came," he said, and it was like a question.

"She wrote they came from the west."

"From Texas. That's the direction this Grant Haskell lives, according to Tom Anderson."

I put the book back in my coat pocket. "Appears that's the logical place to start asking questions."

"Sounds like it," Sam agreed.

"I'll saddle our horses while that bacon's getting ready."

"I knew damn well it wasn't no Comanche killin'," Sam said. "Now we've got proof."

"I ain't all that sure what this diary says will stand up in a court of law, Marshal. We'll need to find something in the way of hard evidence."

Sam nodded, going back to his cooking. "That's exactly what we aim to do, Mr. Dudley."

"A giant won't be that hard to find."

"Maybe," Sam remarked. "We've only got her description to go by. Get those horses saddled. An' while you're at it, make a better effort on that diamond hitch over the mule. It's a wonder we haven't lost all our gear comin' this far with a loose knot to hold everything where it's supposed to be."

I slipped away to get our animals ready with Sam's caution ringing in my ears.

Sixteen

Clear days can be colder than the cloudy variety; and when a wind blows across fresh snowfall, it can chill a man plumb to his bones after a few hours. I'd gotten so cold I put on Clara's red mittens, seeing as how there wasn't anybody to see me in 'em and if I'd had another pair, I would have worn them, too. The panhandle region is mighty flat, so there's nothing to cut off the wind most times. There's hardly a tree anywhere. It's good land for raising livestock, but hard on humans in wintertime.

We rode the river west, blinded by sunlight reflecting off snow. Our animals labored through deeper drifts in places; but for the most part, travel was easy enough if you didn't mind being froze. Toward noon we came to an abandoned mud house, its walls crumbling, on a low rise north of the river. We rode over just to get out of that wind for a spell and to give our animals some rest.

Sam got down from his saddle stiffly, and I knew I would be in for some complaining because his joints hurt. He complained more and more about his knees lately. When his knees hurt, he'd stay in a foul mood.

"Dig a bottle of whiskey out of our packs, Mr. Dudley. This occasion calls for a drink," he said, loosening his cinch around the roan's belly.

I swung out of my saddle, shivering, thankful to have a few moments behind a windbreak. I gave the old house some study as I opened a pack to fetch the bottle. "I wonder why these settlers gave up, Marshal. Looks like they spent considerable time on the house to just move off."

"Maybe they got the same discouragement those folks got back at Antelope Hill. Somebody wants all this grazin' land for his own purposes. Might be more of Grant Haskell's doings, if he's behind what happened there. No way to know for sure yet. We'll be lookin' into it."

I'd been thinking about those murdered settlers all morning. Georgina Cooper's writings still haunted me. I carried the pint over to Sam. "Funny there's no mention of seeing Indians in her diary. Just the three gents who ordered them to move away. I'd say she identified their killers for us. Now all we've got to do is find some proof of it."

Sam downed a large swallow of whiskey, making a face when it burned his throat. He handed it to me. "Whoever the killers were, they didn't leave no witnesses. Provin' they did it won't be easy." He glanced around us at the mud walls. "Same can be said about what happened here, most likely. Comanches might have killed 'em, or cattlemen wantin' this grazin' land. But on the other hand, what's more likely is they fell victim to hard times. Way out here, most anythin' could have done 'em in. Sickness, or a bad accident. Madness can set in, livin' so far from civilization. Folks get stir-crazy after a long spell bein' alone. I've seen people who lost their minds from loneliness on the prairie."

I took a small sip of whiskey, stamping my feet to get some circulation going. "I reckon I'd go crazy out here myself with nobody to talk to."

The marshal took back his bottle. "It's the women you'd be missin', Mr. Dudley. You cut your eyes toward every creature in a skirt, like that Anderson girl. But you'll probably live long enough to regret that inclination, if you don't lose your scalp or stop a bullet doin' this job. One of these days you'll wind up like me, preferrin' the company of a horse to stayin' home so some woman can talk your ears off." He grinned and looked down at my hands. "By the way, those are right pretty mittens you're wearin'. Wish I had a pair just like 'em."

We encountered a herd of cattle at midafternoon, a large bunch of maybe a hundred or so being pushed out of some snowy hills by two cowboys. When they saw us they held a quick conversation and pulled rifles from saddle boots.

"They're reaching for their guns," I warned needlessly, for Sam had already seen what was going on.

"You've got eyes like an eagle," he said, standing in his stirrups while waving to the drovers.

When the cowboys saw Sam's friendly wave, they relaxed a bit. We kicked our horses to a trot in their direction, crossing a low spot where snow was a foot deep. They still appeared uneasy as we rode closer, but they rested their rifles across the pommels of their saddles until we got within shouting distance.

"United States Marshals!" Sam declared. "You can put those guns away if these cows belong to you!"

One cowboy glanced at the other before he spoke. "We ride for the Rafter H! Just bein' on the safe side!"

They were booting their guns when we rode up. One bearded gent wore a green mackinaw with a wool shawl covering his ears, tied underneath his hat. The other had the collar of a dark-blue greatcoat turned up to keep out wind. I noticed a Rafter H brand on both horses, an "H" with a little roof over the top.

We halted our horses in front of theirs.

"We're lookin' for Grant Haskell's spread," Sam began. "I'd judged it was somewheres along this river."

The cowboy in the mackinaw pointed west. "Keep on ridin' in the same direction, Marshal. You'll make the ranch headquarters by noon tomorrow." His brow knitted. "Mind if I ask why a U.S. Marshal is out this way?"

Sam rested his hands on his saddlehorn, sizing up both

men before he answered. "Awhile back some settlers got killed east of here. Just wanted to ask a few questions."

"We heard about it. Comanches on the warpath again. The boss said to keep our eyes peeled for Injuns."

"Have you seen any Indians?" Sam asked offhandedly, like it wasn't all that important.

The other drover spoke up. "Our ramrod said he spotted some a week back. He said he was real lucky they didn't try an' lift his hair."

"Who's this ramrod?"

"Will James. He tol' us he lit out of there like a scalded cat soon as he seen 'em. He was ridin' a good horse or he'd have had hell outrunnin' Injun ponies."

"How many Indians did he see?"

The cowboy in the mackinaw said, "Don't remember if he told how many there was. A big bunch, most likely. We heard they was sendin' the army after 'em. If you ask me, it's high time."

"You been havin' a lot of Indian troubles this summer?"

The men looked at each other.

"We've lost a few head of cattle. The thievin' bastards are sneaky about it. The count comes up short, an' we know they hit us again."

"But have you seen any Indians?" Sam persisted.

They both wagged their heads.

"Maybe one time, back in the spring," a cowboy remembered as he scratched his chin. "Like Burl said, they's real sneaky about it. Time I saw 'em, they was way off in the distance, which is the way I aim to keep things, if I git my way. More distance I keep betwixt me an' them Comanches, the better I like it."

"That was back in the spring?" Sam evidently wanted to be sure of the season.

"Early. I'd say it was in March."

"But you haven't seen any since then?"

They wagged their heads a second time.

Sam passed a glance across the backs of cows moving at the rear of the herd. "This Will James . . . seems I've heard of him a time or two. Does he carry a pistol in a cross-pull holster?"

The gent in the mackinaw nodded. "He sure does. Some of us figure he's real fast with it. He don't act like he's scared of nothin' on this earth."

Sam kept digging for more information. "Somebody told me he hails from up in Missouri."

"That's him. He's the same one, Marshal. He signed on with Grant last fall as ramrod."

When Sam was silent a moment, I asked, "What about some real big feller who don't speak good English? You ever see anybody who fits that description?"

Both men shared a look. "That could be Valdez," one replied like he hadn't oughta admit it. "He's mighty big. A Meskin. He do somethin' wrong?"

Sam was staring a hole through me and I knew I should have kept my mouth shut. "Just curious," I answered quietly, looking off. "Somebody mentioned him working for Haskell. Can't recall just who it was."

Sam asked the next question. "This Valdez . . . has he worked for Haskell quite a spell?"

"He's new," the same cowboy said. "He hired on with Will. Why would somebody mention him to the law?"

"No particular reason," Sam declared, by the sound of his voice angry with me for bringing it up. "Seems I remember they said he was unusual big. We'll ride for the ranch. Be seein' you boys. Watch out you don't run into any Indians. They're liable to be most anyplace out here. A man can't be too careful in Comanche country. Sure as hell would be cold to lose a scalp in this wind. A man's head could freeze."

"You got that right, Marshal. Worst early cold spell I can remember. Our cook claims this'll be the worst winter on record in these parts, on account of how early the cows put on a coat of winter hair."

Sam sounded disgusted when he said, "There's a woman over in Cache who'll agree with him." He lifted his reins and swung his roan back toward the river.

I fell in behind, leading the mule, wishing I'd kept my mouth shut about the Mexican but wondering why it made Sam mad for me to ask. To keep from having him get madder about it, I stayed back as we rode away from the cattle herd. It had seemed like a harmless question.

We hadn't ridden but half a mile before Sam turned back in the saddle. "Sounds like Valdez is the owlhoot that woman wrote about in her diary," he said. "The more I hear about Haskell's operation, the more I'm startin' to think he's responsible for havin' those folks killed. It's gonna be hard to prove; but if we keep pokin' around, maybe somethin' will turn up. How come you're ridin' so far back yonder?"

"I figured you were mad at me for asking about Valdez when we talked to those cowboys. You gave me one of your looks, like I shoulda kept quiet."

"You're bein' too damn sensitive, Mr. Dudley. At times you show you've got a good head on your shoulders, but you've got a sensitive side nearly as bad as a woman's. I gave you that look when I remembered you were wearin' those damn red mittens. Next time we meet up with strangers, I wish you'd take 'em off. It's liable to look bad when folks see me with a deputy who's got on red mittens. As soon as it warms up, I wish you'd toss 'em in that river yonder. They look plumb sissified. We'll tell Clara somebody stole 'em. I'm not in the regular habit of lyin' to my wife, but red mittens are unusual circumstances. Now, ride up here an' hand me that whiskey jug. I'm chilled clear to my toes, an' you've got the only remedy."

We camped for the night on the banks of a frozen creek feeding into the South Canadian. A deep wash helped as a break against the wind. I'd been thinking all day about Valdez, what to expect when we found him. Was he as big as Mrs. Cooper said he was? I wondered.

We had a time of it getting a fire started with wet wood we found in the draw. Sam blew on a pile of tinder until I was sure his lungs would burst. But after a bit, flames licked up a tent of sticks and pretty soon I added larger limbs. I put coffee on and laid out our utensils for supper, the skillet, and a fork with a bent tine.

Just then I heard a sound that made the hackles stand up on the back of my neck. A wolf howled off in the night, its cry so eerie when it broke the silence.

"A wolf," I said, turning toward the sound.

"A big lobo," Sam agreed when no other cries answered the first. "He's lettin' everything else out here know he's huntin'. Even his victims know he's out there. Some folks say that makes a wolf dumb, to be howlin' before he stalks his prey. But I see it the way a Comanche does . . . that wolf is brave enough to let his enemies know he's comin'. He ain't dumb, just so full of courage he can't keep himself from singin' about it. Comanche legend has it that their ancestors come back from the spirit world as a lobo wolf at night. Comanches are superstitious people. They won't kill a lobo wolf at night because it might be some of their kin in another form."

I listened for the wolf to cry again. "There's such a thing as being too full of courage, ain't there?"

"Not to a Comanche. Dyin' bravely is the highest honor any Comanche warrior can hope for. That's why they're so damn hard to whip in battle. They fight like they want to die, which is nearly the truth. Now a wolf, he's smarter. He ain't lookin' to die. That's what makes a wolf such a hard animal to kill."

"I've never gone wolf-hunting."

Sam bent down to pour our coffee. "I'd hate to try an' make a living at it," he said.

"I'll check on the horses," I told him, taking my steaming cup and my rifle. I'd taken off those mittens, believing there was nothing worse for a Deputy Marshal than looking sissi-fied.

Alone in the dark, I listened for that wolf. In many respects Sam Ault reminded me of a lobo wolf the way he hunted down Wanted men.

Seventeen

A sign hanging crookedly on a fence post told us we reached the Rafter H shortly before noon. A blanket of snow lay over a hilly landscape dotted with a few trees. Several windmills were placed near a collection of barns and a rambling house with too many rooms to count, all strung out like boxcars on a train. We had sunny weather, although it was bitter cold while we headed into a wind all morning. Our animals' muzzles were covered with icy whiskers and that red mule looked like he'd had his nose in a flour keg, it was so white. My hands and face were nearly froze too stiff to have any feeling. It was lucky for us we found a place to warm up or I'd have lost the tip of my nose to frostbite and my lungs to the pneumonia.

A dog set in to bark when it saw us cross the horizon above the ranch. "We'll be gettin' some company," Sam said as we saw several men come outside a bunkhouse near one of the barns. "I don't figure they'll let us ride up without findin' out just who we are."

Sure enough, true to Sam's prediction, three men came riding out of a stable before we'd ridden more than a quarter mile. It didn't appear they were unfriendly, just being careful about two strangers showing up in the middle of nowhere. This was country known for its lawlessness, Sam told me, like some parts of Indian Territory. Men on the run from a warrant knew there wasn't much law in this region, away from the bigger settlements.

I watched the three strike a lope in our direction. Two had rifles in their hands. Snowflakes flew from their horses' feet when they hurried them. Sam signaled a halt and we sat as calm as could be until they rode up on us.

A gent on a big buckskin gelding did the talking. He had a suspicious look in his eyes when he looked at me and Sam. "This here's private property," he said. "You passed our sign on top of that hill. State your business or move along."

"We're U.S. Marshals from Indian Territory," Sam began. "I need to talk to Grant Haskell an' his foreman, a man by the name of Will James."

"I'm Ward Haskell," the rider said, and I knew now he was the one planning to marry Anna. "My pa's down at the ranch. As to Will, him an' some of the boys are away on business."

I wanted to ask what kind of business, like maybe getting rid of another bunch of settlers.

"How 'bout a big feller called Valdez?" Sam asked.

Ward's gaze shifted to one side, and he wouldn't look Sam in the eye. "He's with Will. How come you to ask about him?"

"I may have some questions for him. I'll talk to your pa in the meantime."

"What's this all about? Is there Injun trouble?"

"That's what somebody wants us to think. I've got it judged otherwise, maybe. It's cold out here. Let's do our talkin' down at the house."

"Follow me," Ward said, turning his horse. He gave the two men flanking him a nod, then he kicked his dun back to a lope in the direction of the ranch.

I rode up beside Sam as we started downhill. "He don't act all that happy to see us," I said softly.

Sam merely grunted. It was easy to see his mind was on something else right then.

We rode down to the ranch at a jog trot, passing a split-rail fence around the house that was more for decoration than serving any real purpose. The ranch house was made of logs and planking with a roof of cut cedar still covered with a thick layer of snow melting in the sun. We halted at a hitchrail out front and swung down.

"See to their horses," Ward told a cowboy. He motioned us up a set of steps to a stoop at the front door.

We walked in, and I'd never felt such wonderful warmth in my whole life. A big fireplace across a main room gave off enough heat to warm all of west Texas, the way it felt.

A thick-chested man sporting gray sideburns came over to us with his hand extended. "I'm Grant Haskell," he said, as we were shedding our heavy coats.

Sam shook with him first. When I took his hand, it was thick with calluses, like he'd done a sizable share of outdoor work in his time.

"Sam Ault, United States Marshal. This here's my deputy, Leon Dudley. We've got a few questions."

"Help yourselves to chairs," Grant said, indicating several leather-bound chairs near the fireplace. "We're always glad to see a lawman out this way. Don't get many in this neck of the woods. Ward, have Maria bring these men a cup of coffee and tell her we'll be having guests for dinner." His attention went back to Sam. "What sorta questions did you want answers to, Marshal?"

Sam and I took seats near the fire. Sam warmed his hands a moment or two before he looked up at Grant. "Eleven settlers were massacred east of here at a place called Antelope Hill on the South Canadian. It looked like the work of Comanches, so we were told by a feller who dug their graves. Those folks were cut plumb to pieces. Scalped. To begin with, I wanted to know if you knew anythin' about it."

"We heard," Grant said, frowning just a bit like he was set to recall what he knew with a little difficulty. "Somebody told us the army was lookin' into it, that they figured it was

Bull Bear's bunch who done it." He settled into a chair across from Sam.

"Comanches wouldn't scalp young women. They'd keep 'em for slaves or trade 'em to the Kiowas. That's the part that don't add up."

Grant's scowl deepened. "Who else would do somethin' like that? Only a goddamn Comanche cuts up their victims like they owned a butcher shop. I've seen dozens of 'em—men and women—who were cut to ribbons, back before that treaty. I never did make myself believe they'd honor a piece of paper. A treaty don't mean a damn thing to an Injun. When we first came to this part of Texas, they painted these hills with blood. . . . White man's blood was what got spilled. They didn't give a damn about no paper or nothin' of the kind!"

Sam took the outburst in stride. "All the same, those folks at Antelope Hill are dead and we're lookin' into it. We aim to talk to Bull Bear; but first, we wanted to ask you about some of your wranglers."

"Some of my boys?"

Just then, a small-boned Mexican woman came into the room carrying a tray. She brought us steaming cups of coffee and put the tray down on a table beside Sam's chair, then she left and didn't say a word.

I was watching Ward while his pa talked. He stood over in a corner with his hand resting on the butt of a six-shooter he wore on his right hip.

Grant got a frown on his face. "How come you want to ask me about my wranglers, Marshal?"

"We don't know who to suspect just yet, Mr. Haskell. But a woman who died at Antelope Hill wrote down that three men came to their holdings not long before they got killed. She wrote that these men warned 'em to move off, that the land couldn't be homesteaded on account of it belonged to somebody else. Seein' as that wasn't the truth an' seein' that your cattle graze not too far to the west, I wanted to ask you about those three men. One was described as big—a giant, she called him—an' she said he didn't speak good English. We were told you've got a big Mexican who works for you by the name of Valdez. I aim to ask him a few questions, too, only your son tells me he's off with Will James, your foreman."

Grant's gave flickered to Ward, then back to the marshal. "I can vouch for my cowhands. They wouldn't do the sort of dirty business you described, not to nobody. I can't believe you'd even think such a thing. Only a goddamn redskin is capable of that kind of killin'. A white man wouldn't do that to another human being."

"Maybe," Sam remarked, and I knew he didn't believe it. "We can talk to your men as soon as they get back, whenever that'll be."

Grant shifted his weight like he might be uncomfortable. "I sent 'em up to Kansas Territory, to Dodge City, to pick up a few things we'll need before spring. They won't be back for weeks."

It was Sam's turn to frown. "Just when did they leave?"

"Pulled out this mornin', early. Bad timing on your part, it seems. A day earlier an' you'd have had a chance to ask 'em your questions . . . not that it'll do any good. My cowhands didn't have a thing to do with those killings. You're dead wrong, figurin' they could have. It was Comanches, plain an' simple. Whatever that woman wrote, she's wrong about it bein' my men who threatened her people. Fact is, Antelope Hill is just over the line in Indian Territory. Can't nobody own that land besides the government. Only way anybody besides an Injun can use it is to have grazin' permits from Washington. Could be that lady misunderstood. Somebody might have been tellin' her they was settled on government land. It could have been a simple misunderstandin'."

Sam took a sip of his coffee. "That don't explain how they got killed. We aim to find out who did it, one way or another.

If it was Indians, they'll face justice same as any other man who broke the law."

I noticed Grant was getting a little edgy. "It's nearly the same as an insult for you to think some of my cowhands could be responsible for somethin' as awful as that."

Sam remained calm. "I didn't say we believed they had anything to do with it. I only want to ask 'em a few questions."

"But your meanin' is real plain, Marshal. You suspect some of my boys did it or you wouldn't need to ask them questions. I take it kinda personal."

"Tell me about Will James," Sam continued, hardly showing he knew Grant was on the prod. "What do you know about him?"

Grant's face was turning red. "He's a good cowman. He came from somewheres in Missouri, best I remember. He ain't the sort who'd kill innocent people for no good reason, much less cut 'em up the way a Comanche does. You're pushin' me, Marshal, to imply that any of my men could be involved."

Sam wasn't about to back down. I drank that wonderful hot coffee down because I guessed we were about to be asked to leave the Haskell spread almost before our horses could be unsaddled down at the barn.

"Some fellers down south of Elk took shots at us one night while we were headed this way," Sam went on. "My deputy killed a half-breed who slipped up on our camp. Before that, a man who carried a gun in a cross-pull holster rode up an' said it was all a mistake made in the dark. From his description, he sounds like this Will James. It occurs to me that it's right unusual for a cowman to be wearin' a gunfighter's rig, if we're talkin' about the same Will James."

Grant came to his feet abruptly. "The way a man carries a gun don't make him a gunfighter."

Sam knew our welcome was worn out. He downed his coffee and got up. "It don't make him a cowboy, either. We'll talk to him, and to Valdez. Seein' as they're headed up to Dodge City, that's where we'll look for 'em."

"You mean you ain't even gonna question those Injuns first?"

Sam put down his cup and glanced over at me. "After what my deputy found out about what the woman wrote before she died, I've nearly made up my mind to talk to them first. If I'm satisfied with the answers they give me, we'll ride over to talk to some of Bull Bear's people."

Sam towered over Grant Haskell, but his size didn't appear to make much difference to Grant when he was mad.

"The law is supposed to protect decent white folks who are tryin' to make an honest livin' out here, not some god-damn Injuns who've got no respect for the law whatsoever."

"Comanches have their own laws," Sam said. "But if they've broken the white man's law, we'll see to it they'll be punished just like anybody else."

"There oughta be a law against havin' a U.S. Marshal who's a damn Injun-lover," Grant snapped, glaring into Sam's eyes like he wanted to take punch at him.

Muscles in Sam's jaw turned to iron, and I could see cords standing out in his neck. He gave Grant a look as cold as ice. "We're obliged for the coffee, Mr. Haskell. We'll be headin' up to Dodge City so we can have a talk with Will James an' Valdez. If we don't get suitable answers, we'll arrest them so a judge can decide if what's in that diary we found is enough to find 'em guilty of murder. We've got a pretty good description of Valdez, and sometimes a man will point a finger at a few others in order to save his own skin." Sam relaxed a bit. "Maybe Valdez didn't do it, but we aim to find out what he has to say. He looked at me. "Let's go, Mr. Dudley. We've found out all we needed to know here."

I followed Sam to the door. The room was so quiet you could hear the hiss of flames in that fireplace. We walked out on the stoop and went down the steps, turning for the barn without Sam saying another word.

When I looked over my shoulder, I saw Ward standing outside keeping an eye on us, but his pa was nowhere in sight. "Grant got kinda mean about your questions," I said, walking beside Sam through packed snow dotted with hoofprints.

"He's got somethin' to hide. . . . I'm sure of that," Sam said as we neared the barn.

I caught a glimpse of a cowboy looking through a window-pane of the bunkhouse. He backed out of the way when he saw me. I was sure I recognized him and he recognized me. I lowered my voice. "Yonder's the cowhand we talked to yesterday pushing that herd, Marshal. Seems strange he got here before we did. Maybe that's why Will James and Valdez pulled out ahead of us gettin' here, because that cowboy told 'em we were asking questions about the two of 'em."

Sam hardly broke stride when he said, "Good work, Leon. It makes sense now that the gents we want to see ain't here all of a sudden. All the more reason why we're gonna track those boys all the way to Dodge, if that's what it takes to get answers."

Eighteen

We picked up the tracks made by four horses a little to the north of ranch headquarters. Sam appeared to be puzzled by four sets of hoofprints.

"Seems Will James an' Valdez took along some company," he said, guiding his roan along their tracks. He hadn't said much since we left the Rafter H, and I could tell he was still boiling mad over what Haskell said about him being an Indian-lover. Sam had a healthy respect for Comanches, but I'd never have said it was love.

"The diary said three men came to Antelope Hill," I reminded him. "Maybe four came back to do the killing."

"Haskell's behind it," Sam declared. "He got his back up a little too easy when we touched a nerve. I try not to judge a man on first impressions, but in his case I'd almost swear he's got somethin' to hide."

"They way I see it, that cowboy we talked to riding herd was the one who warned 'em. He must have ridden most of the night to get word to Haskell about what we wanted to know."

"I'm glad you had your eyes open when we were headed down to the barn, Mr. Dudley. You're startin' to show good instincts now an' then."

Sam wasn't going to pay me too much of a compliment. I was satisfied with what praise he gave me. "How far is it to Dodge City?" I asked, thinking I'd never been colder in my whole life and a long ride in this weather would only make matters worse.

"Three days of hard ridin'. Judgin' by these tracks we'll never catch up to 'em unless they stop for a considerable spell someplace, which ain't likely. Put on those mittens an' get set for bein' miserable awhile. It's November. It ain't gonna get any warmer."

I chuckled. Only a short time ago he'd been telling me to throw Clara's mittens in the river, and now his advice was to put them on. "If it gets any colder, you'll be wishing you had them," I said.

Sam's expression didn't change when he told me, "My hands won't ever get that cold."

We crossed a snowy ridge and saw miles of white country in store for us, gently rolling land covered with snow. The tracks headed due north. When Sam wasn't looking, I took out the mittens and put them on, wishing I had a second pair for my feet.

This was just like Sam, to ignore the hardships of terrible weather and pretty near everything else when he got his mind made up to follow an outlaw trail. In the past he'd shown a tendency to spare an animal hard use whenever he could, but he acted as if our horses and the mule were having no difficulties.

My bay horse played out just before sundown, its knees so weak they trembled from pushing through so much deep snow. Sam's roan and our mule fared better, owing to the fact they were fresh from Elk and hadn't traveled up from Cache like the bay. We took shelter in a low spot on the prairie, out of the full force of an icy north wind until my bay could travel. I fed our animals some corn and rubbed the bay down with my saddle blanket until my gelding got warm enough to stop shaking.

"We've got to keep pushin'," Sam said. "There's no firewood and no windbreak out here. If we have to, we'll dig for buffalo chips. They make a respectable flame, if they ain't too wet to catch."

"I never remember being so cold before," I said.

"You'll be colder tomorrow unless this wind dies down. If it don't let up, we'll be punishin' our horses more than I can abide. We'll have to find a place to wait out this damn north wind."

I could only guess the temperature was somewhere low in the teens; and with a wind blowing in our faces, it felt worse. "I'd never live in a place like this without no trees. I feel like I nearly went blind today, on account of the sun shining off this snow."

Sam took a swallow of whiskey and handed me the jug. "If I remember the trail right, it'll only get worse the closer we get to Kansas. There's an old sayin' among cowpokes that there are three kinds of suns in Kansas: the one hangin' in the sky durin' the day, sunflowers, an' plain ol' sons of bitches. I'd settle for a little bit more of all three rather than face another day with my feet froze solid like this. If there's any blood in 'em, I ain't able to tell it."

I was too cold to laugh. "If we ever get back to our office, I'll never complain about those cracks in the walls again. Ain't hardly no wind at all coming through, compared to this."

We tightened our cinches and moved on as dark spread over an empty snowbound prairie around us. The wind showed no signs of letting up at nightfall. Resting against the cantle, I remembered Anna's pretty face, just to pass some time.

Stars winked at us from a night sky so clear I figured I could see all the way to Dodge City. We had a slice of moon to guide us, showing just enough of the land to let us know there weren't any trees or cutbanks for shelter. My bay plodded into one drift, then another, until its flanks were heaving with the effort.

My teeth had begun to chatter. No matter what I did to get warm, nothing worked. Rubbing my hands together only made them tingle, and my feet had no feeling. Frost curled away from our horses' muzzles, making them look like fire-breathing dragons in the dark. It was quite possible the temperature had dropped to zero by now.

"I can't hardly stand no more of this without warming up a little," I said, sure that Sam wouldn't like hearing me complain about things.

"I'm hurtin' a bit myself," he replied, slumped over in his saddle like he had a pain in his belly. "We'll have to stop in another quarter hour or so. My knees are killin' me and I never did know feet could hurt so bad. Mainly, it's these animals I'm worried about. They won't have much left in 'em, unless we give them some rest."

I thought about saying I was in worse shape than my horse, only I kept quiet about it.

When I sighted along the horizon, I thought I could see a dark shape against the sky. "I see something out yonder. Can't tell what it is."

Sam looked in the direction I was pointing. "Trees," he said, like he'd seen a fancy hotel with soft beds and a hot bath.

The tracks went a different way, angling northeast, but Sam acted like it didn't make any difference. He turned his roan to one side and made for those trees as straight as he could ride.

We rode up on a grove of red oak, bare limbs sticking up in the sky like the fire-blackened bones of a skeleton. It wasn't all that much of a windbreak; but when we rode in, I was so damn grateful to be out of that wind I didn't care much what it looked like.

When I eased out of my saddle, I couldn't feel my legs, like I was standing on a pair of sticks. Off to the right I found a few dead limbs. "There's enough kindling to get a fire started," I said, my teeth chattering so bad it sounded like rock rattling around inside a coffee tin.

Sam didn't say a word. I saw him leaning against his horse, and then he sort of went to the ground real slow, almost as if he went to sleep standing up. I hurried over to him and found him lying on his back, unconscious.

Hurrying as fast as I could, I took matches from our packs and scooped out a place in the snow for a fire. I had a time of it finding enough dry tinder, but when I cupped my hands around a pile of leaves and struck a match to it, a flame came to life so quickly it startled me.

"Hold on, Sam," I said, knowing he couldn't hear me. "I'll get some coffee going shortly."

I dipped our coffeepot full of snow and set it beside the flames, then I staggered off to gather bigger wood before I made a pallet for the marshal to lie on near the fire. Dragging him over was a chore, seeing as he's so much heavier than me; but I got it done and spread his bedroll out before I rolled him over next to the flames so he'd be warm.

After I put a handful of coffee beans in our pot, I took our horses and tied them off with loose cinches. Our mule turned his tail to the wind and wouldn't budge when I tried to lead him off to one side. I left him there, hobbled, so he couldn't run off. As soon as I got done with the animals, I hurried over to Sam to see if he'd begun to thaw out any.

His eyes were closed and his breathing was shallow, like he was sound asleep. When I touched his face, it felt too cold and it got me real worried. We'd ridden too far against a freezing wind, and it took its toll on Sam. I hoped he wouldn't up and die on me.

Not being brought up in cold country, I didn't know exactly what to do for somebody who's froze. Mississippi is about the warmest place on earth, even in winter. I brought my bedroll over and covered Sam up to his chin. I knew we were in one hell of a fix, way out here in the middle of an empty prairie with nobody to ask for help. About all I could do was tend our fire and keep it built up . . . pour some coffee down his throat if he could wake up enough to swallow. I figured whiskey would help, so I got one of the pints from our packs and splashed some in a cup while I waited for the coffee to boil. That fire felt so good I nearly stuck my hands and feet in it, and pretty soon that small clearing in the trees got warm enough to melt some of the snow close by. I could see Sam's face in the firelight and it wasn't the right color, a little on the blue side. When I touched him, he didn't so much as wiggle or make a sound.

After a bit, when I heard bubbling inside our coffeepot, I poured some in with the whiskey and knelt down beside Sam to lift his head.

"Try to wake up, Marshal," I said real loud, hoping my voice would bring him around. "You gotta drink some of this. It'll warm your insides."

When I touched the back of his head, it was cold as ice; and even raising up his head didn't do any good towards waking him. I was scared he was gonna choke if I poured coffee down him when he was unconscious, but I had to do something—I couldn't just let him lie there and freeze to death.

"Wake up, Sam!" I cried, beginning to get this panicky feeling in my gut.

Yelling didn't do any good. I put the cup down and made a ball out of one blanket behind his head. I was still shivering, only I couldn't tell if it was from the cold or fear that Sam was dying or a little bit of both.

"Damn," I whispered, wondering what to do. So as not to let the coffee and whiskey get cold, I drank it down. If Sam froze to death out here, I'd be in one hell of a mess. I knew I couldn't go off and leave him to look for help, even if I knew which direction to ride. This was the godawfulest empty place without a sign of civilization. The closest help

I knew of was back at the Haskell ranch, and they'd be about as glad to see us as they would a couple of polecats.

"I need to get him warmer," I told myself, thinking that was about all I could do. I pulled down his blankets and took off my red mittens, fitting them over his frozen hands. Then I got up and went to Sam's saddlebags to look for another pair of socks to warm his feet. Taking the saddlebags over to our fire, the first thing I found at the bottom of one bag was a faded tintype in a little brass frame, a likeness of Clara.

I stared at the tintype a moment. "You sure were right, Miz Ault, about this being a mighty cold winter," I whispered, and I smiled a little when I thought about how much Sam complained over the way she fussed at him and how he made it sound like he could hardly wait to get away from her. The tintype was proof it was mostly just talk, seeing as he carried her likeness with him when he was away. I'd never tell him I found it in his gear.

I took out a pair of wool socks and pulled his boots off to put them on. Sam never so much as twitched while I was pulling on his legs, and that worried me all the more.

If he didn't wake up at dawn, I'd have to find a way to get him on his horse and start looking for help. I knew enough about this empty country to know a doctor wouldn't be close.

"Please don't die on me, Sam," I said real quiet, sitting on a blanket beside him.

His face looked peaceful, too peaceful, like he was already nearly dead.

Awhile later I got up and added wood to our fire, building it up as high as I could. Drinking coffee laced with whiskey, I sat there feeling helpless. I'd grown real attached to Marshal Ault and his wife. They were like family to me. If I had to ride back to Cache with the news Sam had died out in this storm, I'd have rather faced anyone besides Clara. It would be about the saddest day of my life, if he passed away. Of all the things I figured might happen to us out in the Territory, the last was that a man as tough as Sam would freeze to death. A bullet or a knife was what I worried about for both of us.

I listened to the wind moaning through the tops of those empty trees and it sounded like a voice singing a sad song, the kind they sing at funerals. I looked up at the stars and said a little prayer, even though I'm not much when it comes to having an audience with the Almighty. It wasn't likely He'd pay much attention to any praying coming from me.

Nineteen

I dozed off sometime during the night. When I woke up, our fire was down to embers and I was cold. I was lying on my side like I'd fallen over sound asleep. A pale morning sky brightened to the east as I sat up and looked over at Sam.

He hadn't moved. I could see his nostrils flaring some with every slow breath he took. His face was the color of bee's wax, almost white. I shook him, relieved to discover he was breathing okay.

"Wake up, Marshal," I said.

He didn't. I got up to gather more wood for the fire, stiff as a board from sleeping in a bad position and being cold. Our horses had pawed through snow where tether ropes allowed them to reach winter grass while the mule, still carrying our packs, had gone a short distance to a tree trunk to gnaw on bark, a habit peculiar to some mules.

I found enough dead wood where limbs had fallen and hurried back to the fire, placing a few just so in order to bring flames quickly. I was starving, my belly rumbling like a spring storm. I took out our skillet and salt pork before I put more snow in the coffeepot.

Pretty soon our fire was crackling and warmth spread inside the red oak grove. A couple of times I went over to Sam and gave him a shake or two, but nothing worked. He slept like he'd been hit in the head with an axe handle, out cold.

When I felt of his skin, it was a little warmer, maybe, but not enough so I could see it made any difference.

I put my mind on what I'd do if I couldn't rouse him by the time breakfast was cooked. I sure didn't aim to tie him over his saddle like he was already dead, which he wasn't yet. Back two summers ago, I'd seen my first travois, a contraption made out of two poles dragging behind a horse with a blanket tied between so someone could lie on it. We had a small woodcutter's axe in one of the packs, so I could chop down a pair of saplings if I wanted to fashion a way to haul Sam to the closest town. It was nearly the only idea I could come up with that wouldn't make him too uncomfortable.

Finding the right small trees wasn't hard since this grove was hardly more than a good start at becoming a forest. Red oak is just about the hardest wood there is, meaning I'd be at the chore a spell, chopping down the ones I wanted. We had plenty of rope to tie the poles together and hold blankets in place. It wasn't something I was looking forward to, but right then it was about the only way I could figure to get Sam away from here if he didn't wake up.

Worst was, deciding which direction to ride. The Haskell ranch was south, and Dodge City at least two more days to the north. West was open range, I figured, being as it was part of the Texas panhandle, which wasn't settled. East was all that was left, and I didn't have any idea what lay east of here, except a few Indian villages where they'd camped for the winter. It was plenty risky to ride through Indian Territory, and so I decided against it. If we could make Dodge City in two days, there was a chance we'd find a doctor there, although I'd never been to Dodge or any other place in Kansas.

I made up my mind that a doctor was what Sam needed most, so riding north was the only selection I had. It meant riding into that same blue-cold wind, not exactly the right thing to do for a man who's already froze.

I began frying up bacon. I couldn't remember when I felt

so all alone. If the decision I made was a bad one to ride north, it could cost Sam his life. Just thinking about it gave me a case of the shakes that didn't have anything to do with temperature. I had Sam's life in my hands. Dozens of times since I'd become a marshal, he'd had my life in his. I discovered this morning that having things switched around sure as hell didn't suit me.

A winter sun was midway across the sky by the time I got two poles cut and trimmed and a travois tied together. I had it fastened to my saddlehorn since I trusted my bay to be gentle. When I was satisfied with the way I had the blanket tied across those poles, I tested it with my own weight. My bay kept turning its head, eyeing this strange bit of human invention as though it didn't quite trust the thing, or me. I would ride Sam's roan, leading the bay, with our mule on the other side. The whole time I was working on the travois, I heard that wind in the treetops, and just listening to it made me colder than I was. Every now and then I'd check on Sam and shake him just a bit; but no matter what I did, he remained unconscious.

Lifting a man weighing almost two hundred pounds is near impossible for someone my size; however, I managed it after what amounted to considerable effort. Sam felt like dead weight, a comparison I didn't want to make, when I hoisted him onto the travois. I wrapped two blankets around him and tied them so the wind couldn't blow them off, then I tied his spare flannel shirt around his head and put his hat under the blankets with him. He looked a bit strange with a red-checkered shirt covering the top of his head, but all I wanted was a way to keep him warm—and it didn't matter since nobody would see him besides me. When I'd seen to the last detail, I cinched up the red roan and collected the mule. After I got a rope around my bay's neck, I was as ready as I was ever gonna be.

"I hope this thing don't fall apart," I whispered, not quite trusting what I'd done, seeing as it was my first time to make a travois. It was an Indian's answer to not having a wagon, and I guessed it would work. The poles were thin enough to have some give in them, making Sam's ride a little softer when we happened to encounter a bump or a rock.

I mounted up and secured both lead ropes, then touched the roan's ribs with my heels. Our travois moved off fairly smoothly across the snow, although my bay kept its ears laid back like it wasn't too keen on pulling it. Sam bounced along on his bed of blankets as we left that red oak grove behind. Right away I felt the wind sting my face again. We were in for a couple of rough days of travel, so I decided I'd better get used to being froze again.

I picked up the tracks again a half hour later and followed them almost due north. I could see for miles that morning, miles of empty white bills stretching in all directions. It was about the loneliest feeling I ever had, being out there with Sam's life depending upon me getting him to the nearest town. When you're in open country like this, miles from civilization without seeing a house or a road anywhere, it can have the opposite effect from what I'd expected. Instead of feeling free, I was beginning to feel closed in, closed in by circumstances. Unless I found help soon, Marshal Ault was sure to die from exposure to the cold.

My luck turned bad after noon. On higher ground, the wind had blown snow over those hoofprints and I'd lose them, forcing us to wander until I found them again on the leeward side of a hill. And off to the northwest loomed a much larger problem, a line of dark clouds—another snowstorm building. Just when I was sure things couldn't get any worse, we faced prospects of being caught in falling snow in addition to the cold. And there wasn't so much as a single tree anywhere in sight to shelter us from it, even though time was too precious to waste for us to wait out a blizzard if one blew in. No matter what else happened, I had to get Sam out of this weather and to a doctor. If it started to snow, I'd have to keep riding. Riding blind if it snowed heavy.

Leaning into the wind, I sheltered my face with my hat brim and kept my hands in my pockets as much as I could to keep them from freezing. The snow we crossed was already a foot deep; and if it snowed again, we'd be down to a crawl getting through it.

I recalled what Clara said before we left, how this was sure to be a rough winter, one of the worst in years. That woman knew a thing or two about weather, no matter what Sam had to say to the contrary.

By the time a couple more hours had passed, those deep-blue clouds were over us and the wind was picking up, blowing loose snow off hilltops in big swirls, adding to our misery and to the difficulty for our animals. When we hit a swale where the wind seemed less, I got down and went back to see about Sam. He lay there like always, sound asleep but still breathing regular. I was fit to be tied, watching that sky darken. Before I mounted up again, the first snowflakes started to fall, sweeping down on us from the west. In a matter of minutes, the tracks would be covered with snow and I'd be guessing as to our direction from here on. I covered Sam's face with a blanket, making sure he could still breathe.

"Seems like everything turned against us," I chattered, my teeth rattling so bad I couldn't keep my jaw clamped shut.

We came out of that swale into a wall of wind-driven snow so thick I couldn't see more than a few feet ahead. That's when our red mule did something I hadn't counted on, making our situation even worse.

That mule turned its tail to the wind and refused to be led in any direction, pulling back on its halter rope for all it was worth.

"Don't sull-up on me now, you son of a bitch!" I yelled as loud as I could, banging my heels into the roan, asking it to pull harder. But the mule wouldn't budge, which is another trait common to mules, and I couldn't leave it there on account of all our food, the tent, and our other gear was on its back.

I gave that mule the evil eye. "You no-good bastard," I said. Experience with plow mules back in Mississippi taught me that, sometimes, cussing them helps. This mule didn't act like it cared either way, because it still wouldn't move the direction we needed to go, humping its back in the wind and snow as though it meant to stay there until doomsday. Snow was falling so hard now that I couldn't see a thing around us. I gave up pulling on the rope and sat there, so mad at that mule I could have shot it dead with a bullet square between its eyes.

"We're gonna die right here," I mumbled, almost too cold for my tongue to form words.

All of a sudden our mule did a strange thing. It started to walk forward with the wind, like it was being pushed. It ambled past me as quiet as you please and Sam's roan took off along with it, pulling the bay and the travois behind. We were moving the wrong direction to be sure, but at least we were moving and it was better than standing still in a howling blizzard, I figured.

Hunkering down inside my coat, I decided to let the mule take us wherever it wanted to go. Not that mules are widely known for having good sense, but it was clear I didn't have any other choice.

With the wind at my back, it felt a little warmer despite a pelting we were taking from snowflakes. I judged we were headed east, maybe a little bit south.

"A dumb animal is gonna get us froze in the middle of Indian Territory when he oughta be headed for Kansas," I whispered. I'd taken to talking to myself lately, with Sam being unconscious. I knew Sam would freeze to death shortly, if he wasn't dead by now. And the same fate would be mine unless we found some cover pretty soon. I was hurting all over from the cold, except for my feet and hands and the end of my nose, being those parts didn't have any feeling in them at all.

I started to wonder what it would actually feel like to die. Would I see angels like in the Bible? I wasn't much on scripture or religion in general, although it wasn't due to any failure to have me exposed on my ma's part. She dragged us to church nearly every Sunday to listen to preaching. Folks around Possumbelly Flats went to church real regular and we weren't no different in that regard. My ma was convinced our souls needed saving from a week's worth of sinning. But the truth was I didn't learn that much from it, so praying wasn't something I was real well-versed in when it came to knowing how it was done.

Right then, I didn't see any way to get out of the mess we were in. We were being led through a snowstorm by a mule, one of the dumbest creatures on earth. I was so cold I couldn't do much besides hang on to my saddlehorn and hope for the best. All we needed was some cover, a place to get away from the wind. After the storm let up, we could try for Dodge City again. I hoped Sam could hang on until then.

I watched that red mule's rump, thinking how ridiculous we'd seem to anyone who happened to be looking. A full-grown man with reasonably good sense following a pack mule, leading a horse with a sick man lying on a travois. On the dark side of things, it was likely a funeral procession we were in, heading toward an almost-certain grave. But there was no changing that mule's mind on the direction, leaving me no choice but to go along.

"I wonder what they'll think when they find us in the spring thaw next year, a marshal and his deputy, froze solid in a snowbank somewhere in northwestern Indian Territory."

My voice was nearly torn from my mouth by the wind, so it was even hard for me to hear it. I was beginning to feel sleepy, in spite of the fact I'd slept the night before. My eyelids got so heavy I could hardly keep them open. Snow was getting deeper on our animals' hooves, slowing them down, making it harder to keep moving.

A time or two, my chin dropped to my chest until it woke me up with a start. Blinking, rubbing my eyes, I knew I was swaying in the saddle. For some reason I remembered a preacher back home warning us against the fires of hell. As far as I was concerned, hell was right here south of Kansas, and it was snowing in the part of hell we were in.

Twenty

How that mule found a ravine in the storm was beyond me, but when my horse stopped moving it startled me and I jerked upright in the saddle, rubbing my eyes. The roan snorted with its ears pricked forward, bowing its neck like it saw something ahead that made it fearful. Just in front of us was a drop-off, a steeply slanted bank leading down into a wide creekbed. I could make out dark tree trunks and barren limbs of slender cottonwoods at the bottom of the draw, growing beside the wandering course of the stream. The best news of all was a hollowed out place where we would have shelter from wind and snow. Before I could pick out a spot to ride down, the mule stepped over the rim and pulled me down a slope right in front of us, slipping and sliding until we got to level ground. I turned back to watch the travois when it dropped off behind my bay, but it came down as nicely as anyone could have wanted.

I didn't need to be shown where our mule was headed, over to a rocky overhang where floodwaters had hollowed out a niche big enough for us to be out of the storm. I slipped out of my saddle and came within a whisker of blacking out when I put weight on my legs, they hurt so bad. When I looked around inside our shallow cave, it was like somebody had prepared a camp for us. Piles of old driftwood were heaped up at the back, perfect for making our fire, enough to last for quite a spell.

I dropped my reins and staggered around gathering firewood, so close to freezing to death a fire was the only thing I could put my mind on right then. When I got matches out of our packs, my hands were shaking so badly it was all I could do to keep from scattering them all over the ground. That wind howled across the lip of the draw like the yelp of a hundred coyotes while I held a match to a pile of dry leaves. Two matches blew out before a bit of flame leapt up. . . . I sure as hell didn't need to blow on it to keep it going. In a matter of minutes I had sticks burning, and the heat felt so wonderful I forgot everything else for a time. Then I remembered Sam and climbed to my feet, dreading the chance I'd find a corpse on the travois.

I brushed a dusting of snow off his blankets and pulled them away from his face. Sam's cheeks were sunk in, and at first there was no sign he was breathing. I touched his forehead, and to my surprise it felt warm, a hell of a lot warmer than my fingers did at the moment.

Then I saw his nostrils flare. "You're alive," I said in a shaky voice, trembling from head to toe from the cold. "Sorry to have to do it, Marshal, but I'm gonna have to drag you over to the fire 'cause I ain't nearly strong enough now to carry you so far."

I untied his blankets and gripped his coat collar, thinking how loudly he'd complain if he were awake to see how rough I was handling him. But I tugged him off one side of the travois and dragged him on his back until he was lying next to the flames.

I covered him up the best I could and pushed a blanket under him so he wasn't lying in snow. Both horses and the mule crowded as close to the fire as they could get, flanks shivering, legs so weak they looked like they were ready to buckle.

I looked over at that red mule. "Sorry I cussed you so bad that time," I said. "I reckon you knew where you was going.

You got my word I won't never cuss another mule so long as I live."

I set about to make coffee and unsaddle the animals. This looked to be a powerful storm that could last for days. I had it figured we'd be staying here for a while; and in order to make the best of it, I intended to erect our tent and make the place as livable as I could. For sure I wasn't going to get Sam anyplace where a doctor could help him until this storm let up. I walked back and forth carrying our gear while coffee was boiling, too cold to do much real thinking beyond what was necessary. We were alive and that was what mattered most. Sam was mighty sick, but he still had a fighting chance if I could keep him warm and dry.

An hour later, I was slumped by our fire sipping coffee and whiskey. This time I didn't mind the taste of whiskey at all, at least not enough to notice. A crackling fire threw off so much heat in that cave I was almost warm, for a change. I'd fed our animals a few handfuls of corn and they seemed content. Overhead, the storm raged like the end of the world was coming. But inside our shelter of rocks, we were warm and dry. I had dipped snow in a little cast-iron pot and put a handful of beans on to cook; and when I smelled beans and fatback, my belly started growling.

Things seemed nearly perfect until I looked at Sam. He lay there, looking for all the world like he was dead, if you didn't notice his chest rise every now and then. I aimed to try to get some coffee and whiskey down him if I could, holding his head up so he wouldn't choke. Other than that, I had no notion of what to do for him besides keeping him warm. Coming from a warmer climate like Mississippi, I was short on experience when it came to a remedy for a man being froze.

I prepared a concoction of coffee and plenty of whiskey for Sam. When I lifted up his head and rested it on my knee he gave no sign of noticing. His eyes were shut tight and I had to pry open his lips to pour some of the mixture into his mouth.

For a little bit it didn't appear he meant to swallow, until I saw his neck move some. One small sip at a time, I got a dose of coffee down him, although he never once woke up or showed any indication he knew I was there. The sky was getting dark by the time I covered him up again. I'd planned to erect our tent while there was still enough light; however, as tired as I was, I decided to sleep by the fire tonight and wait until morning.

I wolfed down half-cooked beans when my stomach told me it was tired of waiting. At full dark, with snow falling so thick I couldn't see anything but white beyond the cave, I checked on our animals, making sure of tether ropes, and fixed my bedroll close to the flames.

I'd no more than laid down and got myself covered when my eyes batted shut.

Sometime during the night I heard a sound. I listened for a while to see if I could identify it above the howl of wind. Then I recognized it, a man's voice coming from the other side of the fire.

I jerked up and tossed my blankets back. . . . It was Sam's voice I heard, only the words didn't make any sense. I got up and went over to him. His eyes were closed, but he was mumbling something and I listened real close to see if I could understand any of it.

"Wake up, Sam," I said, shaking his shoulder. I thought he might be ready to come around.

He couldn't hear me. Instead of opening his eyes, he began to cough, and his lungs sounded wet. He coughed a few more times before he started mumbling again.

I took a half-empty pint of whiskey and held it to his lips. When I poured some, he swallowed, although he still wasn't the least bit inclined to open his eyes or wake up. I gave him more, and he drank it down.

"You said this stuff helps keep you warm, Marshal," I said in a low voice.

He coughed again suddenly, with fluid gurgling deep inside his chest.

"It's the pneumonia," I whispered. My Aunt Grace had died from it when I was a kid.

I lowered Sam's head and covered him again, remembering how Grace had coughed for days, finally coughing up blood before she passed on in her sleep one night. Ma told me there wasn't a cure for the pneumonia, that only folks with a strong constitution got over it.

I gazed down at Sam. "If ever there was a man with a strong constitution, it's you," I said. "If I knew how to pray, I'd say a few words to the Lord about you."

I sat there awhile, wondering what I'd do if Sam passed on the way Aunt Grace did. A grown man ain't supposed to have real feelings for another man who ain't his kin; but I sure did think a lot of Sam Ault and I sure didn't want to be the one who had to bury him.

Sam coughed on and off through the night, waking me up when he did it. He never offered to open his eyes. I gave him more whiskey and coffee at dawn when the sky turned a shade brighter above dark snowclouds hanging over us. There had been no letup in the blizzard. Snow was piled so deep across the creekbed, it would be hard to navigate, either for a horse or a man on foot. We didn't dare travel in weather like this, with Sam coming down with lung sickness. We had food, and another bottle of whiskey if whiskey was a help, enough firewood to last several days if I couldn't get outside. But in the back of my brain the thought kept gnawing on me that Sam had to see a doctor real soon if he was to pull through.

Squatting by the fire, I stared out at falling snow with my mind elsewhere, on what I'd do if the storm didn't let up. I'd forgotten all about the four men we were after, the reason we got in this fix in the first place. Our duties simply had to wait for Sam to get better. I kept wondering how I'd get us all the way to Dodge City with this much snow on the ground. A horse was never intended to be ridden through anything like this.

Sam started coughing again, reminding me how few choices we had. He would die unless we got out of here mighty soon. I sat watching it snow, thinking how rotten our luck turned. If Clara was here, she'd say it was Sam's hardheadedness, not luck, that got us caught out in this storm.

At dusk, as I was making soup out of strips of jerky in hot water, Sam spoke to me.

"Where are we, Leon?"

I jumped up and hurried over to him. "We're holed up in a creekbed waiting for this snow to quit. Worst blizzard I ever saw in my life."

Sam raised his head, and when he did he coughed. "Damn, but I reckon I passed out on you. How long have I been out?"

"A couple of days."

"A couple of days? Why the hell didn't you wake me up?"

"I sure tried, Marshal. I shook you every chance I got, and nothing worked. You were unconscious. I made a travois out of a couple of trees so I could haul you to Dodge City. Only, that's when this godawful storm commenced. Our mule took off like it had a mind of its own, leading us to this draw. Otherwise, we'd have both froze to death."

Sam was trembling with the effort to keep his head up. He lay back down. "I'm weak as a kitten. My lungs are so full of fluid I can't hardly breathe."

"I reckon it's the pneumonia. My aunt died from it."

He scowled at me. "Well, I sure as hell ain't gonna die so soon, Mr. Dudley. I ain't nobody's sickly aunt."

He woke up in a foul humor, which I didn't mind since he was alive. "I'll fix you some soup."

"Bring me whiskey. Soup ain't gonna fix what's ailin' me, not until after I get some redeye down."

"I've been feeding you whiskey, when you'd swallow it," I told him.

His deep scowl didn't change any when he snapped, "There's never been a day of my life when I couldn't swallow whiskey, Mr. Dudley."

I grinned and went over for the bottle. "We've got one more of these in our packs, Marshal. That oughta be enough. . . ."

He took a hand out from under his blankets, and that's when he saw he was wearing those red mittens. "I'll be goddamn if I'm gonna wear these!" he said, glaring at that mitten like it was a coiled rattler.

I pulled it off. "Your hands was cold, Marshal. It was all we had to warm up a pair of hands."

"I'd rather cut both hands off," he said, taking the pint as soon as his mitten was removed. He took out the cork with his teeth and spat it toward the fire. "Fetch me that other bottle. This ain't hardly enough to drown a pissant."

I was still grinning as I went over to the packs. Sam would pull through now, on nothing more than disposition. Maybe my ma had been right when she said only folks with strong constitutions survived the pneumonia. Sam Ault had outlived things a hell of a lot worse in his time.

By the time I got back with a fresh pint, Sam's eyes were closed again. When I tried to rouse him, I couldn't.

I put the bottle beside him and went back to tending to my soup. Before dark I needed to take our horses and the mule out to eat snow, the only water we had. I chuckled again when Sam's outburst echoed through my thoughts.

Just before full dark I led the animals out one at a time

to fill their bellies with snow, turning up my coat collar when cold wind came over the lip of the draw. On higher ground that storm was still blowing something fierce. Down in the streambed we got out of most of the wind.

"Sam's gonna be all right," I said to our mule as it pawed down to a few blades of brown winter grass. "Thanks to you, he's alive. It ain't likely he'll credit you with saving him when you found this place, but I'll always know it was you that done it."

If the mule heard me or understood a word I said, I couldn't tell it. A moment later it raised its head all of a sudden to look east, down the draw, its long ears turned forward, a sure sign it sensed something.

I looked that direction as hard as I could and didn't see a thing. But I trusted that mule now, and I would have wagered a month's pay there was something down there that didn't belong, so I hurried back to the fire and took out my rifle, just in case we had unexpected visitors.

Twenty-one

I spent a restless night, dozing with my rifle beside me in spite of the fact nothing went wrong. It was the way our mule looked downstream earlier that made me wary. Sam mumbled in his sleep from time to time; and when he coughed, it sounded like more fluid was building up in his chest. He didn't wake up until dawn, and it was only for a short while, long enough to open the bottle lying beside him, taking a few swallows without uttering a word.

There was a slight change in the weather. Snow continued to fall, but now it came in flurries with short periods of lighter snow in between. I could see farther down the draw occasionally, a few hundred yards every now and then. The creekbed wound back and forth like a long snake with a broken back, lined with small cottonwoods and an oak here and there. But every time I looked that way, I didn't see anything that should make a mule nervous.

I kept our fire burning high so it warmed the cave as much as possible. Every now and then, when the wind died down, smoke would build up under the overhang, making my eyes water. I fixed bacon and coffee, checking on Sam every so often until all of a sudden, he woke up as I was finishing breakfast. He went into a coughing fit and pushed himself up on his elbows. As soon as I saw him awake, I poured coffee for him, waiting until his coughing spell ended before I handed him the cup.

"Your cough's getting worse," I said needlessly, since he was the one doing the coughing.

"Where the hell are we?" he asked again, like he couldn't remember what I told him. He was groggy, shaking his head to clear it.

"I've got no idea, Marshal. Somewheres northeast of Grant Haskell's ranch, I suppose. That storm blew us off course, so I ain't rightly sure just where we are. We rode north about a day, if you count how long we rode at night. Then we turned east as soon as that mule balked over riding into the wind."

"East is the Beaver River," Sam said, looking fevered in the face, his skin red as a poker. He took a sip of coffee after clearing his throat. "This draw probably leads to the river some place. Most winters a bunch of Kiowas led by old chief Lone Wolf camp along the Beaver, if he's feelin' peaceful. Either way, it will be smarter to avoid 'em. Soon as I can ride, we'll head on up to Dodge City. In case you've forgotten, we've got business up there."

Sam's arms were trembling, either from the cold or weakness or maybe a little of both. "I'm real glad you're awake, Marshal, and feeling some better, but I ain't all that sure we oughta take off riding out in a storm like this. Right where we are, you're warmer. But if we leave this ledge while it's snowing so hard, you'll freeze and maybe get sicker."

He took another sip of coffee and lay back down. "We can't stay here all winter, Mr. Dudley." He set in to coughing again. "If I don't get this fluid out of my chest pretty damn quick, I'll drown sure as hell."

I glanced out at the falling snow. "How will we know where to look for those Kiowas? Maybe they ain't even there. I'd sure hate to run into 'em, just the two of us."

"All we gotta do is stay away from that river," he replied, sounding as though he was getting sleepy again.

My experience with Kiowas hadn't been good. Back when we went down to Palo Duro Canyon, we'd had to fight off a bunch of young warriors on the prod—and up on the Cimarron, those renegades hitting cow herds had been Kiowas, too. Sam said they were called Rope Heads by Comanches, I remembered, because of the way they wore their hair, braided in a single strand hanging down their backs like a length of rope. I recalled they called themselves Ki-was. I damn sure didn't trust them. They were widely known for taking well to a fight at the drop of a hat. "I'm more inclined to wait a spell, Marshal, until we see if it stops this heavy snowing. That way, we'd be able to see those Indians before we ran into 'em, riding blind in all this snow."

He didn't answer me and I saw he'd gone back to sleep.

A letup in the blizzard later that morning gave me an idea. I shouldered my rifle and walked away from the ledge to see if a trickle of water might be under a sheet of ice down at the creek. Snow was nearly three-feet deep where it drifted because of wind, making it mighty hard to walk without sinking down so deep snow was over the tops of my stovepipe boots. Snowflakes were still falling, sweeping over the lip of the wash on gusts of wind; but I could see a good distance in both directions up and down the draw, so I felt better about going. Our animals needed more water than eating snow was giving them, so if the ice wasn't too thick over that creek, I could lead them down one at a time for a drink to keep them from being water-starved.

When I got to the edge of the stream, I could see it was dry, so I walked a little farther east to see if a catch-pool might be frozen over someplace. Where streams make a bend, sometimes a deep spot gets washed out where rainwater collects. I figured it was worth a try, the way our animals were getting so gaunt in the flanks. Otherwise, I'd be taking them out so often I'd be plumb worn out by dark.

I came to a bend about a hundred yards east of our cave and stopped in a stand of cottonwoods where heavy layers of snow were clinging to bare branches over my head. I stopped long enough to button the top button on my flannel shirt, resting my Winchester against my leg. I happened to look downstream before I searched for trapped water, and what I saw brought me up short, holding my breath.

Five or six horsemen rode along the edge of the creek, only dark silhouettes visible through a curtain of white snowflakes. I wasn't expecting to see anyone; and when I did, I just stood there with my mouth open, too surprised to move. They were more than a quarter mile away, whoever they were, riding toward me at a slow, deliberate walk.

I hunkered down behind the largest tree trunk I could find with my heart hammering. When a break in the snow allowed me to see them better, I knew who, or what, they were. "Indians," I said to myself, just about the worst sight I could imagine while Sam was too sick to help me fight them off, if a fight was what they were after.

I counted them carefully. "Six," I whispered, wondering if they were Comanches or Kiowas or maybe something less troublesome. The Territory was full of Osages and Delawares over in the western part. Most were peaceful, unless they were provoked. I watched them as long as I dared, trying to see if I could identify some characteristic that would tell me who they were. Then I recalled something Sam told me a long time ago—that Indians were able to smell smoke for miles, when the wind was right. I knew these Indians were following the scent of our campfire, and it was too late to do anything about it.

Now I could see they were wrapped in blankets and buffalo robes, perched on the backs of wiry little ponies. One who rode at the front was aboard a red-and-white pinto; and when I got a better look at him, I saw a rifle in his hands.

I figured it was either a hunting party who'd picked up our fire smell or a war party out to see who was camped on some of their land. Either way, when they saw how badly they outnumbered us, it would be like an invitation to try to

take our horses and guns and our other gear. The time I'd
spent with Sam, he taught me a number of things about plains
Indians, not the least being how they were inclined to seize
opportunity. With two white men having things they wanted,
six Indians of most any breed were a bit more likely to cause
trouble. Stealing was nearly an art in some tribes. Sam said
they didn't see it the same way a white man does, having to
do with ownership. If something, particularly a good horse,
can be stolen without getting caught or killed in the attempt,
it was considered a test of cunning, not a crime. The only
crime was failing at it, or winding up dead.

I glanced over my shoulder. Our cave was poorly suited
for defense, to say the least. We'd be easy targets, out in the
open with no cover to stop a bullet, and our animals would
be the first victims of any gunfire.

"Our goose is cooked," I told myself quietly. Sam was too
sick to move on his own and I sure as hell couldn't carry
him to a place of safety, even if I found one. My heart was
beating so fast I was getting dizzy.

I wheeled around in a crouch and took off running, stumbling when I hit deeper drifts, my mind on just one thing—
getting Sam awake long enough to help me figure what to
do. We couldn't run and we couldn't stay where we were
without getting killed, the kind of difficulty I sure as hell
didn't care to face on my own.

Dodging back and forth to stay out of the deepest snow,
I was gasping for air by the time I got back to camp. My
sudden movements spooked our horses and the mule so that
they were in high agitation, snorting, ears pricked forward
until they recognized me.

"You gotta wake up, Sam!" I shouted, running over to the
bed I made for him. I knelt down and shook his right arm.
"Listen to me, Marshal! There's six Indians headed up this
draw and one, maybe more, has got a rifle!"

Sam didn't so much as twitch. His eyes remained closed.

"Wake up, Sam!" I cried, feeling more desperate as precious time slipped away. Those Indians would be in sight of the cave in a few minutes.

He groaned when I shook his arm again real hard.

"You gotta listen to me. Six Indians are coming this way, and if we don't do something to discourage 'em, they'll shoot us down and take our horses."

Finally, his eyelids raised just a bit, fluttering. "What's the ruckus all about?" he asked, and then he commenced to cough so hard I was sure his ribs would break. He coughed over and over again, making this wheezing noise every time he took in a breath. "Goddamn lungs are about to bust wide open," he managed to say, strangling on nearly every word.

"Indians. Six headed up this draw on horses. One of 'em has got a rifle, maybe more."

Sam lifted his head off the blankets. He made like he was trying to see them right in front of us. I don't see nobody at all," he gasped. "Have you been in our whiskey, Mr. Dudley?"

"They're coming. Right over yonder past them trees. I'd say they'll be here in less than a minute. I counted six, but there could be more of 'em. I can't tell what breed they are on account of they're wearing buffalo robes and it's still snowing too hard to make them out."

He raised up a little more and got one elbow under him as he coughed again. "Hand me my rifle. Don't do any shootin' until we see if they're friendly. It ain't like 'em to be out in this bad weather. Somethin' got 'em riled up."

"That's what I was afraid of, Marshal," I said, going over to his saddle to take his Winchester from the saddle boot. I was careful to check the firing chamber for a cartridge before I gave it to him. "There has to be a reason why they're out in a snowstorm like this, and I sure as hell hope it ain't on account of us."

Sam sat all the way up, resting his rifle across his lap as he peered out into the snow. "Most important thing to be sure of first is knowin' which tribe they are." He reached down for his bottle of whiskey, taking a healthy swallow, then another, before he put it beside him again.

"You said this was Kiowa country," I wondered aloud.

"It's damn near anybody's country the way things are because of that treaty. I only said Lone Wolf camped along the Beaver in the winter sometimes. They could be Comanches from Bull Bear's bunch." He coughed and wheezed one more time. "I hope it ain't Kotsotekas out in this blizzard. They won't be in the best frame of mind, if that's who it is."

I couldn't help wondering myself why any man, regardless of breed, would be out in this snow without plenty of good reason. I looked back down the draw, expecting to find Indians moving in clouds of snowflakes at any moment. "Can't see 'em yet, Marshal. What are we gonna do if they start shooting at us?"

When I didn't get an answer, I turned around. Sam was lying on his side, unconscious again. I knew there wasn't time to try to wake him up before those Indians got there.

I decided on a dangerous plan, but about the only one that I figured stood any chance of saving our animals. Without the use of our horses, we were as good as dead anyway, so far from help of any kind.

I raced over to my saddlebags and grabbed a box of shells for my Winchester—and Clara's mittens to keep my bare hands from freezing; then I took off running toward those trees at the bend, determined to keep our visitors from getting past me if I could. As soon as they saw two horses and a mule, with only two white men defending them, they'd think we were easy pickings. If I could keep them from finding out I was the only one they'd have to fight, maybe they'd ride on.

I ran so fast my eyes were tearing by the time I got to the first tree trunk; and at the same time I saw them less than fifty yards downstream, grouped together like they were having a talk. I slipped and caught myself against a cottonwood, then I put on the mittens and levered a shell into the firing chamber, making sure I could use a finger on the trigger by stretching the yarn on my right hand.

They saw me, and right away they started pointing, and as soon as they did, all six began bringing rifles up.

Twenty-two

All at once, all six ponies were moving in different directions, bounding away at full speed with riders clinging to their backs. I saw an Indian with a lone eagle feather tied into his hair swing a rifle to his shoulder as he urged his pony across the creek. Before I could bring my sights to bear on him, a shot cracked. A ball of lead struck the tree where I was standing, a sound that made me flinch involuntarily. Bark chips flew a foot higher than my head, as limbs on either side quivered with the bullet's impact. Snow on the ends of branches dropped to the ground with a soft plop I was scarcely able to hear because of thudding pony hooves. Snowflakes kicked up by speeding ponies swirled, dancing on the wind like ghostly apparitions until they fell back to earth. I was tempted to fire at poor targets, although I resisted those urges for now, waiting for a shot that wouldn't miss. But due to my hesitation, in a matter of seconds all six warriors were well out of range, racing back down the creekbanks on both sides, their ponies' manes and tails flying in the wind.

My mouth was suddenly bone-dry. I watched the Indians gallop away into spits of windblown snow farther downstream. I tried to slow my breathing and my heart. Only one shot had been fired, and none of the warriors had shown much inclination to continue our brief encounter with more shooting.

"Maybe they won't come back," I said softly, peering into a veil of white to see if they were doubling back, or splitting up to flank me.

I understood the weakness of my present position immediately when I glanced both ways across the wash. They could easily have me in a crossfire by riding along the top of the draw, shooting down at will, using the rim for cover if they came for me on foot later on. I had to get up on top, on the ledge above the cave. It was the only spot I could find where I'd have a view of every possible angle of attack.

After a final look downstream, I took off running for all I was worth to climb the bank above our camp, stumbling through one deep drift after another. My lungs got so full of icy air it was painful to take a breath. I reached the bottom of the incline in record time and started up, slipping and sliding, struggling for a purchase in loose snow wearing slick-bottomed leather boots not made for climbing.

I glanced over at Sam. He was where I left him, lying on his side near the fire, unconscious. There wasn't time to pull him away to the back of the cave where he was less likely to be hit by a stray bullet.

I made the top and looked along the rim when I saw a pair of Indians galloping toward me through falling snow. I dropped to my knee and held my Winchester steady. I could hear the thump of hooves growing louder. I fixed my gun sights on one of the Indians and a second later, I drew the hammer back. I was gasping for air, and it was hard to steady the muzzle. Sam warned me not to start shooting until we knew who these Indians were; but a shot had already been fired at me, and as far as I was concerned, I had enough to be satisfied they meant to kill us.

"A little closer," I whispered, shivering, trying to catch my breath. Even the best marksman would have trouble hitting me from the back of a moving horse when it was snowing so heavily. I waited until I knew I couldn't miss.

I squeezed the trigger. That .44 caliber Winchester packs a hell of a kick; and when the cartridge exploded, it rocked me back while the sound was like thunder in my right ear.

Yellow flame spat from the barrel. The roar of the shot echoed from the far side of the wash.

For a split second I couldn't believe I'd missed, until my target fell back across the rump of his speeding pony. His legs went up and he rolled like a ball off the rear of his horse with his robe fluttering around him. He appeared to float in midair for a moment before he fell, toppling into a snowbank, sending a cloud of white flakes away from the spot where he landed. His dark pony shied, bolting off to the left without its rider in an all-out run.

I was levering another shell into the chamber when I heard a shout, a yipping cry like Indians sometimes make when they enter into a fight. Far to my right, across the draw, a gun roared in the distance. I could hear a slug whistle overhead, high and too wide to the left.

I turned my sights on the second warrior, guessing he'd make a swing in another direction rather than continuing straight at me. But I guessed wrong. He was pounding his heels into his pony's ribs as hard as he could, yelling at the top of his lungs. I saw a muzzle flash and heard the crack of a rifle. Ducking as low as I could, I held my gun steady.

He was almost on top of me before I fired because he stayed down near his pony's neck and I didn't want to shoot an animal if I could help it. My finger nudged the trigger when the Indian was barely twenty yards away. My rifle slammed into my shoulder so hard I felt it all the way to my toes, and the noise left me momentarily deaf as a stone.

I saw the Indian's head jerk backward. In the same instant, his pony swerved. He went off one side of his horse so quickly I would have sworn he'd vanished altogether until I saw him land, skittering across the snow, twisting this way and that with arms and legs windmilling. He slid to a halt where snow drifted deep and sort of bunched up, his knees under his chin. He lay there a moment while I was chambering another round before his legs fell flat. I noticed then he had a single braid of hair, making him a Kiowa. Sam would be glad to know we weren't facing Comanches, if he ever woke up long enough to realize we were in a fight.

A shot from across the creek sent me diving flat on my belly with my face buried in snowflakes. When I rolled over on my side, I saw an Indian on foot, standing in front of his pony with his rifle smoking. I swung the Winchester to my shoulder, resting on an elbow, trying to see through spits of snow making it hard to be sure what I was aiming at. I blinked snow from my eyes, but before I could clear them, the warrior was aboard his horse at a dead run away from there.

"Damn it," I hissed, clenching my teeth to keep them from chattering. I watched that Indian disappear into the storm with a thankful feeling. He'd had a perfect shot at me, and I'd been so careless I hadn't even noticed him before he got off a shot. I knew I couldn't count on being so lucky again.

It was then I realized how out in the open I was, lying on my belly at the top of the creek. If any one of them got a good shot at me, I'd be a sitting duck.

I crawled backward, inching through powdery snow, feeling a wet, chilly sensation down my chest where snow had gotten inside my shirt, melting with the heat of my body. Now I could hear the wind moaning overhead and feel gooseflesh pimpling my skin. If I was forced to stay up here very long, I'd freeze. But where else could I find a vantage point where I could protect our camp and our horses?

Looking around, I discovered I had no other choice but to hold my present position as long as I could. As I was taking stock of my situation, a gun banged to my left. When I heard the noise, I couldn't be sure of its direction; and like a fool, I'd been taken completely by surprise.

I flipped over to find where the shot came from, clutching my Winchester close to my chest. The bullet had gone so high I didn't hear it; however, the sound was close, too close for me to relax and get my wits together

I made a turn on my belly and shouldered the rifle, sweeping its muzzle back and forth, searching for anything I couldn't be sure of that looked like it could be a target, I saw a riderless pony plunging into a snowdrift north of the draw, trailing its rein. In a few seconds it went out of sight into sheets of snowflakes, leaving me without a clue as to where the shot came from. For what seemed like an eternity, I remained frozen there, looking across the tiny metal sight at the end of my rifle with nothing to shoot at.

A movement on the far side caught my attention. An Indian rode brazenly along the western edge of the creek, out in plain sight like he wanted to draw my fire. I was ready to oblige him just then, until something moved on my side of the stream.

A galloping pony appeared through the whirling snow-flakes, and for a moment I was sure the little horse ran loose without a rider. Until I saw a darker shape clinging to the sorrel's high withers, a Kiowa with a rifle.

There was no time to get ready for a clean shot—I had only a second or two to aim and fire. I held the Winchester's stock to my shoulder as tightly as I could and brushed the trigger with a finger enclosed by a half-frozen red mitten.

The blast drove me backward. When the shell went off, my toes weren't dug in to keep me from moving. I slid back as a puff of smoke billowed from the muzzle; and in spite of myself, I closed my eyes when the sound was so loud it felt like it threatened to break something inside my right ear.

I missed. I knew it the minute I fired. Working the lever as fast as I could, I readied another shell; and at the very same instant, a chilling scream came from the Indian bearing down on me. I saw him working a bolt on a single-action carbine, and I suppose the fact that he had an older weapon must have spared my life—he took too long getting ready to shoot, just long enough for me to fire first.

My Winchester belched flame. The Indian was so near I could see a tuft of brown fur torn from his buffalo robe where the slug went through his shoulder. He shrieked, twisting on the withers of his charging pony to reach for his shoulder wound, at the same time tossing his carbine in the air. That's when his mount stumbled over some object hidden beneath deep snow. It went crashing on its chest, legs flailing, making a grunting sound as it fell.

The Kiowa was tossed forward through the air, kicking his feet helplessly as though he meant to run as soon as he hit the ground. He was coming straight at me, propelled toward me by his pony's fall, so close I could see the wild expression on his face and even the whites of his eyes. There was no time to eject my spent cartridge and chamber another. I scrambled to my knees and swung my rifle like a club as he was falling on top of me.

The barrel struck bone midway through my swing. I heard a snapping noise and felt the shock of the blow clear down to my shoulders when I hit him across his skull. The angle of his dive changed suddenly when I knocked him to my left with every ounce of strength I had. He tumbled to the snow-bank with blood squirting from his head, groaning, landing disjointedly the way a man does when he's out cold. Blood was spreading around him so fast it colored the snow crimson, like someone spilled a bucket of red paint.

I gathered my wits while I rocked back on my haunches to get another cartridge chambered, looking around me as the empty shell went spinning away into the snow. The sorrel pony struggled to its feet and snorted once before it whirled and galloped off into the storm.

Before I could collect myself from such a close encounter, a shot rang out across the wash. The whine of lead screamed above me, forcing me to dive down on my belly again. I caught a brief glimpse of a buckskin pony racing through a curtain of snowflakes before a gust of wind swept snow in front of my eyes, temporarily blinding me. It looked like the Indian was aimed for our camp as hard as he could ride.

I crawled to the rim as rapidly as possible with my rifle in both hands, bringing it to my shoulder the minute I had a view of the streambed. The mounted warrior urged his buckskin across one last drift at the bottom of the slope, forcing it to run where no horse could without floundering. Deep snow was slowing the pony just enough for me to draw a bead on its rider.

My arms were trembling when I pulled the trigger. The sharp report of my Winchester popped, a noise like snapping timber. At almost the same time, a fraction of a second before I fired, that buckskin sank to its knees in the drift. My bullet kicked up a big cloud of white on the slope behind the Indian's head, a wide miss, way off its mark.

I chambered again quickly while the buckskin got to its feet and shook itself. The warrior clinging to its back attempted to fire up at me. His rifle roared a split second before mine.

I felt a breath of air whisper past my right cheek. My gun exploded, kicking, ramming the butt plate against me. I blinked and shook my head.

Down below, a robed figure atop the buckskin slid off one side of his pony as the little horse was dashing toward our cave at full speed. I saw him fall into the snow, losing his rifle. It had been a difficult shot, but I'd made it.

The Kiowa rolled a few times before he came to a halt with his arms and legs landing loose. I couldn't tell where I hit him from this distance. He was out of the fight for now, and that's what mattered.

I worked the lever with cold-numbed hands only to discover my Winchester was empty. . . . I'd fired six shots, which was the way we kept our rifles, so the chamber was empty just in case a horse happened to fall, it wouldn't go off accidental.

My spare ammunition was down in the cave. I'd downed four Indians, leaving two more who might still be looking for more fight.

I came to my knees quickly and cleared my coattail out of the way to get at my pistol. As I was getting up, I thought I heard a sound behind me, a quiet footfall in the snow.

Twenty-three

I whirled, reaching for my Colt when a dark blur came at me from behind. A Kiowa with a gleaming knife in his hands made a dive for my chest, wielding his blade. I'd clawed for my gun too late to bring it up before the warrior fell against me, driving his knifetip downward.

I blocked the sweep of his weapon with my forearm as we fell heavily in two feet of snow. His weight knocked all the air from my lungs. I reached for his wrist with my free hand, the tip of his blade only inches from my neck, beginning a vicious arc that would slice open my throat. I was able to catch his wrist with a hand encumbered by a mitten, the same predicament preventing my right hand from using the gun trapped underneath me. The suddenness of the attack caught me off guard, and I wasn't able to think, merely react to what was happening above me. I grunted, sucking badly needed air into my mouth while staring into a pair of fierce black eyes alight with hatred.

I arced my spine in an all-out attempt to throw him off my chest, clinging to his wrist, summoning every bit of strength I had to halt the downward sweep of the Kiowa's blade. But he was stronger, with the advantage of being on top of me, and no matter how hard I tried to throw him to one side, I failed. He drew his lips back across his teeth in a snarl. I could smell his stale breath and feel drops of spittle falling on my face as he brought the knifetip closer to my neck. Our arms shook with effort, his as well as mine. I was losing a battle of strength. Any second now, his steel blade would penetrate my windpipe.

Planting my right foot in the snow, I made a desperate lunge to throw him off, twisting while I lunged. He swayed, giving me a moment of slight advantage. I turned the other way and threw all my strength into a final effort to dislodge him.

He went forward unexpectedly, pushing his knife up toward my face. I drove my knee into his groin for all I was worth.

His eyes bulged with pain. He went sailing over my head as his blade swept across my left cheek, slicing into my frozen skin before I could push it away. Raw pain flashed over that side of my face like I'd been branded with a red-hot poker. In spite of it, I rolled over, releasing his wrist when he fell beyond reach as my right hand jerked up with the gun.

The Kiowa tumbled and rolled, scrambling to his feet in only an instant. He crouched and sprang at me like a cougar, knifetip sweeping. Blood splattered from my cheek over my arm and wrist, down the front of my coat as my finger curled around the Colt's trigger while I was falling backward to escape another bite from razor-sharp iron.

I fired. . . . The pistol bucked in my mittened fist only half a foot from the Kiowa's head. I collapsed on my back, watching the Indian's snarling teeth disappear. As he leapt toward me, a plug of coal-black hair flew away from the back of his skull into the air above him. His head jerked back in midflight as though he'd run into some invisible wall. Bits of skullbone and drops of blood fell on us when he landed on my chest like a lead weight, pinning me to the ground. I gasped and tried to crawl out from under him, staring into his lifeless eyes, noticing that my slug had shattered his front teeth on its way through his mouth.

I lay there stunned, too terrified and weakened to move for several seconds, with a dead Kiowa warrior crushing my ribs and belly. I needed a moment to gather my senses; but with his face so badly distorted by my bullet and blood all over me, I couldn't wait a moment longer.

I pushed him off and sat up unsteadily, still clinging to my pistol with an iron grip. I looked down the creek where my first victim had fallen and found that he was gone. Now I knew how the Kiowa had gotten so close before I was aware of him. I could see a blood trail in the snow coming toward me. The wounded Indian had crawled up behind me with a knife while I was shooting at the one down below. It looked like the rest of them had pulled back for a spell. There was no sign of them anywhere, and the longer I waited, the more convinced I became that they intended to have a talk before they rushed us again.

I touched my cheek. Blood was dribbling down on the front of my coat from the knife wound. Wearing a mitten, I couldn't tell yet how bad it was, but it sure hurt like hell. All around me I saw blood, the Kiowa's and mine. I was lucky to be alive.

I got up on my knees to pick up my rifle, peering over the rim to see if any more of them were near the cave. I needed more ammunition for the Winchester quickly, before they came back to make another try for our horses.

I stood in a crouch and picked up my hat where it had fallen off in the snow, dusting it off, taking note of the blood spots on the crown and brim. I happened to glance down; and when I saw the back of that Indian's head, I wished I hadn't. There was a hole at the base of his skull half the size of my fist. Flinty white bone and brains were exposed, and right away, my belly went to churning.

With my rifle in one hand and my pistol in the other, I went to the edge of the draw and started down, keeping a close eye on the Kiowa I'd felled in front of the cave. He wasn't moving at all, with a patch of bloody snow encircling his upper body. I didn't need a reminder how close he'd come to getting to Sam or our horses.

It had begun to snow harder, making it more difficult to

see downstream. As I was walking back to camp, I groaned
inwardly as I remembered the spare box of shells in my coat
pocket. I came to a halt and simply stood there shaking my
head, wondering how I could have forgotten something so
important. About the only kind of excuse I could come up
with was I'd had a chilled brain that didn't work right when
it was cold.

Holstering my pistol, I continued toward the cave to check
on Sam before I went back on top. I pulled off a mitten with
my teeth and fingered the slice in my cheek. It wasn't all
that deep, although it was bleeding some. The stinging was
less, but I knew it would take some time to heal and would
leave an ugly scar.

I fished into my coat and got out the spare shells, thumbing
six into my Winchester's loading gate before I put the box
back in my pocket. I knelt down beside Sam and covered
him with a blanket. I was puzzled why the other two Indians
had pulled out of our fight. Had losing four of their number
been enough to discourage them?

"You've been asleep through one hell of a fight, Marshal,"
I told him quietly, certain he couldn't hear me. "There's four
dead Kiowas lying around in this snow, and two more are
still out there—looking to steal our horses, I reckon."

I added some driftwood to the fire and peered out at more
snow falling into the wash. If this storm didn't let up, we'd
be up to our asses in snow pretty soon. This cave our mule
found had saved our lives, for the present. . . . if a band of
Kiowas didn't claim our scalps before it was over.

I crept back out in the snow and started up to the rim on
the balls of my feet, giving both sides of the draw real careful
looks as I climbed higher. Before I got to the top, I crouched
down, making sure I didn't have any company up there.
While I was waiting, I heard a noise and it startled me. Until
I knew what it was. Sam was coughing again.

Shivering, I put those red mittens on to keep my hands from
freezing and eased along the edge of the rim. A dusting of

snow covered the Kiowa with the hole through his head, and for that I was thankful. I didn't want to remember him, or how close he'd come to slicing my throat. If his friends came back looking for my scalp, I'd be reminded soon enough.

I settled down on my haunches to watch the draw with thick snow billowing around me. As far as I was concerned, this was the worst winter I ever hoped to see. If it never snowed again in my lifetime, it would be just fine with me.

With my back turned to the wind, I kept a roving eye on my surroundings, resting my rifle across my lap. If this storm got any worse, I wouldn't be able to see my hand in front of my face, much less another attack by those Kiowas. I thought about how curious it was that I was sitting out in the middle of the worst blizzard imaginable trying to keep Indians from stealing horses and a mule. Of all the occupations I ever considered for myself, putting my life on the line for a few head of livestock had never crossed my mind. At the District Office back in Fort Smith, they failed to mention same of the duties required of a U.S. Marshal out in the Territories. Otherwise, I might have given this job some serious second thoughts.

I was frozen to the bone when the sky got dark as night came over our camp. I couldn't see a thing with so much snow falling, and I figured it was time I built up our fire and thawed out some before I froze to death. There had been no sign of Indians after the two survivors pulled out. If they were as cold as I was, it wasn't likely they'd come back, leastways not until sunup.

The fire had almost burned out when I reached the cave. I piled more wood on the coals and set about to make coffee and fry bacon. Sam was sound asleep, looking peaceful enough under those blankets with his shirt wrapped around his head. I noticed the bottle of whiskey was nearly half gone, the last one we had.

While coffee was making, I led our animals out to eat

snow, cradling my rifle as I did it, staying watchful for Indians. It had snowed so much during the day, another foot
of white covered the ground, making it almost impossible to
walk in spots where it was deepest. As the last bit of light
faded in the sky, I got the roan horse put away for the night.
I gave them corn and tied them away from what light there
was coming from the fire, to make it as hard as I could for
an Indian to see them from a distance.

I squatted down by the fire to cut strips of bacon, sipping
coffee, applying a little bacon fat to the cut on my face, an
old remedy my ma believed in for cuts and burns. I kept glancing in Sam's direction from time to time, wishing he'd wake
up or show most any sign he was feeling better. His face felt
hot when I touched it, a fever I couldn't do anything about
other than feed him whiskey. But far more than worrying
about Sam's sickness, I was worried what I'd do if those
Kiowas came back tonight. I'd need to stay away from the
fire's light so I wouldn't be silhouetted by it, making it too
easy for one of them to take a potshot at me from the darkness.

I remembered the four Indians I killed. . . . One was lying
out in the snow, maybe fifty yards from the cave. But the one
I was remembering most held a knife just inches from my
throat before I shot him at close range. I'd been so close to
dying myself that I knew I was justified in what I did. He was
sure as hell trying to kill me. But no matter how justified
killing another man can seem, it still lingers for a spell on a
conscience.

A couple of hours after dark, Sam woke up. He commenced to cough something awful, sitting up all of a sudden
like something brought him right out of his deep sleep. He
saw me and gave me this bewildered look.

"Where the hell are we?" he asked, as though he didn't
have any recollection.

"Same place, Marshal, stuck in this hollowed out creek-
bank in a snowstorm," I replied.

He reached for the shirt tied around his skull. "What the hell is this?"

"Your spare shirt. When it got so cold I couldn't figure no other way to keep your head warm."

He pulled it off and looked at it. "That's plumb silly, Mr. Dudley, to tie a man's shirt around his head while he's asleep." He tossed it down and reached for the pint; but when he saw what had happened to my face, he came up short. "What did you do to yourself there?" His voice was softer.

"An Indian tried to cut me with a knife."

"An Indian? When did it happen?"

"While you were sleeping. Six of 'em came at us, and I had it figured they meant to steal our horses. They fired the first shot. I killed four, including the one who almost got me with a knife."

"While I was asleep? I didn't hear any shootin'. . . ."

"You've been out cold for several hours, Marshal. That bad cough you've got is likely the pneumonia."

"Damn," he whispered, frowning. "Were those Indians Comanches?"

"Kiowas, judging by their hair. Like you showed me a long time back, they had their hair tied like a rope, just one braid."

"Kiowas," he agreed, and now he took a drink of whiskey as if he needed it to calm his nerves. "You held off six of 'em all by yourself?"

I nodded. "It got kinda scary for a while. They came at me from all sides. It kept me pretty busy. They rode off east down this draw, the two who got away. Hadn't seen no sign of 'em ever since middle of the day."

Sam looked out at the snow. "They'll come back with a few of their friends tomorrow," he told me gravely. "I 'spect they came from Lone Wolf's band on the Beaver. When they report what happened here, we could be in for some real trouble. Lone Wolf don't take kindly to an ass-whippin'."

"You know him?"

"As well as any white man will ever know him, I reckon. He hates a white man worse'n a preacher hates sin. The Medicine Lodge Treaty didn't suit him none. He's been goin' along with it lately, but we better not count on him stayin' peaceable after he lost four warriors here."

"What else was I to do, Marshal? They shot at me first, so I fired back."

It took Sam awhile to come up with an answer. "You did the only thing you could."

Twenty-four

I spent a long night worrying and listening to Sam cough in the wee hours before dawn. I dozed from time to time, although I never really slept soundly, thinking about the possibility Lone Wolf would come back to have his revenge for the warriors I shot yesterday. Every now and then I'd look out at a lump in the snow where one dead Kiowa lay, and the sight of it made me all the more jittery. I never was good at having dead men on my conscience, even though those Indians had been the ones to start our fight. On the good side of things, it was snowing less when a streak of gray brightened the eastern horizon; however, my brief celebration was over the minute I could see down that draw well enough to recognize forty or fifty Indians riding slowly toward our camp.

I scrambled to my feet holding my rifle. My heart began to thump. "Wake up, Marshal!" I cried, edging over near his pallet, never once taking my eyes from that fierce-looking party of Kiowas moving along both sides of the creek until I was close enough to reach down and shake Sam's shoulder. "Better open up your eyes if you can," I added quickly as a sinking feeling got started in the pit of my stomach. There were so many Indians, I knew we could never stand them off.

Sam stirred underneath his blankets. "What did you say, Mr. Dudley?" he mumbled sleepily, rubbing his eyes.

"I said you'd better sit up. There's at least fifty Indians out there." I was only guessing at the number.

Sam sat up quickly, focusing on what he saw riding toward us in dawn's pale light. He coughed once and spat a mouthful out in the snow. "Hand me my rifle," he said softly. "An' whatever you do, don't fire a shot unless I tell you to." He put on his hat and came slowly to his feet as I was handing him his Winchester.

"There's too many of them," I said.

Sam tugged the brim of his hat low over his eyes. "It's a comfort to know you can count, Mr. Dudley." He buttoned his coat and turned to me. "The one ridin' the piebald roan stud is Lone Wolf. It's gonna take some fancy talkin' to get us out of this."

He made it sound like I was to blame. "I had to shoot back yesterday or they'd have killed us both and taken our horses. I didn't see no other way out."

Sam didn't offer an opinion, watching Kiowas ride closer to our cave. I paid attention to the one he identified as Lone Wolf, riding a colorful roan pinto stallion. Shrouded in his buffalo robe, he made a fearsome sight. He carried a rifle with an eagle feather tied to the stock, resting it across his pony's withers. His face was as hard looking as nearly any Indian I'd ever seen, with the possible exception being Quannah Parker. Quannah's pale eyes gave him the meanest expression, but Lone Wolf had his own fierce look, fixing us with a cold stare as he rode in front of his warriors. They came toward us like they knew we didn't have a chance against them, appearing real confident, unafraid of our repeating rifles. I was cold before I saw them, but now I felt a chill all the way down my spine.

Sam walked away from our camp, balancing his Winchester in the palm of his left hand. His stride was a little unsteady as he crossed all that snow, and I knew it was because he'd been so sick he hadn't eaten right for days. But he still managed to carry himself like he had pride, walking straight out to face a half-a-hundred armed Indians without showing any visible signs of fear. I had to hand it to him. . . . If he knew we were gonna die, he damn sure didn't let on to those Kiowas.

He stopped about thirty yards from the cave and raised his right hand, making sign talk while Lone Wolf and his bunch kept coming toward us. I watched Lone Wolf real close to see if he answered back with a sign. He didn't, and that convinced me all the more that me and Sam were in the last fight of our lives, as soon as the shooting started.

Lone Wolf rode his pinto right up to Sam, with warriors on either side of him. When Lone Wolf stopped, so did the others.

Sam said something, words I didn't understand. When he was speaking Comanche or Kiowa, it sounded more like grunting than making words, most of the time. He told me once that Comanche and Kiowa are nearly the same language and that the two tribes were almost kin. I listened as close as I could, waiting for Lone Wolf to answer.

"Pe-she-pah Mah-e-yah," Lone Wolf said, and then he pointed right at me, staring like he would kill me any second now. Then he uttered another string of words, spitting them out so rapidly they all came at once.

Sam looked over his shoulder. "Come here, Mr. Dudley. Be real sure you don't act scared or go for a gun. No matter what he says or does, just stand still an' don't act like you're the least bit afraid of him."

My heart quit beating entirely for a second or two. "You want me to come out there?"

The look on Sam's face told me it was a dumb question. I'd heard him right the first time. I took a big breath and started walking toward Sam and the Indians, wondering if these might be the last steps I ever took. I kept my rifle pointed down at the ground, but my eyes were on Lone Wolf. If I could, I aimed to see if I could stare him down.

The closer I got, the more it appeared that Lone Wolf was in a killing mood. He watched me without a trace of expression on his face, but his dark eyes said enough, a mouthful. He gave me one of the meanest stares I've ever seen until I was standing to the left of Sam with my feet spread slightly apart.

Sam spoke to me first. "He wanted to get a good look at you up close, Mr. Dudley. Just stand there 'til he satisfies himself about you. Don't look off, an' whatever you do, don't make any kind of move with a gun. He's curious about you. The two boys who rode back to the village told Lone Wolf you had a pair of red hands. They also said you were a brave warrior, that you fought with a lot of courage. He wants to see if you're really all that brave-lookin'. If we're lucky, all he'll do is look. Those boy-warriors who traded lead with you yesterday were young, out on a huntin' trip, when they smelled our smoke. When they saw you an' those damn red mittens, they figured you were somethin' evil from the spirit world."

I didn't dare look down at my hands after what Sam told me. "He'll know they're only mittens, won't he?"

Sam lowered his voice. "I'm hopin' he won't ask."

"Pe-she-pah Mah-e-yah," Lone Wolf said, and it sure didn't sound friendly, giving me the eye so hard I felt near naked. I sensed the other Kiowas were listening real close, but I never stopped looking up at Lone Wolf.

"He's given you a Kiowa name," Sam went on, "and a while ago he asked how you got that cut on your face. He's callin' you Red Hands, on account of those mittens. So far so good, Mr. Dudley."

I spoke to Sam without looking at him. "I suppose you could tell him I didn't have no choice in that fight with his hunters."

"I don't intend to tell him a damn thing he doesn't want to know," Sam answered. "He knows he can kill us anytime he takes the notion. Showin' we ain't afraid is the smartest thing we can do. Kiowas are like Comanches when it comes to courage. They understand that, sometimes, it's all a man has."

Lone Wolf spoke to a warrior seated on a sorrel pony beside him. He said just a few words, then he made a circular motion with his right hand. When he looked at me again, he closed his fist over his heart.

I didn't know what to do. I waited for Sam to tell me what Lone Wolf meant. Some of the Indians on either side of us turned their ponies away.

"He made the sign for a brave heart in battle," Sam told me.

I wasn't sure I understood. Before I could ask, Sam spoke again.

"He's payin' you about the highest compliment an Indian can pay a white man. It also means he won't take our hair today. He knows your hands ain't really red, that they're just some bit of clothing a white man wears. The warriors who came yesterday were young and they'd never seen anything like 'em before. Lone Wolf is gonna punish the other two for startin' a fight before they had his permission. Those you killed have already been punished. He asked to take back their bodies so their families can hold a burial ceremony. We're free to ride on anytime we want."

I was looking up at Lone Wolf while Sam was talking and an idea occurred to me. "How about if I offered to give him these mittens as a way of showing we're friendly? That we didn't mean no harm when his warriors rode up and started shooting at us."

"He'd be a fool to take 'em, ugly as they are."

I put my rifle down in the snow and pulled off Clara's red knitting, then I held them out to Lone Wolf. "Tell him we're making him a present out of these," I said, although I figured the Kiowa chief already knew what I was doing.

Lone Wolf looked to Sam for an explanation, not making any move to take what I was offering him. Sam said a few words and made a looping motion with his hands.

I saw the chief's gaze return to the mittens. He grunted and urged his stallion forward until he could reach down to take them. He looked me in the eye right after that and said something. For some reason I wasn't afraid of being that close to him now.

Lone Wolf wheeled his pinto away and rode off into the snow with his warriors following close behind. Several Kiowas had begun to load the stiffened corpse of the warrior lying near our cave onto the back of a pony.

As I was bending down to pick up my rifle, Sam made what he thought was a joke.

"He'll be the only Indian in all of creation wearin' a pair of bright-red mittens. Serves Clara right for sendin' those damn things along. They nearly caused us to get scalped. I aim to tell her what happened, next time she gets her knittin' needles out."

I noticed how Sam was still a little shaky on his feet, and I said, "Maybe you oughta go back and lie down, Marshal. It looks like you've still got a touch of fever."

He turned to me and snapped, "When I need a nursemaid, you'll be the first to know. Let's get saddled. If we ride hard, we can make Dodge City in a day or two, if we ain't completely lost due to followin' a lame-brained mule." He staggered across a deep drift with his rifle slung over his shoulder like he was sure he could walk all the way to Kansas if he had to. I watched him go a few feet farther until he began to cough, sinking slowly to his knees. He dropped his Winchester to grip his sides, coughing so loudly it startled a few of the Kiowas close by.

I ran up to him and held his shoulder. "Let me help you to the fire, Marshal. Maybe it ain't such a good idea to saddle up just yet."

Pride wouldn't let him admit he couldn't ride. He spat a mouthful of clotted spittle into the snow and wagged his head. "Saddle the damn horses, Mr. Dudley," he said, wheezing between breaths. "I can lie on that drag you made as easy as I can lie on frozen ground."

"But it's still snowing, and the snow's mighty deep. Our horses will have a time of it plowing through."

When Sam looked up at me then, I knew I'd argued one time too many. "It's wintertime," he said evenly, biting down around each word. "It could snow from now 'til spring. The longer we stay here, the less chance we've got of findin' those boys who ride for Haskell. He'll get word to 'em and they'll hightail it out West some place where we'll never find 'em. I haven't gone through all this misery to let 'em get away. Help me up, an' then put me on the travois, even if you have to tie me there. The last thing I need from you is a bunch of coddling."

"I was only saying how you're still sick."

"I sure as hell ain't gonna get no better layin' here. Now help me up an' get those animals ready to travel."

"I'll make us some coffee while I'm at it," I said, avoiding the way he stared at me. I glanced up at the sky. It wasn't snowing quite so hard now. I took Sam's arm and helped him climb to his feet, picking up his rifle afterward when I saw he could stand on his own.

As we were walking toward the fire, I noticed several Indians up on the rim above our cave loading frozen bodies on the backs of horses. I didn't want to remember that Kiowa I shot through the mouth, only I couldn't help it when I saw them hoisting him over a pony's rump. If I could, I wanted to forget the entire affair quickly. Only my mind just doesn't work that way when it comes to killing. Sometimes I dreamed about men I killed in the line of duty, seeing their faces up close.

I helped Sam to his blankets and put snow in our coffeepot along with a few beans. When it was nestled in the coals, I went over to our horses to begin saddling. I sure wasn't looking for more days riding through that north wind, but Sam wasn't hearing of anything else.

I led our animals out to eat snow when the last Kiowas rode off to the east with their dead. Sam was coughing every now and then, sipping whiskey to quiet it. Above the rim, wind whipped snowflakes into the air like millions of tiny feathers, carrying them off. We were in for another rough ride, and I had no choice but to make the best of it.

The last thing I did was tie the travois poles to my bay's saddlehorn, fixing a blanket between them with ropes. I tested it myself before I went to the fire to fill my belly with coffee for the day's ride.

That was when I noticed Sam had passed out again.

Twenty-five

When I caught sight of Dodge City, as bleak as it was, I'd never seen a sight so beautiful. Stretched out across a plain as flat as pancakes, snow-covered buildings caught rays of sunshine, making rooftops sparkle like new copper pennies. We'd ridden for almost two days through snow that was three-feet deep in drifts. It had stopped snowing the end of the first day, making for much easier travel while we were warmed by the sun. Sam was in pretty serious shape, coughing his head off, having trouble breathing at times. We arrived in Dodge none too soon for his sake. He lay on that travois like he was half dead, if you discounted how he was given over to coughing fits so often. A north wind kept him and me so cold I didn't think we'd ever thaw out. He woke up now and then after we left that cave and we'd talk some about where we were, how far I thought it was to Dodge, but not for more than a few minutes at a time, long enough to eat a bite of bacon and drink a few sips of coffee. His fever seemed worse and he made that same wheezing sound when he gulped air. I was hoping we'd made Dodge City soon enough for a doctor to help him.

We passed a sign reading *Front Street* on our way into town that second afternoon. Rows of saloons sat along several narrow streets, a cowtown like Fort Worth catering mostly to the cowboy trade with whiskey and gambling and such diversions as trail hands needed after a two-month cattle drive. Somewhere in one of those buildings I expected to find Will James and Valdez. I made plans to talk to the local sheriff as soon as Sam was attended to by a doctor.

The town looked pretty quiet, this being an off time of year for cowboys up from Texas. In the summer and fall, this place would be crawling with cowherds and drovers. A few horses were tied to hitchrails up and down Front Street, and an occasional buggy went plowing through rutted snow carrying better-dressed men and women across town. I saw buildings with all manner of signs hanging on them advertising elixirs and tonics and various other wares, but no sign showing me where to find a doctor until we rode past a big two-story saloon named *Varieties.* Right next door was a tiny shop with a sign that read *Dr. Rufus Thompson, Physician and Steam Healer.* I didn't know about steam healing, never having heard of such a thing, but I rode right over to the building as soon as we got there.

Tying off the roan and mule, I went back to check on Sam before I went inside. Several people came to store windows to look at the travois and whoever was lying on it. Sam's eyes were shut, so I left him to run inside and inquire about seeing Dr. Thompson. His office windows were foggy from having so much heat in there, and I wondered if maybe this was the steam healing he advertised.

I climbed a freshly shoveled boardwalk cleared of snow and went in without knocking. In a room lined with chairs, a potbelly stove gave off so much heat it felt like summertime. In a room at the back, I saw a man standing over a table where a cowboy in chaps and boots lay groaning.

The gentleman I assumed was Dr. Thompson turned away from his patient. "Be with you shortly," he said.

I smelled ether. "I've got a real sick man outside, Doc, and if it's okay by you I'd like to bring him in where it's a little warmer. I'm of the opinion he's got the pneumonia."

"Bring him in," the silver-haired doctor said, looking back down at his patient's stomach.

"He's too heavy for me to carry," I replied. "I'll ask next door to see if somebody'll help me."

Dr. Thompson turned to me again. "That might not be such a good idea, mister. I'll lend you a hand in just a moment."

I wondered why going next door to Varieties wasn't a good idea, but I didn't ask. Half a minute later, the doctor closed the front of the cowboy's shirt and came from the back.

"Let's bring him in," he said, giving me the once-over as we headed out the door. "You say he's got pneumonia?"

I led over to the travois and pointed to Sam. "He coughs so hard it sounds like his ribs oughta break and he's got a fever."

Dr. Thompson started helping me untie the ropes. It could be a number of things," he mumbled, looking closely at Sam's red face.

We carried him in, struggling up the steps to a second tiny room off the back of the doctor's office. We put Sam on a table padded with quilts; and just then, maybe because it was so warm in there, Sam woke up with a start.

"Where am I?" he asked.

"I'm Dr. Rufus Thompson. Lie still so I can examine you."

As the doctor was listening to Sam's chest with a cup made of metal having a nipple on the end fitting in his ear, I backed over near the door. "His name's Sam Ault, Doc, and he's the U.S. Marshal for the Western District of Indian Territory. We've been out in this cold for several days."

Thompson waved for me to be silent. Then he took his ear away from the cup and said, "Steam with eucalyptus should help in this case. I'll get the steam tent ready out back. A mustard plaster for his chest will draw some of the fluid out."

Sam had been listening. He looked over at me. "Find the sheriff's office, Mr. Dudley. Tell him why we're here, an' ask if he's seen James or Valdez. I'll be up an' around in a couple of hours, soon as this sawbones is finished with me, an' then we'll look for those Rafter H boys ourselves."

Dr. Thompson raised a hand in front of Sam's face. "I can

assure you that you won't be going anywhere soon, Marshal Ault. You have a very high fever and congested lungs. Rest is the only thing you'll be doing for some time."

"Like hell," Sam growled, making like he meant to get off that table right then. He raised his head and shoulders until his eyelids sort of fluttered. He fell back, unconscious.

"He should sleep for a while," Thompson said. "I assure you, he won't be going anyplace. I suggest you take care of whatever brings you to Dodge City by yourself. This man is quite ill."

I figured the same, that Sam was lucky to be alive. "Is he gonna be okay, Doc?"

The doctor didn't sound so sure. "If he responds well to the treatments. Time will tell." He started to leave the room.

"Can you direct me to the sheriff's office and a livery for our horses?"

"There is a stable at the end of Front Street run by Old Man Jenks. Masterson's office is two blocks west. You can't miss it because of the sign on the roof."

"I'm obliged," I told him, leaving Sam in the doctor's care to see to our horses and mule before I took care of legal business.

Sheriff Bat Masterson was reading the *Ford County Globe* when I entered his office. He looked up at me like he didn't want any interruption. Masterson wore a business suit, dressing more like a dandy than a lawman. His mustache had waxed ends and I could see he had a high opinion of himself by the way he took so much care with his appearance. His office was furnished with expensive chairs and a polished desk, which the sheriff had his feet propped on when I came in.

"Can I help you, son?" he asked.

I closed the door. "I'm Deputy United States Marshal Leon Dudley from Indian Territory. Marshal Sam Ault is over at Dr. Thompson's office. We've been tracking some men this direction and got caught in the blizzard. Marshal Ault wanted me to ask you if you've seen 'em."

Masterson took his feet off the desk, offering me a handshake without standing up. "Always glad to be of service to a Federal Marshal. Tell me who you're lookin' for." He waved a hand toward a vacant chair across the desk.

I took a seat, bone weary after so many days in a saddle and being so cold. "One's named Will James. He carries a gun across his belly. The other's a big Mexican named Valdez. We were told they had two more cowboys with 'em from the Haskell ranch down in Texas. Marshal Ault suspects they may have been involved in the massacre of eleven settlers, maybe on orders from Haskell himself if Sam's hunch is right."

Masterson looked down at my badge when I opened my coat in a warm room. "I've seen a big Mexican, only I never knew him by name. Will James is a gunfighter, a dangerous man. He's wanted in Missouri for two killings. I've got a description of him on a Wanted circular someplace, but I don't think he's one of the men with the Mexican. Hell, they look like simple cowhands to me."

"They ain't," I said. "Leastways Marshal Ault don't think they are. We had a run-in with 'em earlier, and Grant Haskell acted mighty suspicious when Sam started asking him questions at the ranch. Where did you see the Mexican, Valdez?"

"He was at a little place north of the railroad tracks near the cattle pens. It's called *Mickey's*. That was maybe two days back. I can't recall seein' him since; however, if you're of a mind to, we can ask around."

I wasn't looking for a confrontation with James or Valdez until I'd had some real sleep on a bed in a room with four walls and every comfort. "I'll hire a room for the night and get a few hours of shuteye, Sheriff. We've been camped out on that prairie so long I'm due for some sleep. I'll drop by in the morning and we'll look around then. My mouth's been watering for some real home cookin', if you can recommend a place."

"Down the street at the Blue Plate Eatery. Best grub in all of Kansas Territory. The best hotel is the Cowman's Roost over by the tracks. They've got hot baths, and drinks are two for a quarter in the bar downstairs."

"Sounds like heaven to me, Sheriff. I'm obliged for all the help and I know Marshal Ault will feel the same."

"He's at Doc Thompson's?" Masterson asked.

I nodded as I got out of the chair. "He's getting a steam treatment right about now, I reckon. Never heard of such a thing before."

The sheriff stood up as I was leaving. "Maybe I'll look in on Marshal Ault later this evening. Come by tomorrow, and we can ask around at the stockyards for Will James and the others."

Waiting until tomorrow was about the best I could do, even as serious as the charges might be against James and Valdez. I gave Bat Masterson a wave and went outside, casting a hungry eye on the Blue Plate Eatery a few blocks away.

Hoisting our saddlebags and a bundle of clean clothing I got from our packs, I trudged down the street toward my first square meal in days. It wasn't until then I realized how tired I was, or just how glad I was to be off a horse's back for a spell. I hoped the doctor could work his wonders on Sam, but right at the moment I needed a cure for what ailed me . . . an empty belly and a brain needing sound sleep, for which Dodge City had remedies to fix both conditions.

I ate the best plate of beef stew I ever tasted in my life at the Blue Plate, served to me on a blue plate just like a sign above the door said. I washed it down with several cups of dark coffee and ate bread pudding for dessert. That good food was a reminder of how Bonnie Sue Miller's cooking tasted, and I had to admit I missed seeing her just a little, although I'd never say such a thing to her face.

After I paid my bill, I strolled down toward the doctor's

office before I hired a room, seeing as it was still early, not sundown yet. With my belly full, I got to worrying about Sam. If he was awake, I'd tell him about Sheriff Masterson seeing Valdez at a place called *Mickey's*.

When I went in, I found Dr. Thompson pulling a tooth from a cowboy's mouth in a back room. He saw me come in and let go of the tooth with a pair of long-handled pliers.

"Marshal Ault is resting comfortably," he said, nodding in the direction of a closed door where the padded table was. "I gave him something to help him sleep. Come back tomorrow. He should feel somewhat better. By the way, Sheriff Masterson came by inquiring as to his condition."

"I'll look in on him tomorrow, Doc. It's good to know he's feeling better." I went back outside, turning for the Cowman's Roost over on the north side of the stockyards. My legs were so weary they were hardly able to carry me.

Crossing the business district of Dodge City, I gazed in a few windows, feeling full and more content than I had in quite a spell. Tomorrow I'd be facing some dangerous men, according to Bat Masterson, but tonight I aimed to sleep and forget about the past few days riding a frozen prairie, pulling a travois over so many miles of bitter-cold trail. Times like this, I didn't take too well to a Deputy Marshal's job. After fighting half-a-dozen Kiowas, almost freezing to death in a blizzard, living out of a saddle for better than a week, I couldn't find much about it that would cause a man to want more of the same.

"Maybe I will give some thought to taking up carpentering," I said under my breath, remembering those remarks Sam made back at Cache before we rode off into this misery. Having a hammer hanging from my belt instead of a gun was sounding more and more like a better idea.

I walked past the stockyards, rows of corrals with loading chutes to drive cattle into railroad cars, all empty now. This city wasn't much to look at during the winter. Farther down a snow-rutted road I saw a few small saloons past the hotel where I'd be staying.

"One of 'em will be Mickey's," I told myself. Were Valdez and Will James still in town? I wondered.

I'd find out tomorrow morning, after I took a hot bath and slept like a bear until the sun came up. I walked up the hotel steps like a man headed toward pure happiness.

Twenty-six

I heard a noise. When I opened my eyes, that hotel room was so dark I couldn't see my hand in front of my face. I'd been so sound asleep I hadn't moved since I lay down on the bed after a hot bath and a shave, being careful to miss the angry red scar on my cheek. I lay there listening for the sound to come again, but everything was quiet out in the hall, even downstairs in the bar where a piano had been playing before I went to sleep. It being the slow season in Dodge, the hotel was almost empty and the bar only had a couple of patrons when I came upstairs after I took my bath.

As a precaution I sat up and took my revolver from a small washstand beside the bed, cocking an ear toward the door leading into the hallway. Gradually, as my eyes adjusted to bad light, I could see shadows on the floor cast by a sliver of moon, spilling through a window beside my bed. I didn't have any idea what time it was, only it must be late because things were so quiet.

I decided, after a bit, I was hearing things, maybe in some sort of dream. That room was so warm and the bed so comfortable, I was asleep minutes after I lay down. I couldn't even be sure of the kind of sound I'd heard, only that it woke me from a deep sleep. I got up and tiptoed over to a tiny dressing table and struck a match to an oil lamp, turning the wick down so low it was only a pinpoint of light burning inside the globe, just enough to let me see where I was going as I got back under the covers.

I lay back on a soft feather pillow with my gun resting on the mattress beside me. I figured so much had happened over the past few days, I'd gotten too jumpy, expecting more trouble.

"Won't be no Indians on the prowl in Dodge City," I whispered to myself, closing my eyes, feeling mighty snug and warm in my clean longjohns under a pile of quilts. I thought about Sam, hoping he was feeling better after his steam treatments and the mustard plaster.

Before I drifted off to sleep again, I felt a little bit of nervousness, thinking about meeting up with Will James and Valdez and whoever rode with them. I was counting on Sheriff Masterson to be there to back my play when I questioned them. I had that diary belonging to Georgina Cooper with me, a piece of evidence we hadn't counted on. It might be enough to convince a judge those men were guilty. I'd have felt a lot better about things if Sam was there tomorrow, but he wouldn't be. I'd have to handle it on my own. I'd been lucky he was strong enough to talk to Lone Wolf that snowy morning. Otherwise, events might have happened very differently, with our scalps hanging on a Kiowa lodge pole somewhere in Indian Territory.

I bolted straight up in bed when I heard something rattle in the lock on my door. I'd hardly gotten my eyes open when someone burst into the room, a blacker shape among black shadows, only this one was moving, rushing toward me. Half asleep, I dove off the mattress when that dark blur became the silhouette of a man lunging for my bed with a knife in his hands—the biggest bowie knife I'd ever seen, gleaming in moonlight from the window as it swept downward toward my pillow.

I rolled to the floor, scrambling away from the bed almost before I landed, watching that knife being stabbed into the place where I'd had my head only a half second before. As

I jumped up, I got my first look at the man wielding the knife, a big bearded gent with long shaggy hair hanging to his shoulders.

Goosefeathers flew away from the pillow. I heard a ripping noise, then a grunt when the shaggy owlhoot saw he'd missed me. I barely got my feet under me before he whirled, crouching down as though he meant to spring over the mattress after me, brandishing his knifetip, drawing circles in the air.

"Who are you?" I cried, backing away. I'd left my gun on the bed when I jumped off so quick. He had me cornered against the wall of my room with no place to run.

He spat something in another tongue sounding like, *Pendejo!*

I backed up until I was touching the wall, my mind racing to find a way out of this fix without being carved up like a turkey on Thanksgiving.

He started around the foot of the bed and I knew I'd run out of time. Our Winchesters stood in a corner, well out of my reach even if I'd had the time to chamber a shell. I had nothing with which to protect myself from the arc of his blade when he came at me.

I jumped over to the dressing table just as he bunched his muscles for a lunge. I grabbed that glass lamp, the only thing within reach, and threw it as hard as I could toward his face.

He tried to duck. I suppose because it was dark he didn't see it coming until it was too late. First the glass globe hit his forehead, shattering, but it was what happened next that he wasn't expecting and neither was I. The lamp's glass coal-oil tank broke against his arm when he tried to shield his face and eyes, and that's when fire erupted like a giant orange ball down the front of his coat and in his scraggly black beard.

He straightened up and shrieked for all he was worth, at the same time dropping his knife to paw at the fire sizzling in his chin whiskers. Burning coal oil spilled on the floor around him, licking up his legs, catching his pants on fire.

I drew back when that ball of flame ignited, nearly blind

in its sudden bright glare. Then my head cleared and I leapt over to the mattress, grabbing my gun in one hand, a heavy quilt in the other.

I threw the quilt at him, trying to smother the flames while keeping my gun aimed at his chest. "Smother it!" I shouted as a terrible smell filled my nose—burning hair and clothing, maybe a bit of flesh. The whole room would go up in flames unless I got the fire put out.

He staggered back, spreading fire when he did as more oil dripped to the floor. He screamed again, knocking the quilt away to paw his flaming beard. I saw his eyes rounding with pain and fear. He wheeled toward the window, his head and chest and legs engulfed in flames, illuminating the room as bright as if it were daytime.

What he did next had to be a product of fear. He ran to the window and dove through the glass pane head-first, smashing it to pieces. He had to know it was a second-floor room since he'd come upstairs to knife me. He plummeted out into the darkness with a strangled scream caught in his throat and fell down to the street below. I heard him thump when he landed; but right then I was so busy gathering more quilts to put out flames dancing all over the floor, I scarcely noticed when he fell.

The edge of the mattress burst into flame. My bare feet got so hot I yelped like a scalded puppy, then I started to scream as loud as I could, "Fire! Fire! Somebody help me!" I pounded the floor with one quilt, tossing my Colt aside to grab another cover so I could smother flames with both hands. For a few seconds the fire got the best of me until at last I got all of those puddles of oil burning on the floor put out.

I started beating my mattress as hard as I could, using both quilts to suffocate flaming bed-sheets. In a moment the last bit of fire was snuffed, leaving only sparks here and there and a room full of smoke so thick I could hardly see a thing. That's when I heard boots running down the hall behind me and voices shouting back and forth. I was completely out of breath by the time two men got there carrying lanterns.

"What happened?" an older gent asked, peering in at all the smoke.

I was standing there holding two smoldering quilts and it didn't seem like events needed an explanation. "The room caught fire," I gasped. "Some gent busted into my room and tried to cut me up with a knife. . . . It's lying over there on the floor. He went out that window yonder. Somebody run fetch the sheriff while I get dressed. His face and clothes was on fire when he jumped and he's gotta be burnt pretty bad. I'm a Deputy U.S. Marshal, and I aim to arrest him for attempted murder."

"Who was he?" another man asked, standing out in the hallway looking over the other's shoulder. "An' how did this fire get started?"

I didn't give all the details. "A lantern broke. I'll tell Sheriff Masterson all about it soon as he gets here. Leave one of those lanterns so I can see to get dressed. I reckon a bucket of water tossed on this bed wouldn't be such a bad idea, 'cause there's a few sparks still burning."

One of them took off at a trot while the other handed me his lantern. I limped over to the dressing table on scorched feet to put on my denims and boots.

"Who woulda been tryin' to kill a U.S. Marshal?" the old man asked me again, walking into the room to stamp on a piece of bed-sheet glowing red on the floor, gazing out the broken windowpane for a moment. "The sumbitch had to be crazy to jump so far. Every bone he's got is liable to be broke." He went over and stuck his head out the window. "Don't see nobody down there. . . ." he added.

I got dressed in a hurry, strapping on my gun before I put on my coat and hat. "He won't get far," I promised, taking one Winchester along. "Keep an eye on that bed until somebody gets here with a bucket of water. I'll see to that big bastard who tried to carve me up."

He went over to my nightstand for a pitcher I'd forgotten about, taking it over to the mattress. "This'll help some 'til Jesse gits back with a pail." He poured water on a smoking pile of sheets and stood back, wrinkling his nose.

I left the room at a brisk walk, moving down a darkened hall as fast as I could without being able to see. My mind was on the owlhoot who tried to kill me, wondering who he was. Why would a robber pick my room to make his play? Some of it didn't make any sense.

On my way downstairs I remembered the killer called me some foreign word or name when he missed me with his knife. I started to put things together all of a sudden, if I was guessing right. "That was Valdez," I whispered, shaking my head in disbelief when I got to the bottom of the staircase. "He found out we were in town and tried to kill me." That could mean he'd also made a try at killing Sam down at Dr. Thompson's office, and Sam wouldn't be in any shape to stop him if Valdez had come for him first.

I ran over to the hotel's front door and unlocked it, seeing as the lobby was dark. When I rushed out on the front porch, I drew my gun, expecting to find Valdez out in the snow with broken leg-bones, lying directly under my window. But when I got there, to my surprise, I didn't see anyone.

I walked over to the spot right below the busted window-pane with my breath coming from my nose and mouth in frosty curls. There was only an impression where somebody had landed, and then a set of footprints leading away toward those cow pens beside the railroad tracks. Somehow, possibly because the snow was deep enough to break his fall, Valdez had gotten away. It took a minute for things to sink in as I stood there covering a wallowed-out place in the snow with my pistol.

I looked toward the stockyards. Valdez was probably there now with burns on his face and body, trying to find a way to give me the slip.

"How the hell did he know I was here?" I asked myself out loud.

There was just one answer. The only person in Dodge City who knew where we were staying was Sheriff Bat Masterson. But was I ready to believe the sheriff was in cahoots with men like Valdez and Will James?

I had two choices. Either I ran down to the doc's office to make sure Sam was okay before I went after Valdez or I started tracking him from here, hoping I had been the big Mexican's first target tonight.

A commotion in the hotel kept me from making up my mind what to do right then. A man wearing a nightshirt came outside with a lantern. I recognized him as the hotel clerk who rented me that upstairs room.

"What's all the ruckus about?" he demanded. "I'd nearly swear I heard a window break an' then somebody yellin' about a fire. My wife claims she can smell smoke. . . ."

"A man broke into my room and tried to kill me," I said. "A lantern got smashed, but the fire's out now. He dove through my window, only I can't find him. Yonder's his tracks, heading for the cattle pens."

"You right sure the fire's out?" he asked, turning quickly to go back inside.

"A couple of men showed up. One's gone to fetch a bucket of water from out back. Another gent is up there keeping an eye out for sparks. When the sheriff shows up, tell him what happened."

The clerk was on his way inside, his mind clearly on another matter upstairs. "I'll tell him," he said, disappearing through his front door. Before he closed it, he said, "By the way, there was a feller askin' fer you earlier tonight. I told him you was already retired for the evenin'."

"What did he look like?" I asked.

"Big feller. A Meskin. Couldn't hardly understand him. He stunk worse'n high heaven. Needed a bath worst I ever smelled." At that, he closed the door and hurried across the lobby.

I decided to go after Valdez, with a fresh trail to follow. With a bit of luck Sam was sleeping soundly at the doctor's place and I'd be wasting precious time running down there first.

I took off at a jog trot down a deeply rutted road packed with snow, levering a cartridge into the firing chamber of my rifle. It was a clear night with stars overhead and a piece of moon showing me the way. I was still troubled, thinking Valdez could only have learned where I was from the Dodge City Sheriff. There was no other way to explain how Valdez had known where to ask for me.

Twenty-seven

Loading chutes and plank corrals rose up against a night sky when I reached the railroad tracks. A tiny depot sat between two sets of rails, looking dark and empty with a touch of frost on a windowpane in its door. His prints led straight for the building; and when I saw this, I slowed to a walk. I couldn't be sure he didn't have a gun—his knife was back on the floor of my room, but he'd meant to kill me quietly. There hadn't been time to see if he was carrying a six-shooter.

A row of telegraph poles carried silver line to the east of Dodge City, icicles sparkling in light from the moon and stars, a pretty sight if I hadn't been on such deadly business.

I crept closer to the depot, annoyed when my boots made a crunching noise in old snow Valdez would hear, if he were close by. I was sure he'd keep moving until he found a safe place or some help from his friends, Will James and the other two Haskell riders. I started to wonder if I was in over my head, stalking Valdez by myself.

I made a half circle beside the depot when I was fifty feet away, looking behind each corner until I was sure no one was back there waiting to jump me. I was cold, starting to shiver, with painful feet reminding me of the fire. It was quiet around the stockyards, and dark as pitch where the moon made shadows below wood fences. Farther down the tracks I saw a three-sided barn where hay and feed were kept for cattle during busy seasons. I walked past the depot, creeping along a stretch of fence with my rifle leveled, looking for Valdez's tracks. I'd lost them at the depot somewhere and I'd have to double back to pick them up again unless I happened across them elsewhere.

When I turned around, I thought I saw something over on the far side of a corral, a darker shape amongst shadows along the bottom of a fence. The longer I looked, the surer I was that it was someone hunkered down behind a corral post. I'd have to go through the corral to get there, leaving me out in the open most of the way. I decided on a safer way to find out what, or who, it was.

Moving over to the closest fence, I rested my rifle on one of the planks chest-high, sighting along the barrel. I thumbed the hammer back carefully, figuring the shot would be no more than eighty yards. I'd won plenty of shooting contests when I was a kid back in Mississippi. Shooting a long gun with accuracy was one thing my pa insisted on since we didn't have any extra money for wasted shots back then. I wasn't meaning to kill him, if it was Valdez hiding behind that post. It was never my nature to shoot at a man unless he fired at me first, but it was easy to make an exception after he tried to kill me while I was sleeping. The sound of a shot would let him know I was after him, if I'd guessed wrong, although I was pretty sure what I saw was a man crouched down to make himself as small as he could.

"Stand up with your hands in the air or I'm gonna shoot!" I shouted, gripping the rifle harder than was needed when my nerves got the best of me. There was no answer.

When I was satisfied with my aim, I nudged the trigger very gently. In the dark, with total silence all around me, I heard a soft click when the hammer fell, then an explosion roared through the night. In the same instant a cry sounded, a shout of pain so intense it sounded much closer than it was.

The shape of a man went spinning away from the fence, grabbing his shoulder, the exact spot I'd aimed for if what I saw was the outline of a man. Proof I'd been right was there before my eyes, a shout followed by a wail, then the crunch of feet running in snow.

"Hold it right there or I'll kill you with the next one!" I yelled, levering another shell, aiming as fast as I could for a moving target between fence planks. "I'll blow your head smooth off! From here I can't miss!"

He ignored my warning and kept on running. I aimed down for his legs and fired another shot. The Winchester recoiled against my shoulder, banging loud enough to wake everyone in Dodge.

I saw him stumble and fall; and when the roar of the gunshot faded, I heard a groan.

I climbed the fence and took off running in his direction as fast as I could, ejecting my spent cartridge, loading another one with a swift jerk of the lever. I saw him try to get up again while I was midway across the empty corral—only when he did, he fell back on his belly.

"Hold still!" I commanded, staggering over a deep spot where snow covered a frozen bog. I kept my balance and ran over to the next stretch of fence, panting like I'd run a quarter mile.

"Dios!" I heard him say in a deep voice.

I was climbing the planks before he got it out of his mouth. Another thirty yards from him, I saw him struggling to come to his hands and knees in spite of my second warning.

I ran up to him and covered him with my rifle. "Lie still or I'll shoot you in the other leg," I said, smelling burnt hair and clothing. You've got a lot of explaining to do. Don't force me to shoot you again."

He rolled over on his back while I was talking, and I swear I never saw nobody any bigger. Or any uglier, besides he got burnt in the fire. His beard was burned off to stubble and part of his hair had been burned short. When he looked up at me with those big black eyes full of hate, I'd have agreed he was the devil's own disciple. He had about the meanest look on his face I'd ever had the misfortune to see.

"Bastardo," he snarled, and I didn't need to know Spanish to know what he said.

Right then, I don't know what came over me. I got mad as all hell thinking about those women and kids he gutted back at Antelope Hill. . . . We didn't have proof he done it yet, but I was satisfied he did. So I leaned over him, showing him the muzzle of my rifle real close to his forehead.

"I oughta kill you, you no-good son of a bitch," I said in a low voice. "Nobody'll ever know. I can say you tried to run off again." My heart was beating so hard I could almost hear it, not from running after him, but from thinking about what I was nearly ready to do. "One bullet would scatter your damn brains all over this snow. There's some who'd call it justice, for what you done to those women and kids."

I reckon he realized what I'd made up my mind to do, because he started wagging his head. "Do not kill me, *señor.* I want no more fight with you."

"Then start talking," I said. I was still of a mind to kill him until better judgment began to creep inside my head. Even as lowdown as he was, he deserved to stand trial for what he did instead of being shot like a crippled horse. "Tell me who paid you to cut up those settlers down in Indian Territory. Not that me and Marshal Ault ain't already got it figured out. We know it was Grant Haskell, but I want to hear you say it. Tell me all of it or—so help me—I'll blow your brains all over this ground."

"Señor Haskell say make look like Comanche. Cut off scalps. Cut bellies open *también.* We go *en la noche* . . . when is dark. Do what *Señor* Haskell say."

"You killed 'em all. Butchered 'em like sheep."

Valdez groaned. *"Sí.* Is what he tell us."

Now I knew for sure what Sam had already guessed. "Who was with you? Tell me their names."

He appeared to hesitate a moment.

"Tell me, Valdez, or I swear I'll kill you!" I moved my rifle until the muzzle was right between his eyes. "It'd be a

hell of a lot easier on you if you cooperate. Maybe the judge
will show a little leniency in your case."

He closed his eyes briefly, and when he opened them, I saw
something I'd never seen before in the eyes of a man. Granted,
it was dark so I could have been mistaken, but it looked for
all the world like I was staring into the eyes of a snake.

"*Señor* Will is *jefe* for *Señor* Haskell. He give orders. Two
more *gringos* ride with us. One is called Billy. One is Ike."

"Will James. He's the one who carries his pistol across
his belly," I said, although I already knew who he was, "then
there's two more, Billy and Ike."

"*Sí,*" Valdez replied, closing his eyes again. "*Por favor,* I
have much pain, *señor. Mucho dolor.*"

"Where are they now, Will James and the others?"

He didn't want to tell me right at first. He watched me
through slitted eyelids. His face had a number of dark burns
above his whisker stubble and his eyebrows had been burned
off completely. A bullet wound in his left shoulder oozed
blood on the snow where he lay, and another dark-red stain
leaked around his right calf muscle. Valdez was proving he
could take a hell of a lot of pain.

"Tell me!" I insisted, aware of a deep silence around us
after the shooting stopped. Off somewhere in town I could
hear men shouting. I figured Sheriff Masterson had been
summoned, which didn't give me long to get to my next
question. "I want you to tell me where they are and then tell
me how you knew where to look for me tonight. Somebody
told you I was at the hotel."

Valdez heard the distant voices, too. "Maybeso is Señor
Will coming now," he said, and I'll be damned if he didn't
give me a one-sided leer. "He will kill you, señor. He is *un
malo hombre* with a *pistola.*"

I got mad all over again when he said that. "I figure he'll
try, only it ain't gonna matter to you, Valdez, 'cause you're
as good as dead already, unless you tell me what I need to
know. It will be easier just to blow a hole through your damn

head so we don't have to take you all the way back to Cache."
I took a half step back like I meant to shoot him, sighting
down my Winchester.

"No, señor," he pleaded, raising both hands in front of his
face.

"Then tell me where they are and tell me who told you
where to look for me!"

He swallowed hard. *"Una casita.* Little . . . house. *Una
casita de las putas.* I no can say *en Ingles."*

"A little house? There must be a hundred little houses in
Dodge . . ."

"Las mujeres. How you say . . . women?"

"A little house where women live." I looked over my
shoulder when those voices grew louder. I could see men
with lanterns headed our way. "Now tell me how you knew
where to look for me. The sheriff was the only man who
knew where I was staying, so it has to be him. Somehow."

Valdez could hear the voices, too. He gave me that same
leer again. *"Señor* Will *es un amigo de* Masterson. He say
we go now. Two men look for us. *Señor* Will say I kill you.
He no afraid of two *gringos."*

"So I had it figured right," I said softly. "Masterson was
the one who warned you, only Will James wouldn't listen.
Instead, he sent you to kill us. . . ." Shouting men interrupted
me before I could ask about Sam, if Valdez had gone there
first.

"Over here!" I cried when men carrying lanterns came to
the depot. I backed away from Valdez, still keeping my rifle
ready, just in case.

I waited while five men crawled over fences. Most carried
rifles or shotguns. Sheriff Masterson was with them; and
when he saw me standing over Valdez with my Winchester,
he came over to me and started talking before I could get a
word in edgeways.

"I see you got the Mexican," he said, sounding out of
breath when he spoke. "I asked around to see if anyone knew

they were still in town. Someone said this fellow tried to kill you in your hotel room." He had his hands shoved in the pockets of a long greatcoat.

With other men standing around us, I didn't tell Masterson what I knew quite yet. "He did. I had to shoot him in the leg and shoulder to keep him from running. I imagine he'll need a doctor. He got burned when a fire started up in my room. I'll tell you all about it later, Sheriff, after I see how Marshal Ault is doing. In the meantime, I'm asking you to lock Valdez in a jail cell. I'll be filing formal charges against him tomorrow morning by telegraph with a Territorial Judge."

"I'll be more than happy to cooperate," Masterson said, only I could tell by his voice he wasn't all that happy to see how it turned out.

Before I accused Masterson, I wanted to talk to Sam about it and see what he had to say. More pressing was tracking down Will James and his partners before they hightailed it out of town. "I reckon you'll have to carry him," I said, pointing down to Valdez with my rifle. "I shot one of his legs out from under him."

"He's too damn big to carry," one of the men with Masterson complained. "We're gonna need a wagon."

"I'll attend to it," the sheriff replied. He kept giving me this strange look, I suppose wondering how much Valdez told me before he got there, especially the part about him and Will James being *amigos*.

I started to turn away. "I'm gonna inform Marshal Ault of what happened tonight," I said when Masterson didn't have any more to say.

He nodded. "Did you see any of the others you were looking for, this James character, perhaps?"

He'd gotten right to the point. "The Mexican was by himself as far as I could tell. He gave me a full confession for those murders down at Antelope Hill, and he implicated Grant Haskell as the man who ordered the killings. It's enough to put Haskell behind bars . . . maybe even send him to a gallows. That'll be up to a judge and jury."

"I see," the sheriff said thoughtfully.

I could tell by the look on his face he'd seen more than he wanted to see.

Twenty-eight

I knocked on the door of Dr. Thompson's office as hard as I could. I didn't see lamps burning behind windows in any of the rooms when I walked around back. I banged on his front door for a half minute or more, and a lamp finally came on somewhere in the rear of the place. There was no sign of a forced entry around either doorjamb, allowing me to breathe a sigh of relief. By all appearances, no one had broken in before I got there. It had occurred to me that Will James might make a try to end Sam's life while Valdez was taking care of me. On the way over I'd worried about it some.

Dr. Thompson came to the door carrying a lamp, clad in his nightshirt and cap. He peered through his front glass at me for a moment before he unlocked the door.

"It's five o'clock in the mornin'," he said.

"Sorry to wake you, Doc, but there's been some trouble. If Marshal Ault can wake up, I need to tell him about it. I take my orders from him."

"Very well. Come in, but don't keep him too long. He's a very sick man. He was feeling a little better tonight before I went to bed."

He let me inside and locked the door behind me, showing me to Sam's room with his lamp. Dr. Thompson went in first to place the lamp on a bedside table, adjusting the wick so there was just enough light for me to see Sam's face.

"Wake up, Marshal," I said, touching his shoulder. "I need to tell you what's been going on."

Sam's eyes flew open. "Is that you, Mr. Dudley?"

"It's me. Sorry to wake you, but Valdez came up to my room awhile ago. He tried to stab me with a bowie knife, only he didn't get it done. He dove out the window after this fire got started. I followed him down to the stockyards. I had to shoot him to get him to stop, but I only winged him in a place or two. I got a confession outa him. He told me Grant Haskell was behind the whole thing down at Antelope Hill, paying him and Will James and two more men named Billy and Ike to cut up those settlers to make it look like Comanches done it. It's enough to put 'em all behind bars to stand trial, only there's one more bit of news I ain't told you yet."

Sam was frowning before I got to the middle of my story. He sat up in bed and asked, "Where's James an' the others?"

"I ain't rightly sure. Valdez told me they were at this little house some place, a little house where women live. He was saying something in Spanish, only I didn't understand. But that ain't the part I was gonna tell you . . ."

"I'll get dressed," he said, swinging his legs off the cot. Before his feet hit the floor, he set in to cough. His coughing fit lasted several seconds, making his face turn beet red.

"Not so quick," Dr. Thompson warned, stepping between me and the marshal. "You're too ill to go out in this cold night air. It could kill you. If your deputy needs assistance, he can ask our town sheriff for it. You mustn't get out of bed so soon."

Sam gave me a quizzical look. "Did you ask the sheriff if he knew about James an' his bunch?"

"I sure did. His name is Bat Masterson. Sheriff Masterson was the only one who knew where I was staying. Valdez told me that Will James and Masterson are *amigos*. There may even be a connection between Masterson and Haskell. I didn't mention it to the sheriff when he showed up to haul Valdez off to jail."

Now Sam was really frowning. "That don't make a hell

of a lot of sense, but it wouldn't be the first time some crooked lawman got his hands dirty. Until we can prove it, don't say a word to Masterson. Sounded like Valdez was talkin' about James bein' at a whorehouse." He looked over at the doctor. "Is there some little house full of whores in Dodge like Leon just described?"

Thompson said, "That would be Belle's. It's on the western edge of town not far from the tracks. Some call it *Shantytown* because most of the houses are shacks. When the big herds come, it does a thriving business, catering to poorer cowboys who don't have much to spend." He addressed Sam again. "You have pneumonia, Marshal Ault. It could kill you to breathe cold air. I'm sure your deputy and Sheriff Masterson can handle this."

Sam gave the doctor one of his looks as he stood up to put on his pants. "It sounds like Bat Masterson has already given us the wrong kind of help, Doc, an' I'm a hell of a long ways from bein' dead just yet, so save your lectures." He slipped on his denims and stepped into one boot. "We've tracked these bastards too many miles to let 'em get away. I'll try not to breathe any more cold air than I have to." Putting on the other boot, Sam sleeved into his flannel shirt and buckled on his gun before he took his hat and coat from a wall-hook. "Let's go, Mr. Dudley. We'll stop by Masterson's office to see what he has to say first, an' then we'll head for Belle's." A sudden spasm of coughing gripped him as we left the room.

"Remember, I warned you," Dr. Thompson said.

Sam looked over his shoulder. "I'll have Mr. Dudley put it on my tombstone that you gave me fair warnin'."

We walked out into the night side by side up Front Street before Sam spoke again, buttoning his coat under his chin. "If Masterson don't have a real good explanation for how Valdez got to your hotel, I'll wire up to Fort Hays for Max McCoy, the U.S. Marshal there. If he ain't somewheres else, Max will give us a hand as quick as he can get here."

"I figure Masterson already warned James and his boys to pull out of town. I'd have gone after 'em myself, only I needed to make sure Valdez didn't come after you while you was asleep."

"I can take care of myself," he said. "You've got a duty to arrest the men we're after 'stead of lookin' out for me, only I guess you did the right thing, comin' to me first so you'd have somebody backin' you up, seein' as Masterson ain't inclined to help none."

After my run-in with Valdez I didn't see anything wrong with saying, "I think I've proved I can handle myself. I didn't come here to fetch you because I was afraid of going after Will James alone."

Our boots crunched softly through the snow for a time before Sam spoke. "You've done just fine, Leon. Fact of the matter is, I don't think I could have done any better myself."

I was mighty proud of that compliment, only I didn't say any more about things right then, listening to Sam cough every few paces. While I was real glad to have him there in case we ran up on James and his men, I sure was hoping Sam didn't get any sicker because of it.

When we came in sight of the sheriff's office, there was light in the windows and smoke curling from a stovepipe on the roof. I could see men huddled around the potbelly warming their hands.

"We'll borrow a shotgun from 'em," Sam said. "You've got a rifle. If we get James trapped in that whorehouse, surrounded, I don't look for him to put up much of a fight."

I wasn't so sure, and I had this feeling Will James wouldn't be there by now, warned off by the Dodge City Sheriff. "The way I see it, we've got enough to arrest Haskell either way, after I got that confession from Valdez. If James and the others get the jump on us, we can have warrants sent out for their arrest."

Sam didn't disagree, keeping an eye on windows in Masterson's office until we got near the door. He coughed again real hard as we climbed the steps and went in.

Two gents who were with Masterson when they came for Valdez nodded as I was closing the door.

"Mornin' boys," Sam said. "I'm U.S. Marshal Sam Ault an' this here's Deputy Marshal Leon Dudley. Which one of you's Bat Masterson?"

"He ain't here just now," one said, glancing to the other. "He went on home after we locked up your deputy's prisoner. He's in a cell in the back. Bat said he'd send for Doc Thompson."

"Are you boys deputies?" Sam wanted to know. They had on heavy coats and didn't show badges.

"Part time," the other man said. "Bat ain't got no regular deputies 'til spring, when it's busy. The town council claims we ain't got enough money."

"I need to borrow a shotgun," Sam went on, sounding like he wanted to cough up more fluid. "We're headed to a place called Belle's to arrest three more of the same gang. We could use all the help we can get."

"I'll go, he said. "How 'bout you, Wyatt?"

"Got nothin' better to do," the second man replied, starting over to a gun rack on the wall.

He handed Sam a double-barrel twelve-gauge and a handful of shells, then he took one for himself and gave the other deputy a shotgun. He was a hard-faced type, this deputy named Wyatt, with a handlebar mustache and odd-colored eyes.

"Who's this you're after?" he asked Sam as we all started for the door.

Sam walked out and stood on the stoop to load his shotgun. "A feller by the name of Will James. Two more with him named Billy an' Ike. They're wanted in Indian Territory for murderin' eleven settlers, mostly women an' children. The Mexican was one of 'em. I aim to see to it they all hang."

Wyatt went down the steps. "Let's go the back way, Ben, in case somebody is watchin' the street."

We took off to the west, walking shoulder to shoulder, as a faint streak of light brightened the horizon at our backs. A few windowpanes in Dodge were already showing lanterns lit, casting yellow squares of light across the snow outside. We were headed into a section full of shacks, just like Doc Thompson said, not far south of those railroad tracks ending at the stockyards. As I walked along beside Sam it occurred to me Masterson hadn't gone straight home, most likely. He'd probably headed for Belle's place first, so Will James and his men would have a good start on us out of town.

Sam commenced to coughing hard. The deputy named Ben gave him a look.

"Sounds like you're ailin', Marshal," Ben said.

When Sam didn't answer, I told him, "He's got the pneumonia. Doc Thompson said he ought not be out in this cold weather. It's bad for his lungs."

Wyatt pointed to a small house off to itself sitting beside the tracks. "That's Belle's."

Sam ran his sleeve across his mouth. "Everybody spread out so we'll have all sides covered. I'll cover the front door. As soon as I yell for 'em to come out, be ready to shoot any son of a bitch who don't have his hands in the air."

I checked my rifle, loading more cartridges as we got closer to the house. Ben and Wyatt breeched open their shotguns and put shells into the tubes.

"I'll take the side nearest the tracks," I said, swinging off to walk north a ways with Ben following close at my heels.

Sam and Wyatt forked when they were three hundred yards off as I hurried to get around to the back. The house was a couple hundred yards from its closest neighbor, a fitting distance I supposed for a whorehouse to be from everybody else in this part of town. Dawn was brightening things, so we would be able to see who we were shooting at.

I took off at a run to cross the railroad tracks, aiming for a pile of crossties covered with snow almost directly in back of the house. I heard Ben's footsteps coming behind me for a ways.

As I ran across the rails, a dog started to bark. It was a spotted cur chained to a timber on the back porch of the place, a little stoop with a slanted roof keeping snow off the steps. The dog would alert everyone inside that we were getting close.

I ran the rest of the way to that pile of railroad ties and got down behind it, looking over the top, clearing off a layer of snow so I had a better view of things. I rested my rifle on top of the ties, waiting. Curtained windows of the house had lights burning behind them, only the curtains kept me from seeing what was going on inside.

I saw Ben hunker down when he came to a rotted tree stump a hundred yards from the east side of Belle's. The distance was too great for his shotgun to be much good, but I couldn't hardly blame a part-time deputy for not wanting to be in the thick of things.

The dog kept barking, raising more noise, and I knew anyone inside could figure someone was close by. From what I was told earlier, there would be women in there, whores. We'd have to be careful shooting or we'd hit the wrong target.

I settled in to wait for Sam's next move, listening to that dog keep up a ruckus. Ben looked over at me and waved, keeping as low as he could behind that stump.

For a spell it didn't appear Sam was ready to call them out, even after Wyatt took up a spot behind a hog-lot fence next to a neighbor's house. The three of us were set, but Sam kept quiet, making me wonder.

Then I heard him coughing when the dog quieted some.

At a back corner of the house a curtain parted just a bit, and someone looked outside. Right after that a lantern went out so it was dark in the corner room.

"Hello, the house!" Sam bellowed.

His voice set off the dog again, fighting its chain while it barked fiercely.

"Come outside with your hands in the air!"

For half a minute or so, nothing happened. Until a windowpane was smashed on the side where Ben was watching. The muzzle of a gun poked through, and then all hell broke loose at once.

Twenty-nine

Two pistol shots rang out, one from the front and another on Ben's side, ending the morning stillness with a pair of cracking explosions. Before Ben could return the fire, Wyatt blasted away with his shotgun, breaking out a window on the west wall, sending fragments of glass tinkling to the floor inside.

A woman screamed, her voice muffled by interior walls. The dog lunged against its chain, trying to get at Wyatt, unafraid of the shotgun, snarling, snapping its jaws.

Ben fired. When his shotgun thundered, it made such a racket I thought the whole side of the house would fall down. Instead, more breaking glass convulsed inward on a window at the front of Belle's. Another scream followed the shotgun's deafening roar.

Three answering shots came from windows, popping almost in unison. A bullet whined above Ben's head, sending him diving for cover behind his stump.

Wyatt fired again, blasting pellets into thin clapboard walls with flame belching from one muzzle of his twelve-gauge. Someone shouted, "What the hell's goin' on out there?" from the front porch of a shack down the road.

Sam's shotgun discharged, riddling the door and both front windows with buckshot, shattering glass. I sighted along the barrel of my rifle, waiting for a target I was sure of, taking no chances I might hit one of the women by mistake. All over that part of town, dogs commenced barking. I glimpsed people peering outside from the safety of half-open doors, trying to figure out what all the shooting was about.

Ben raised up a little and blasted a shot into a back-corner window where I'd seen a gun muzzle before, buckshot tearing into the windowframe and whitewashed walls. Then I saw him hurrying to reload just as Wyatt's shotgun thundered again.

"Come out with your hands in the air!" Sam yelled during a short lull in the shooting.

A reply to Sam's demand came in the form of three rapid gunshots, the lighter chatter of pistols dwarfed by shotgun shells discharging as soon as the handguns went off. And still nothing moved at the rear, affording me nothing to shoot at.

I'd been wrong about Sheriff Masterson warning James and his companions to clear out . . . unless James was so sure of himself he chose to ignore Masterson's warning. The killers we were after had brazenly stayed put at Belle's as though they had nothing to fear.

The back door opened so quickly I barely had time to draw a bead on a figure racing out on the stoop; but when I saw a woman in a hoop skirt leap off the porch, I held my trigger finger still and breathed a sign of relief. I'd almost killed a woman because of jumpy nerves.

Only a second later, I saw another figure rush outside to jump in the same direction, and this time it was a bowlegged cowboy with a pistol in his fist. I put my sights on him, following his dash for the edge of the stoop before I squeezed off a round at a fast-moving blur.

My Winchester bucked into my shoulder, spitting out fire and lead. The noise of igniting gunpowder made me flinch. I saw the cowboy jump sideways like he'd been swatted with an axe handle in midleap. He crashed into the side of the house, reaching for his shoulder, tossing his gun into a pile of snow. A splash of crimson appeared on whitewashed boards behind him as he slid down to the ground on his rump, clutching his right shoulder. His hat lay in the snow beside him.

The woman was crawling through snow on her hands and knees, trying to escape flying bullets, screaming as loud as she could for us not to shoot at her. I crept over to a corner of the crossties so I could wave her in my direction, yelling, "Over here, lady! You'll be safe over here!"

A bullet fired from a window struck a hog in one of the pens behind Wyatt. The wounded pig made an awful racket, squealing for all it was worth, bounding around in half-frozen mud until it crashed into the fence and fell over on its side, kicking. The noise frightened all the other hogs and they began milling in a circle, making a similar ruckus, squealing so loudly I couldn't hear the woman's frantic cries, nor could she hear me yelling at her to come this way to safety.

Ben's shotgun blasted into a side window, shredding curtains hanging beside the glassless windowframe, turning wood into bits of sawdust and splintered kindling. Before the noise subsided, a voice inside cried, "Where's Ike?"

The shrieking woman scrambled on toward Wyatt with her hoop skirt high in the air behind her. Her long black hair was in her eyes, apparently blinding her until she crawled headlong into the hog-pen fence where she collapsed on her stomach, sobbing. I saw Wyatt rise up over the top plank to offer her his hand when just then a pistol barked from a side window of Belle's, sending Wyatt ducking back down behind cover.

The cowboy I shot came to his knees. Even in the pale dawn light I could see blood pouring from his shoulder, darkening snow underneath him. Using the side of the house for support, he got partway to his feet when a deadly shotgun blast from Ben's hiding place knocked him down flat on his back.

"I got the son of a bitch!" Ben cried, reloading as he took a peek over the top of his stump. The cowboy had been bleeding badly, but I figured he might have lived if Ben hadn't shot him.

Around in front, a pistol snapped twice, sending stray lead

whining across the road into the door of an outhouse sitting to the east of a shanty with darkened windows. Someone gave a yell inside, then the door opened and a man in overalls crawled out on his stomach as fast as he could, scooting across the snow toward his shack.

"Come out with your hands in the air!" Sam bellowed again. "We've got you surrounded!"

For a moment there was no answering fire from the house, a silence that seemed peculiar after so many explosions ended the morning quiet so abruptly. The woman in the hoop skirt jumped to her feet and dove over the fence into a hog pen, landing in mud and ooze on her hands and knees, sending those pigs into another frenzy of racing around in circles, squealing.

"Hey, Billy!" that same voice cried from a front room. "How come Ike ain't shootin' no more?"

"He's dead," another voice answered, softer than the first.

More silence. The hogs settled, and now it was so quiet you could hear a feather fall. Someone, a woman, was sobbing in one of the back rooms.

"Give it up!" Sam demanded. "Toss out your guns!"

He didn't get an answer. I edged back behind the middle of those stacked railroad ties with my Winchester aimed at the back door. I told myself Will James would see there was no way out of this alive unless they gave themselves up. I also kept wondering if maybe I'd been wrong about Bat Masterson, that he warned James last night we were coming for them. I still couldn't explain how Valdez had known where to find me if Masterson was innocent of any wrongdoing. Valdez had come to exactly the right room, meaning someone had to tell him where I was.

A woman shrieked inside one of the rooms, then a voice said, "Shut up bitch or I'll kill you!" I could hear heavy footsteps on a wood floor.

"What the hell's goin' on in there?" Wyatt shouted. "Can't see anybody movin' around, but I can hear 'em."

Ben answered him. "I can't see a damn thing either. Keep your head down."

"Surrender your guns and come outside!" Sam cried, then he broke into a coughing fit lasting several seconds.

I kept my eyes glued to the back door. Something was afoot in there. I could almost smell trouble coming . . . if only I knew where and when.

The sun crept over the horizon. Shafts of golden light came from the east, bathing whitewashed walls with false color, making shadows on the snow behind Belle's and every shack around us on a snow-covered road running through Shanty-town. Curious residents watched us from a safe distance, peering around corners of houses and livestock sheds to see how things would end. An eerie quiet lingered, broken only by the soft sounds of a woman crying in the hog pens and an occasional grunt from a restless pig.

"They're up to something!" Wyatt called out from his hiding place behind the fence and I knew he could sense it, too, that something was about to happen.

We waited for what seemed an eternity. Every now and then I heard Sam cough. Ben acted nervous, working his hands around the stock of his shotgun. I could see Wyatt's hat rise up above the fence once in a while. At last the woman close to Wyatt stopped sobbing.

We all heard noises coming from the front of the house. I couldn't see what it was, but I heard what came next loud and clear.

"Don't anybody shoot or I'll blow this woman's head off!" a voice cried.

Footsteps clumped out on Belle's front porch, so many I was unable to guess the number of people who made them. Then I heard Sam's voice.

"Let the girl go!"

"Like hell! She's our ticket outa here. Anybody takes a shot at us, an' I'll blow a tunnel through her head. We're gonna walk down to the livery to collect our horses. Soon as we're mounted, I'll set her free. Anybody follows too close before we get to our horses an' I'll kill her. Where the hell is Bat?"

"The sheriff ain't here!" Ben answered, staying down behind his stump.

Then I saw them—two men and a woman in a dark-red dress. One of the men held a pistol to the back of her head and I could see plainly it was cocked, ready to fire. They moved cautiously around a front corner of Belle's, keeping the woman in front of them. The gent with the gun had his left fist knotted into the woman's blonde hair. The other cowboy held his six-shooter with the muzzle aimed at her spine. They meant to use her as a shield all the way to the stable. If any of us fired a shot, she would be killed.

"Let her go!" Sam demanded again.

Now that it was light, I could see the owlhoot with his gun to her head wore a cross-draw holster. "So that's Will James," I muttered, keeping my rifle sights on him, on his back. "If he's such a tough character, then how come he's using a woman to get him out of a jam!" I could kill him with one shot, but there wouldn't be time to get another round off before the second gent shot her in the back. And there was a risk that when I shot him his gun might go off. Muscles sometimes worked even when a man or an animal was nearly dead, the way a squirrel kicks after it's shot—or a dying Kiowa with a bullet through his mouth.

"I can't take the chance," I whispered to myself, following James with my sights. The other man would be named Billy.

They walked real slow away from Belle's, angling for the road leading to the middle of town.

"You won't get far," Sam warned, only now his voice lacked conviction. "You've got my word I'll follow you to the gates of hell if I have to."

"It'll be warmer," James remarked, pushing the woman along to the edge of the roadway, keeping his head turned in Sam's direction.

The one named Billy kept his eyes on us, on me and Ben, as he walked behind the woman. He couldn't see Wyatt because of the house right then.

When I looked over at Wyatt for just a moment, I saw him come up with his shotgun. He looked at me and I wagged my head to tell him it wasn't smart to try anything.

I sighted down my Winchester again, hoping for a bit of luck before they got out of range. If something happened to distract them, I'd have a small chance of dropping them both before they could shoot their female hostage.

They proceeded east along the edge of the road with the girl stumbling in soft snow wearing high heels. Ben and Wyatt stayed behind cover, I reckon waiting until James and Billy were out of pistol range.

I looked down the railroad tracks toward town. I recalled running after Valdez along these rails when I got to the stock pens. Will James said they were headed for the livery to get their horses. I remembered what I could about the stable where our own animals were kept.

I got an idea, remembering a hayloft above stalls where the horses were fed. I straightened up and called softly to Ben.

"Tell Marshal Ault I'm headed over to the livery ahead of them. Tell him to follow them, only stay back so they don't get nervous. I've got this idea that might work."

I took off, running down the side of the tracks, keeping as low as I could, balancing my Winchester in my left hand. I'd have plenty of time to get to the stable ahead of them and climb up in the loft. But then it would be up to Lady Luck to give me the opportunity I needed.

I ran through snowdrifts, tripping where footing was bad in places the wind piled snow deep. Pretty soon I was out of breath from running. I kept glancing over my shoulder to see if James or Billy noticed me, although by the time I thought to look I was well past them, headed for town.

I was taking a big gamble; and if it backfired, I'd have to

answer to Sam, as well as my conscience, if the woman got killed. It was just a hunch, but I was hoping Will James and his partner would be too busy keeping an eye on Sam and the sheriff's deputies to pay much attention to a hayloft.

Thirty

The barn was surrounded on three sides by pole corrals where loose livestock, mostly mules and harness horses, were fed. When I ran up to the back of the place, I saw the liveryman forking hay over a fence into one of the pens. He saw me running toward him carrying a rifle and it spooked him. He stepped back and made as if he meant to run the other way, tossing his pitchfork aside.

Then he recognized me, remembering I was a Marshal, and that made him hesitate.

"Better clear out of here," I said, rounding a corner of one corral out of breath. "There's liable to be trouble."

"What's all the shootin' about?" he asked, casting a look in the direction of Belle's.

"Ain't got time to explain, mister. They're headed this way, and if I was you, I'd make myself scarce," I told him, running to the hallway of his barn, then to a ladder climbing into the loft.

As I was going up the ladder, I saw the stablekeeper take off at a run toward Front Street. I was glad he hadn't stayed around to ask more questions or he could be caught in a cross fire.

I reached a musty loft and took a quick look around for a position that would give me a view of the street below. Over at the front of the barn I saw a pair of small doors where bundles of hay were hoisted into the loft. I hurried across a layer of old bedding straw to the doors and opened one just a crack so I had a view of the road out front. I backed into a shadow and hunkered down to catch my breath, knowing I'd have to be quiet up here when they got close to keep from being discovered. I took off my hat and leaned out so I could see up the road leading to Belle's, and that's when I saw them coming. Will James still had his gun to the woman's head while Billy had fallen back a few steps to keep an eye on Sam and the pair of deputies. Off in the distance I could see Sam and Ben and Wyatt holding a talk in the middle of the street, deciding what to do. I was hoping Ben remembered to tell Sam what I said about staying back so James and Billy wouldn't get too edgy. The only way my plan would work was if I got just the right chance to take them by surprise. If they saw me first, I could count on ducking a bunch of lead and the woman would be the first casualty.

I unbuttoned my coat and pulled it off so I'd be able to move around as quietly as possible. I drew my .44 and put it beside me on the straw, in easy reach. When things started to happen, they would happen fast and I needed to have both guns ready.

I peered out again, keeping my head back in the shadow, and now I could see them hurrying a little, walking faster to get to their horses. The sun was halfway above the horizon, making for glare off snow covering everything around the stable. I'd have a slight advantage here, being east of them. They'd be looking directly into the sun to see where I was. Figuring my chances, I would have just one opportunity to take a shot at Will James, if he relaxed for a moment with his pistol away from her head. I'd have to make my first shot count and then be ready to take Billy down before he got the woman. It would take split-second timing and a hell of a lot of luck for my idea to work.

I couldn't keep from thinking about what I was planning to do right then, even though it was the wrong time to be having any second thoughts. If I got the chance, I would try to kill two men like some sort of executioner, shooting them down like rabid dogs without giving either one a chance. Granted, they were wanted for eleven brutal slayings, and I'd heard one of them confess to the murders firsthand. Yet there was something about killing a man from hiding that didn't sit in my mind quite right, no matter what the two of them had done to deserve it.

"There's no other way," I told myself quietly, watching them walk down that rutted, snow-packed road. The sun was in their faces just like I knew it would be. They wouldn't be able to see me unless they knew where to look.

I raised my Winchester to my shoulder, making sure the shell tube and barrel were out of direct sunlight. My pistol was next to my right boot, in case I needed it in a hurry. Things were as ready as I could make them. Now, all I needed was the opportunity.

I eased the hammer back. When I heard it cock, something in my belly twisted. "This is damn sure the wrong time to get cold feet," I whispered, banishing everything else from my mind.

I watched them across my rifle sights. James was pushing the woman as fast as she could walk in those shoes. Billy kept looking over his shoulder, staying back a few paces with all his attention on Sam and the sheriff's deputies. Billy was short and wiry, with a rounded face and ruddy skin. Will James stood over six feet, I judged, with gangly arms and a lantern jaw. This was the first good look I'd had at them in daylight. If I got what I wanted, it would be the last time I saw them alive. I couldn't let myself think about it, what I was about to do. Instead I set my mouth in a line and waited for Lady Luck to take a hand.

I could hear the woman sobbing now, and the crunch of feet in snow. They were less than a hundred yards from the stable.

"Please let me go, Will," the woman whimpered.

I was surprised to learn she knew his name.

"Shut up!" he snapped, jerking her hair roughly. "If you're a good girl, I'm gonna let you go real soon." He looked backward a moment. "Watch 'em, Billy. When we get to the barn, I'll stay out front with her so's they can see me an' her. You saddle two of the best horses and lead 'em outside."

Billy merely nodded, keeping his eyes on the three lawmen in the distance. A moment later, he said, "I coulda swore there was four of 'em, Will, shootin' at us from all four sides."

My hands started to sweat in spite of the chill. I steadied my rifle on James. They were fifty yards away.

"Hurry up an' fetch them horses," James said.

Billy turned his attention to the barn. He took off at a trot for the stable door, never once looking up at the loft in his hurry to get the horses saddled. He ran right underneath me and didn't glance up. I heard his boots thump down the hall between stalls, then the rattle of curb chains and cinch buckles.

A horse snorted somewhere in the stable. I kept my attention on James and the woman until they stopped a little less than thirty yards from the door.

James looked back toward Belle's. He kept his pistol to the base of the girl's skull like he meant to leave it there forever. It was beginning to look like my break wouldn't come. James was being extra-cautious.

I risked a glance over my right shoulder down at the stalls beneath the loft. Billy had his back to me, swinging a saddle on the back of a dappled gray gelding, getting it done as fast as he could. His pistol was holstered. I could shoot him in the back from where I was . . . and it occurred to me all of a sudden that he was in the perfect spot for me to get the drop on him and disarm him. I'd be gambling that he wouldn't yell to warn his partner I had him covered, but it would reduce the odds by one. If he was made to believe I'd kill him if he made any noise, I might just pull it off.

I crept over to the ladder and aimed down. I spoke to him

very softly. "Raise both hands in the air, Billy. I've got a .44 Winchester pointed at the back of your head. If you so much as twitch, I'll decorate that saddle with hunks of your brains."

Billy froze. His head turned slowly. He looked up at me with the biggest surprise I ever saw on a human face.

"It's your choice, Billy," I said, keeping my voice down.

He stared into my gun muzzle just a fraction with both hands still wrapped around his cinch-strap. "Don't kill me," he said with his chin quivering.

"Take your pistol out real slow with your right hand. Grab it by the butt. If I even think you're gonna do something stupid, I'll pull the trigger."

"I swear I won't," he stammered, taking his right hand from the latigo strap as slow as molasses pouring from a winter jug. He lifted his gun by its grips and tossed it on the floor. His eyes were so big they looked about to pop. "Listen, mister, Will's gonna shoot that gal. He's cold-blooded mean. She don't mean a damn thing to him. I know him. He's gonna kill her anyways, no matter what."

Now that I had Billy out of the fight, I had no idea what to do with him and I was running out of time. James would figure something was wrong pretty quick if Billy didn't show up with the horses. "Keep saddling that gray," I said, inching over to the ladder, starting down it backwards with my rifle covering Billy the best I could.

Billy turned around and finished tightening the cinch as I reached the floor. I picked up his gun and stuck it in my belt before I glanced behind me. The alleyway between stalls was dark enough to hide us from someone outside if they weren't close to the entrance. James and the woman were too far away to see me.

I formed a desperate plan without really thinking it through all the way—what I needed was something to distract James long enough for me to get the drop on him. Or kill him if I had to.

"Mount the gray," I said. "Ride out of this barn like your tailfeathers was afire. Don't stop for anything."

"You gotta be crazy, mister," Billy exclaimed, raising his voice more than I wanted. "Will's gonna think I'm runnin' out on him. He'll shoot me."

"Not if I get him first," I said, motioning toward the gray with my rifle. "You've got two choices . . . ride out of here as fast as you can or take a bullet from me. At this range I can't miss. The other way, you've got a running chance."

Just then a voice cried out, "What's takin' so goddamn long in there, Billy?"

I aimed the Winchester square between Billy's eyes. "Get on that horse or you're dead," I whispered.

Billy nodded quickly. He looked past me. "I'm comin' out, Will!" he shouted, sticking a boot in the left stirrup, swinging over the saddle.

I handed him the reins. "Keep riding," I warned, knowing I was letting one man go to get at another. "When the shooting's over, it'll go easier on you if you give yourself up. Now ride."

He heeled the gray gelding into a bounding lope. I made a dash for the barn door right behind him. Billy galloped out into daylight, bending low over the gray's neck, reining hard to the east, toward town. I ran to the stable door and slid to a halt, leaning around the corner of the barn with my rifle shouldered.

"Where the hell you goin', Billy? You runnin' out on me?" James cried.

He turned just a bit to take a shot at Billy, and that was all I needed.

I fired at his shooting arm. I was so close, it was hardly a tricky shot at all—maybe thirty yards, which ain't a distance at all for a practiced shooter. My Winchester cracked, jarring me with its kick. I knew I'd hit what I was aiming at well before the explosion died down when Will James let out this real loud yell and spun around, grabbing his elbow.

The woman shrieked and fell flat on her face in the snow as soon as her hair was free of his grip. James bent over double in an awful lot of pain, dropping his pistol as he groaned and sank to his knees. Blood squirted from his torn coat-sleeve, making a red splash on the snow around him. I ran over and kicked his gun away, even though it was plain there wasn't any fight left in him now.

Then I swung around and fired a shot over Billy's head while he was galloping hard toward Front Street. "Hold it there!" I shouted, chambering another cartridge, aiming lower this time to bring him down if he didn't stop.

Billy sawed back on the horse's reins and threw his hands in the air. For a moment I didn't quite know what to do. Just as quick as that, it was over.

I heard feet running toward us. The woman sat up and looked at me, but my attention and my rifle were on Billy. Sam and the deputies ran as hard as they could to get there. I could hear Sam wheezing and coughing from all the exertion until he trotted up to the front of the stable, trying to catch his breath. He gave Will James a lingering stare, then he motioned for Wyatt and Ben to go after Billy. He was too winded to say what he wanted at the time, what with his lungs being in such bad shape.

I lowered my rifle and helped the woman up. She was too overcome right at the moment to do much more than give me a weak smile. Then she took a step back from James and said, "Got what you deserve, you sorry bastard!"

Sam was looking at me in a strange way, so I asked him what was on his mind. "You act like something's wrong, Marshal. We got 'em all, by my count."

"We did at that, Mr. Dudley," he agreed. He coughed again and spit a mouthful into the snow. "I reckon you had a reason for lettin' that short feller ride off like you did. It had all the appearances of forgetfulness, until you fired that shot over his head."

I was a bit too shaken by events just then to explain it all to him. "I had my reasons," was all I said, grinning, even when a grin didn't quite fit the mood I was in. "I reckon we oughta get this gent to Doc Thompson before he bleeds to death. After all we've been through, I was sorta counting on seeing him stand trial for what him and the others did."

"He'll hang," Sam said hoarsely, giving James another steely stare. "I can promise you that."

"You should get out of this cold air, Marshal, or you'll be sicker than ever."

He looked at me real hard then. "When I'm in the market for a nursemaid, Mr. Dudley, you'll be the first to know. Get this owlhoot on his feet so we can march him to jail. A busted elbow ain't gonna prevent him from walkin'."

I knew Sam wasn't being as tough on me as he sounded. That was just his way. I was used to it.

Thirty-one

The day we rode in at Grant Haskell's ranch early in December I think he knew we'd come for him before Sam ever got a word out of his mouth. Haskell's face got mighty pale when he saw us ride up to the house. We'd waited for a break in the weather to head back down to Texas; but more than anything else, Sam needed the time to get his health back. We sent our prisoners by train over to Springfield in the custody of U.S. Marshal Max McCoy and a pair of deputies. Valdez was a sight, with burn scars covering his face and two bullet wounds, chained up hand and foot, looking more like some half-wild animal than a man. Will James faced two murder charges back in Missouri, and that's where Marshal McCoy took him to stand trial while the others faced murder charges in Federal Court at Fort Smith for the massacre in Indian Territory. Sam said Judge Isaac Parker was known as the "Hanging Judge" in Fort Smith and there wasn't any doubt he'd hang Valdez and Billy Wilson for their crimes. We buried Ike Young in Dodge City after notifying his relatives in San Antone. Bat Masterson denied he was a friend to Will James, even though Sam and I knew better. Masterson swore he didn't tell Valdez or James where I was that night; but since we couldn't prove anything on him, Sam let it go. We found out Masterson had conveniently left town that night, after arresting Valdez and putting him in jail. Seems he found pressing business in a neighboring town that came up real sudden.

What mattered was getting the man behind everything; and when we rode up at the Rafter H with a warrant for Grant Haskell's arrest, he came peaceable. We put him in irons and took him to Amarillo to stand trial, along with signed confessions from Billy Wilson and Benito Valdez saying they worked for Haskell, that he paid them to get rid of those families at Antelope Hill. It was blind luck that gave us Georgina Cooper's diary to help prove our case. That woman's last written words led us straight to Valdez and the rest of the killers. I'd gotten the first confession from Valdez at gunpoint, with him believing I meant to kill him unless he talked. He and the others deserved to hang for the bloody deed they did, but the real culprit was a greedy rancher who set out to get what he wanted at any cost. Me and Sam figured Haskell's son Ward was in on it, too, but we couldn't prove it and Grant wasn't about to give us anything that would implicate his boy in eleven murders-for-hire. Grant Haskell would go to the gallows, which was about all the justice we could hope for.

We got back to Cache just before another blinding blizzard struck the Territory. A day after we arrived, it started snowing so hard I couldn't see across the road to Miller's General Store. Clara Ault's grim predictions about the weather came to pass with a vengeance. Howling winds whistled through those cracks in our office walls like nothing could slow them down. Snow was a foot deep before noon that first day of the storm.

Sam same riding up to the office looking like he was dipped in a bucket of whitewash, covered from head to toe in snowflakes. He dusted himself off out on the porch after he put his horse in the shed, stamping his feet to knock off caked snow before he came inside. He nodded to me as he was hanging his hat on a peg, then he took a dispatch case from his coat pocket and opened it over by the stove.

"Mornin', Mr. Dudley."

I was pouring him coffee before he asked for it. We had a regular morning routine that included several cups of coffee. I handed him a cup. "Morning, Marshal. I see you dropped by the fort on your way in."

"I sent a wire to Fort Smith, tellin' them we made it back. Major Donaldson has been collectin' our telegrams and mail for us while we were up north."

"I reckon you told him about Haskell, that it wasn't Comanches who done it."

A trace of a smile crossed his face. "I did, with a great deal of pleasure. He didn't have much to say. He ain't one to admit he was wrong." He opened an envelope and began reading a letter.

"I hope that means the army won't go looking for Bull Bear. No reason to round them up if they didn't do anything wrong, is there?"

"You can't tell what the army will do. I asked Donaldson to send a full report to his superiors, correcting the mistake. He isn't looking for a reason to send men out in weather like this."

"It is mighty cold," I agreed. "I never saw it snow so hard before."

"Appears it'll be up to our asses if this keeps up. By the way . . . Clara asked that you come for supper tonight." He peered over the top of the letter. "She's bakin' a dried-apple pie for you."

I groaned softly. The first thing this morning, Bonnie Sue Miller informed me she was baking me an apple pie to celebrate my being home again. "Bonnie Sue's baking an apple pie," I said. "I didn't ask her to."

Sam shook his head. "Appears we'll also be up to our asses in apple pies, Mr. Dudley. It might help if you quit tellin' all these women apple pie was your favorite."

"Being polite can give the wrong impression, I suppose. I'm gonna be having a double dose of apple pie, looks like. To tell the truth, after eating bacon and beans so long, a dozen apple pies don't sound all that bad."

Sam tossed the letter on the desk and opened another, taking out a few Wanted circulars. "More bad actors," he mumbled as he thumbed through them.

"I sure hope you won't get a burr under your saddle to go off in this storm looking for 'em," I said, remembering how set he'd been to take off for Antelope Hill last month. I'd never be able to forget how cold we got or how near we were to freezing to death if it hadn't been for a smart red mule. I said, "That red mule might not save our necks a second time."

Sam was still a little bit embarrassed that he'd gotten sick and needed help. He didn't say anything.

A funny thought struck me. "While I'm on the subject of red things, what'll we tell Clara if she asks what happened to those red mittens?"

He looked up and narrowed his eyes. "We'll lie to her, Mr. Dudley, which is what a man has to do sometimes when a woman has the gall to think she can tell a grown man he oughta wear a pair of red mittens. We can't tell her we gave 'em to a Kiowa chief called Lone Wolf who thought he needed 'em worse than we did."

"But that's the truth," I said.

"She wouldn't believe it. Think of something else."

We heard footsteps on the porch. Before I could ponder who would be coming out in a snowstorm like this, Bonnie Sue Miller burst in carrying a pie pan with a napkin over the top. She gave me this real big smile.

"The pie's done," she said, nodding politely to Sam. "I got it right out of the oven just so's you could have some with your coffee."

I gave Sam a sideways look. "You know apple pie's my all-time favorite," I said. There are times, like Sam said, when a man just has to tell a little white lie to a woman.